DAYMOUTH

DAYMOUTH

MALCOLM MACKLEY

Copyright © 2023 Malcolm Mackley

The moral right of the author has been asserted.

Apart from any fair dealing for the purposes of research or private study, or criticism or review, as permitted under the Copyright, Designs and Patents Act 1988, this publication may only be reproduced, stored or transmitted, in any form or by any means, with the prior permission in writing of the publishers, or in the case of reprographic reproduction in accordance with the terms of licences issued by the Copyright Licensing Agency. Enquiries concerning reproduction outside those terms should be sent to the publishers.

This is a work of fiction. Names, characters, businesses, places, events and incidents are either the products of the author's imagination or used in a fictitious manner. Any resemblance to actual persons, living or dead, or actual events is purely coincidental.

Matador
Unit E2 Airfield Business Park,
Harrison Road, Market Harborough,
Leicestershire. LE16 7UL
Tel: 0116 2792299
Email: books@troubador.co.uk
Web: www.troubador.co.uk/matador
Twitter: @matadorbooks

ISBN 978 1803135 922

British Library Cataloguing in Publication Data.
A catalogue record for this book is available from the British Library.

Printed and bound in Great Britain by CMP UK
Typeset in 11pt Adobe Garamond Pro by Troubador Publishing Ltd, Leicester, UK

Matador is an imprint of Troubador Publishing Ltd

Dedicated to my wife, Margaret

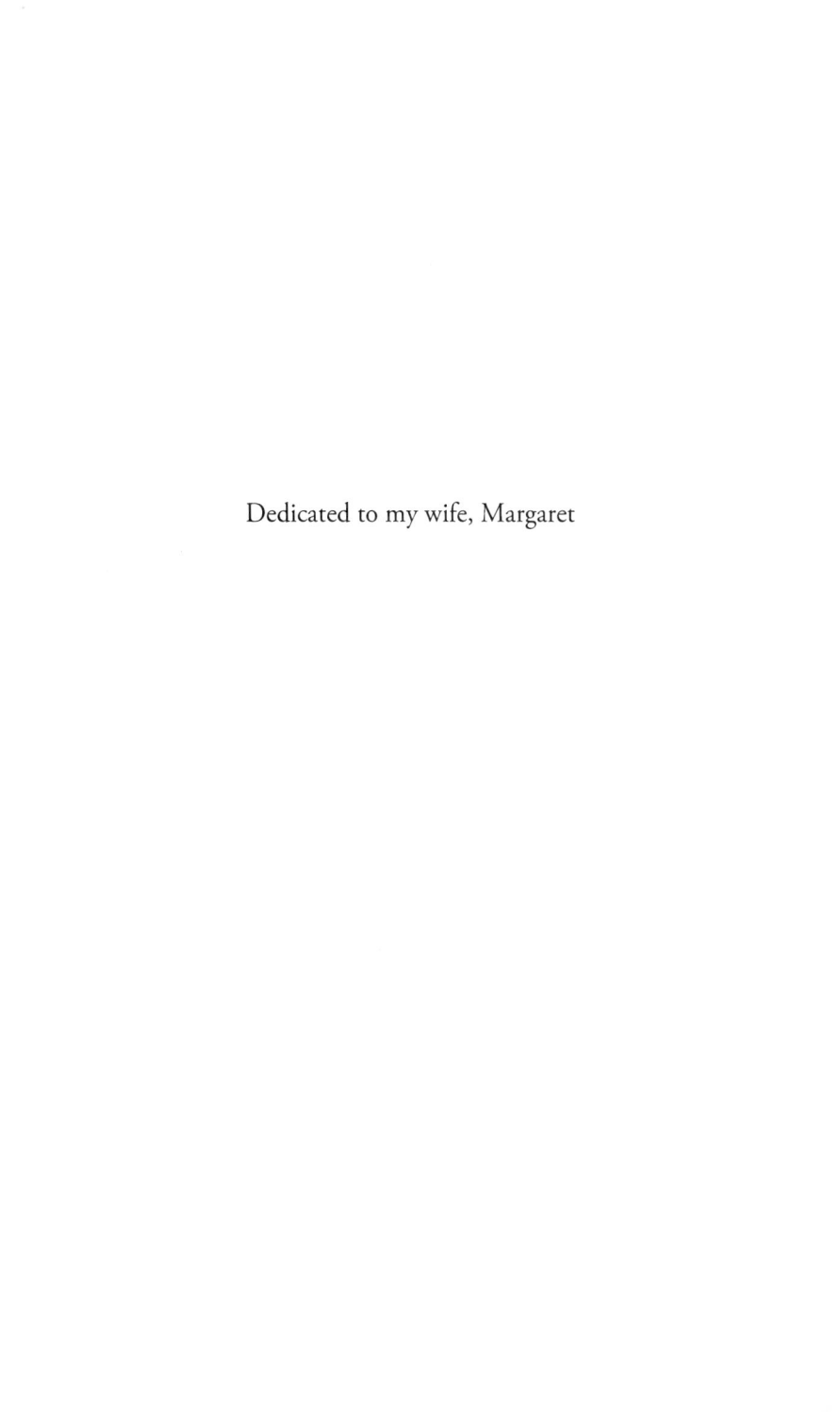

ACKNOWLEDGEMENTS

I would like to thank my wife, Margaret, for her continued support writing this novel and checking the script as it progressed chapter by chapter. I have been fortunate to live in Devon for the last ten years and would like to thank Chris Winzer, Chris Kemp and Robin Hodges for valuable conversations in relation to RNLI lifeboat operations.

I am most grateful to Alan Warren for providing the front cover drawing of Daymouth and Jean Francois Agassant for introducing me to the Côte d'Azur and the wonderful panoramic view from Fort de la Revère above the Principality of Monaco. Finally, I would like to thank the Sutherland brothers for permission to include the lyrics of their song 'Sailing' and Troubador Publishing for successfully guiding me through the process of turning a manuscript into a published book.

CHAPTER 1

His rucksack was feeling uncomfortable, but as Adam took the path down to the golden sands of Taylor's Cove, the glorious sight of Daymouth on the other side of the estuary immediately raised spirits. He had set Daymouth as the target destination for today's coastal walk and decided that he would spend the night there.

The tide was nearly low, and this meant he was able to walk from Taylor's Cove along the sandy foreshore towards the point where the ferry landed to collect foot passengers taking them across the estuary. The holiday season was not yet in full swing and so there were only a few people enjoying the late afternoon sunshine on a beach that was one of the jewels in the crown of the Daymouth estuary. Adam just soaked up the view and the atmosphere of the place as he headed to the landing point.

The ferry was waiting for him. Harry Payne, the ferryman, had seen Adam approaching from a distance along the beach and, because it was a relatively quiet time of the year, he was able to hold the wooden boat until he arrived.

'Many thanks for waiting,' said Adam as he climbed aboard.

'Pleasure,' replied Harry. 'We're here to provide a service. That will be £1.50, thanks.'

Adam and Harry had a friendly chat as they took the short three-minute journey to the town pier on the Daymouth side of the estuary.

'So, what goes on in Daymouth?' Adam asked, having to raise his voice above the noise of the chugging diesel engine.

'Well, it all depends,' replied Harry. 'In the height of season, the place is crazy and we're running three boats continually across the estuary, but in the winter months it's very quiet. Daymouth needs the tourism business to survive. In the 19th century it was all about wooden boat building, now it's holiday homes, leisure boating and a small crab and lobster fleet.'

Just then, there was the sound of a loud klaxon that momentarily obliterated conversation.

'What's that?' exclaimed Adam.

'That's the warning sound for the lifeboat,' said Harry, and a short time later the Daymouth RNLI all-weather lifeboat, the ALB, emerged from its mooring off the harbour quay and swept past the ferry as it made towards the mouth of the estuary and out to sea.

'That's impressive,' said Adam. 'What a sight.'

'Yes, those guys are very brave, they're all locals and some have families and kids. Ted Sandringham is the coxswain and I would back him every time. The weather is good at the moment and so let's hope it's not something too serious. Maybe a fishing boat with a fouled propeller or a boat engine failure.'

Harry expertly brought the ferry up to the pier on the Daymouth shore and as Adam was getting off the boat, he looked at Harry and said, 'Many thanks, that was great. I hope we meet again.'

Adam then climbed the steps and arrived at the busy Main Street where a rather weather-beaten elderly lady was nearby and he asked, 'Excuse me, but can you direct me to the Waterside Hotel? I'm told it's the only hotel in town.'

She took a long look at Adam. 'Along the road and on the left. It's very posh and caters for the well-off visitor. You might find it a bit expensive.'

'Thanks very much,' and after a pause said, 'are you local?'

'Oh yes, lived here all my life. Can't you tell from my Devon accent?'

The woman was happy to engage Adam in conversation and he replied, 'Well, I suspect you can guess I'm not local and probably think I sound as though I have a London accent. I guess also from my walking boots, rucksack and shorts that you think I am not the sort of person who can afford somewhere like the Waterside Hotel.'

'London accent?' came the reply. 'Possibly, but I thought I detected a bit of East Anglian in your speech. Rich or poor? I just couldn't say; in Daymouth, anything's possible. We have a mix of super rich, not so rich and also poor. Most of our visitors are quite well off and those that stay at the Waterside Hotel definitely need to be very well off.' She smiled at Adam and said, 'By the way, my name's Beryl and I'm the local gossip. My husband died ages ago and if you want any more information, you can find me at the Smugglers Inn most days. They do B&B; it's not posh, like the Waterside Hotel.'

Adam thanked Beryl for the cheerful chat and set off in the direction of the Waterside Hotel. On his left there were beautiful views of the estuary looking across to the golden sands of the Eastside shore. He passed the imposing building of the Daymouth Yacht Club on his right and within a couple of minutes arrived at Beryl's posh hotel. He found the main entrance and went up to what indeed was a smart reception desk and receptionist.

'Good afternoon, sir, can I help you?'

'Yes; have you a room for one night or maybe a few days more?'

'Let me have a look for you, sir. You are aware that we have a certain evening dress code, sir?'

'Yes,' replied Adam with a smile.

'The only room I have for one or possibly up to three nights is a guest suite at £300 per night with dinner, and breakfast as a separate charge.'

'That's fine, I'll take it for one night with an option for the other two if I may and yes, I can look respectable. I've just walked twenty miles along the coast path to here.'

The receptionist completed the formalities and directed Adam to the lift. 'Your room is 302 on the third floor, sir. I presume you have no car or further luggage?'

'Correct,' replied Adam with a smile.

When he opened the door to room 302, he was met with a fantastic panoramic view of the estuary looking seawards towards the estuary rocks and the sea beyond.

'Wow,' he said to himself, 'that is some view.' This was the sort of view that made Daymouth so attractive, and as he went out onto the balcony, he spent some minutes just taking in the whole panorama.

Adam was captivated by the view. He took a quick shower, dressed into casual clothes that he had in his rucksack, raided the minibar for a beer and then went back out onto the balcony where he sat by a table and just absorbed himself in the vista. The sun was beginning to settle in the west behind the hotel and this produced wonderful colour contrasts across the south-facing estuary. There was still some pleasure-boat activity and a few crab and lobster fishing boats coming and going out to sea.

After about half an hour, he spotted the red colour of the returning RNLI lifeboat, and it was towing something back into the estuary from the sea. As the boats got nearer, he could see that the ferryman had been right. The boat being towed was a fairly large fishing boat, a crabber maybe, that presumably had suffered some form of engine damage.

Later, as the evening closed in, Adam decided it would be more interesting to dine out rather than alone in the Waterside Hotel, and with Beryl's Smugglers Inn on his mind, he set off in search of a pint of beer and a meal.

The hotel receptionist gave him simple directions on how to reach the pub. 'Go out of the hotel, turn right and then just keep going along Main St until you get to the Smugglers Inn, which will be directly in front of you at the point where the road turns right towards the lifeboat station.'

Adam followed the instructions and, within five minutes, he was opening the door of an authentic-looking pub that was already very busy. He edged his way to the bar, caught the eye of an attractive woman behind the bar and asked her, 'Any chance of a pint of local beer and a meal later this evening? This place seems incredibly busy already. Is it always like this?'

'Hi. How about a pint of Daymouth Gold? And yes, we can sort you out with a meal later. We're very busy this evening because the lifeboat has just towed the crabber "Impala" in; it got ropes caught around its propeller. The "Impala" crew are now buying drinks for the lifeboat crew and that includes me.'

'Do you mean that you are part of the lifeboat crew?'

'Yes, that's right. You must be new around here; my name's Laura.'

'Nice to meet you, Laura, and yes, this is the first time I've been to Daymouth, I've just walked here along the coastal path and I'm staying at the Waterside Hotel.'

'Oh, you must be a DFT then! That's short for someone who has come "Down From Town".'

After Laura got Adam his beer, he made his way to a corner bench and table and spotted Beryl smiling at him.

'I thought I might see you again. Do come and join me if you'd like to talk to an old gossipy woman.'

Adam smiled and sat down beside her. 'Thank you for the invitation. My name is Adam and I seem to have come at a busy time.'

'Yes, you have. I saw you talking to the lovely Laura and could see she took a shine to you. Laura is an angel; works behind the bar, serves on the lifeboat and generally keeps the whole town happy, even in winter, and that isn't easy. I can lip-read and saw that she had you down as a DFT. We don't necessarily see that as a bad thing, but you're much more likely to be accepted here in the Smugglers Inn and Daymouth as a whole if you become a local. Are you planning on living here?'

'Whatever made you think of that?' exclaimed Adam.

'Just a feeling. From time to time, I get these feelings. Sometimes they're rubbish, but sometimes I'm right!'

As the evening progressed, Adam bought Beryl and Laura further drinks. He also enjoyed an excellent meal and ended up talking and sharing drinks with various fishermen from the 'Impala' and the lifeboat crew.

It was near midnight when he finally tracked back along Main St heading for the Waterside Hotel and a good night's sleep.

*

On the following day, Adam rose early and before nine o'clock he was walking from the hotel into the town with both a clear head and a plan. He went into Devon County, the local estate agents' office in the centre of town, and spoke to a woman sitting at her desk. 'Good morning, my name is Adam Ranworth and I'm interested in either buying or renting a waterside property in Daymouth.'

'Well, you've certainly come to the right place, Mr Ranworth. My name is Mary Burns and I've been selling properties in this area for the last twenty years. Can you be a bit more specific about what you would like and the price range you have in mind?'

'To be frank with you, I only made the decision last night to have a base here and so I'm very much open to different options. My finances are very sound and so price isn't a major factor in terms of a purchase or let. I'm single but would want something with reasonable space and a few bedrooms.'

'OK,' replied Mary, 'let me think.' She looked at Adam and quickly tried to assess the sort of person he was. Mary was acknowledged throughout the area as being extremely shrewd and an expert estate agent who had an uncanny knack of valuing and selling properties. 'Maybe I do have something that might interest you. The property isn't exactly in Daymouth but it's on the other side of the estuary. Do you know the passenger ferry? The cottage is adjacent to the landing stage on the Eastside side of the estuary.'

'Yes, I used the ferry yesterday after walking the coastal path.'

'Excellent, let's take a walk to the pier and you can view the property from this side of the estuary.'

While they walked from the estate agents' to the pier, she explained the current situation. 'It is all a bit complicated, but a family have owned 1 Eastside Cottages for many years and used it as a holiday home. Circumstances have changed and they've asked us to either put it up for long-term letting or for sale. The cottage is in fact quite large and it's strategically located with a waterside terrace and running mooring. As you can see, it's a prime location and the sale price would be around two million pounds. I do hope none of that information puts you off?'

'No. Let's have a look at it.'

Two hours later, Adam and Mary were standing on the waterside terrace of 1 Eastside Cottages admiring the view of Daymouth and the estuary. 'This looks fine,' said Adam. 'I think this is the sort of place that would work for me. Who is the next-door neighbour in number 2?'

'Ah, that's Admiral Lord Tom Blechard, who all the locals call "The Admiral". He is a bit of an eccentric but basically a very nice person. Would you like me to introduce him to you?'

'Maybe a good idea,' replied Adam, and Mary leant over the dividing terrace wall and shouted, 'Admiral, are you in?'

The Admiral appeared within seconds, as he'd clearly been aware of the activity at number one.

'Yes, here I am, Mary and who's your friend?'

'This is Adam Ranworth and he's interested in the cottage. As I told you last week, the property is being put on the market.'

The Admiral looked at Adam and said, 'Nice to meet you,' and after a pause continued. 'If you take the cottage on, I am afraid you will have me as a neighbour and I'm not totally sure I would really want myself as my own neighbour. I'm harmless but, well, I was a naval Sea Lord. I was a great man. My wife died ten years ago and now I have come to die here by the sea at Eastside. I drink a bit and enjoy conversation, but yes, I am an eccentric and you need to know this if you're serious and want to spend time here.'

'Good to meet you, Admiral,' said Adam. 'I do hope I can call you that. Maybe we can have a drink together in the future to establish whether we would make mutually compatible neighbours?'

*

Within three days, Adam had agreed a price for the cottage including the current furniture and moved in, initially as a tenant for one month before formalities could be settled for the purchase.

'I have to say that I have never had such a fast purchase,' declared Mary as she passed the keys of 1 Eastside Cottages to Adam. 'You are certainly decisive and have a very firm control of your lawyers!'

'Thanks for your help, too, you've been very efficient. In the last three days I have in fact done a bit of homework on Daymouth, the Admiral and the cottage itself and I feel comfortable that certainly for the moment I've made a sound decision. At this stage I can't yet say if it is the right decision, but we'll just have to find out how things develop.'

'Well, I'll leave you now as I can see the ferry coming across the estuary and if I hurry, I'll catch the boat back to Daymouth. By the way, as I explained earlier, Jasmine Sanders will contact you in the next few days and it's entirely up to you as to whether you employ her as a housekeeper. There aren't many people on this side of the estuary who can look after the property. Jasmine's very reliable and did an excellent job with the previous owners. The Sanders are a local Eastside family and know nearly everyone on this side of the estuary. Anyway, must rush now if I'm going to catch that ferry!'

Adam was left alone in his waterside cottage and he took a can of beer that was in the fridge onto the outside waterside terrace and sat down on one of the large chairs.

'So, this is it,' he said to himself. 'My new home; a new phase of my life and an opportunity to mix with a completely different set of people, places and challenges.' He looked across the estuary towards Daymouth and saw the iconic setting of houses fronting onto the water and covering the hill behind. He saw the bustle of boats, some of which were fishing boats and others pleasure boats of different shapes and sizes. His apartment in London had been in Putney with a view of the river Thames and so he already felt at home with water nearby; however, this was different. The colours were vivid and blue, the water sparkling and the whole atmosphere of the place a complete contrast to the Thames.

*

It was 8pm when the doorbell of 1 Eastside Cottages rang and Adam opened it to be confronted with the Admiral. 'Good evening, Adam; would you care to share a large bottle of good wine with me? We can either drink it here or at my place next door?'

'OK, let's do it here, Admiral,' and he ushered him into the cottage and out onto the waterside terrace.

Adam found two large glasses and the Admiral filled both with the red wine.

'Good luck, Adam. I hope you'll be happy here,' said the Admiral. 'If you're going to call me Admiral, I'm going to call you Adam. I know you're over thirty, maybe even forty, but from my stage in life, you're just Adam. I'll not interfere with your life and pester you, however, I thought it right that we try and get off on the right foot. In the summer months, like now, there's lots of activity. But the winter on Eastside is long and you'll not see many people on this side of the estuary. Yes, there is still some life in Daymouth during the winter, however, even there, the place is pretty quiet in those cold months.'

Adam and the Admiral consumed the bottle of wine on the terrace of Adam's cottage, which overlooked the beautiful Daymouth estuary, and both were careful not to probe each other's background too closely.

'Time to go,' said the Admiral. 'I suspect we will have plenty of time in the future to get to know each other properly. Anyway, good luck and enjoy Eastside. If you want advice at any point, I am happy to give it. Equally, if you prefer, we can live entirely separate lives. Eastside is a very small and close community that you will need to work out for yourself.'

*

The following morning, Adam woke early, saw that it was low tide and went for a jog along the sandy foreshore. As soon as he had seen the cottage, he realised the potential for beach jogging and that seemed so much better than the routes he had taken before when he was in both New York and London. Running barefoot, he enjoyed the experience of taking the sandy waterside run past Sandy Beach, Taylor's Cove and then Sunny Corner. At Sunny Corner, he paused to look out to the magnificent view of the sea and then he backtracked to the cottage for a cereal breakfast and coffee.

At just after 9am, the doorbell rang and he opened it to see an attractive woman who had a smile on her face.

'Hi, I am Jasmine Sanders and I understand that Mary Burns from the estate agents' has recommended me to you?'

'Yes, that's right, come in and we can have a chat.' They walked through the cottage and sat down at the table on the waterside terrace.

'I'll be quite honest with you,' said Jasmine, 'I'm desperate for work and in Eastside there are very few opportunities. I look after a couple of second homes on this side of the estuary and I'm a home help and cook in a few private houses. I've two young children and so I need work nearby.'

'Do you have a husband and does he work?'

'I am afraid Jack's away at the moment,' and after a pause she said, 'well, to tell you the truth, he's in jail for a bit; nothing serious but he got in with the wrong people and was had up for selling drugs in Daymouth and Princewater, the town at the top of the estuary.'

'Hmm, that doesn't sound too good. Mrs Burns didn't say anything about that.'

'Eastside is a very small place and I was afraid it wouldn't be long before you heard about Jack and so I thought it would be better to tell you upfront. Please, Mr Ranworth, I'm very honest, very hard-working and do a very good job; I'm sure Mrs Burns and the previous owners of this cottage will vouch for me. They were very good to me and I did a good job for them.'

Adam was unsure how to respond. He had barely spent forty-eight hours in the cottage and was now faced with a tricky decision. 'Maybe I need to think about this before making a decision. You've put me on the spot and perhaps I should make a few enquiries first.'

'Mr Ranworth, I know every nook and cranny of this house and I can keep it spotless for you. Please, can I make you a cup of tea or a cup of coffee and explain the situation?'

Jasmine had beautiful blue eyes, she was clearly attractive, intelligent and she had a charming way of handling people.

'All right, go ahead. You can then tell me about you, your family, Daymouth and Eastside.'

Jasmine made the tea and brought it out to Adam who was sitting outside at the waterside terrace table. She also sat down and then explained that her parents were both from the village and that, at the age of eleven, she went to Princewater Secondary School at the top of the estuary. Her father worked as a gardener for one of the big houses overlooking Taylor's Cove and her mother worked at the local village shop. By the age of twenty-one, she had two children, Jamie and Sally, and had married Jack, who was from the nearby village of Tordon. Jack worked at Benson's, a local Daymouth boatyard, but unknown to her, got in with a group who were selling drugs in the area. A year ago, things went really wrong for her family when Jack was arrested for selling drugs and two months later her father drowned whilst night-fishing off a small pier at Eastside beach, just along from the cottage. His body was recovered the following day on the beach and the coroner certified the death as accidental. Jack was sentenced to two years in jail, partly as he wouldn't tell the police or her who supplied the drugs to him. She visits him in Dartmoor Prison, but she can't forgive him for not saying where the drugs came from.

The previous owners of the cottage had been very kind to her and supported her and without their regular cash she wasn't sure how she could have made ends meet. They had been fortunate, as she and Jack had bought one of the very few 'affordable' houses that were built in Eastside; however, the mortgage took nearly every penny they could earn. She was not complaining, as she knew the troubles were of their own making, but she did hope Adam would at least continue from where the previous owners left off.

When Jasmine had finished her story, Adam reflected and looked across the table saying, 'Mrs Burns may have told you that I've no family or children and yes, it would be good to meet your own children, Jamie and Sally, sometime. I'm sorry to hear about your troubles, but I'm not sure I can help that much; apart from saying… let's continue for a bit on the same basis as the previous owners and see how it works out. Maybe cleaning once a week and helping out when needed. I'm not really a very good cook and so if I have guests I wonder if in the future you would cook a few small group meals. If you leave me your bank details, I will transfer a small retainer over to you and we can work rates out later.'

'Oh, Mr Ranworth, thank you so much,' cried Jasmine and she got up, gave Adam a big hug and burst into tears.

Adam shied away from her. 'This is business, Jasmine, and I am not used to being hugged like that.'

'I am so sorry, Mr Ranworth, and I won't do it again, I was just so grateful.'

'OK, and if we are going to work together and be friends, you should call me Adam.'

CHAPTER 2

The next few weeks involved Adam disengaging from his Putney apartment and establishing himself in his new home at Eastside Cottage. He quickly discovered that there were significant logistic issues about living on the east side of the estuary as road access was very challenging. A car journey to the nearest town of Princewater at the head of the estuary could take up to thirty minutes along very narrow single-track roads and to go to Daymouth by road would take forty-five minutes by car, when it was only three minutes by boat. He did have the option to get to Daymouth by boat using the ferry and he planned to obtain a small outboard boat to be kept on the cottage running mooring, which would then give him independence from the ferry.

Adam wanted to move forward from his previous life as swiftly as possible and he made the decision not to even return to Putney where he had lived before and just leave his apartment together with his possessions as it was. After his life-changing involvement with a Putney Bridge incident that had occurred some four months earlier, he was adamant that his whole life and lifestyle would change.

Before starting his coastal path walking adventure, he had dissolved his City trading company 'Ranworth Sole Traders' and advised the management company who oversaw his apartment block that he might not be returning for some time. Now that he had made Eastside Cottage his new home, he asked the management company to look after his Putney apartment, car and possessions on a semi-permanent basis. He would start his life again at Eastside Cottage using the furniture already there and buy any additional things that he needed. He also decided to buy a vehicle that was suitable for the local conditions and ordered a small four-wheel drive Skoda Yeti that could handle the very narrow local roads.

He asked David Young, an ex-Cambridge University and London friend, to dispatch his beloved racing and touring bikes to his new home. Whilst at Cambridge, David and he had taken up triathlons, involving cycling, swimming and running, and when Adam was working from London, they had maintained their friendship by competing in regional events around the capital.

In terms of water transport, Laura Clift, the barmaid at the Smugglers Inn and RNLI crew member, introduced Adam to a boatman, Ben Lewis, and he found a suitable outboard boat for Adam to put on the Eastside Cottage running mooring. Ben had said, 'You need something about 14ft that is not too smart, otherwise it'll only get nicked, and with a not-too-powerful, but reliable, outboard engine.' He sourced a boat named 'Greta' and gave Adam an extensive driving lesson and some boat-handling training. 'At some stage you need to go on a proper RYA powerboat course,' said Ben. 'It looks as if you've not had any previous power boat experience. You may be a fantastic swimmer and very fit, but you need proper training on boat handling.'

From then on, Adam found he was using Greta nearly every time he crossed the estuary and he only rarely went on the passenger ferry. Greta was great fun and enabled him to explore the whole of the estuary that extended up to Princewater, and he was even able to take the boat onto the open sea when the weather was suitable.

*

Within a month, he had settled into something of a routine in his new home. He would wake early and, providing the tide was suitable, jog to Sunny Corner and back along the beach. He took long cycle rides exploring the peninsula taking him to Totnes and, on a few occasions, Dartmoor. He would also take a daily swim providing the weather was suitable. Although he could swim immediately in front of his cottage, he generally chose to swim and surf from Sunny Corner at the mouth of the estuary or the beach at Neath, further round the coast towards William's Point. Afternoon walks also became an important and pleasant part of his life as he found that they had a therapeutic effect, giving him time to absorb the countryside and clear his mind.

His contact with local people had been relatively minimal. Jasmine came twice a week to clean and help in the cottage. Adam had left her to her work and they were both being careful not to become too chatty. His neighbour, Admiral Tom, had also stayed at a distance and they'd kept conversations to pleasantries with no probing questions on either side. Laura Clift had seen quite a bit of Adam in the Smugglers Inn, as he had spent a number of evenings both eating and drinking there. She'd told him a lot of information about the RNLI and he met a number of the crew, including the coxswain, Ted Sandringham. Beryl, the 'Daymouth Gossip', had also been surprisingly good company at the pub, filling Adam in with the latest Daymouth news and also factual history of the town.

It was on the fourth Sunday after his arrival at the cottage when Admiral Tom knocked on Adam's door and invited him to supper that evening. Adam was happy to accept and went next door to Tom's home feeling relaxed and happy to have been asked.

'Adam, I thought it was about time we both got to know each other,' said Admiral Tom as they sat in the evening sunlight on the terrace outside the cottage. There was a large bottle of excellent wine on the table and the Admiral was clearly set for a good evening's drinking.

'So, who goes first? You or me?'

'Why don't you go first?' replied Adam. 'You're older than me!'

'OK, fair enough,' he said. 'My life actually restarted in the 1980s because of Margaret Thatcher. She decided we would go to war with the Argentinians and that meant me captaining a destroyer, 'Lionheart', to the Falklands. She was one of the ships that was bombed by the Argentine air force at Port Stanley and I lost the boat and over a hundred of my crew. A terrible tragedy and I was never the same again. However, the whole thing made me more determined to try and do something useful with my life and I guess that's why I became a Lord Admiral. Shear bloody-minded determination.'

'What about your wife? You said when I first meet you that she died ten years ago?'

'Yes, you're right. Edith and I were as one for thirty years, we had two boys, both of whom are now in the navy. Very proud of them, although I don't see much of them. As I also said, I came to Daymouth to die and that's what I'm going to do. I'm now a spectator, not the action man of the past. I'm now someone who still thinks of the lives that were lost on the 'Lionheart' and the families that were, and still are, affected by that. I'm someone who would be happy to talk to you from time to time and someone who you could trust; however, I am now very old and maybe wouldn't be much help.'

Adam was somewhat lost for words as they both drank their wine looking out across the estuary towards Daymouth. Finally, he thought through a response.

'Tom, that's a very strong story and I'm troubled as to how to reply; however, there are aspects of your life that resonate with me and so I'll tell you my own tale, although I feel a need to sort of start from the beginning.'

'Fine; I'll drink my wine, close my eyes, and you can just go ahead.'

'Born in Norwich and went to Norwich Grammar School. My father died of an asbestos-related cancer when I was thirteen and my mother died six months later. I was never told what my mum died of when she was in hospital, but I've always thought it was connected in some way to grieving over the loss of my father. After that, an uncle acted as a guardian to me. I was an only child. I went to Cambridge and graduated in mathematics. Cambridge was OK, I had a few girlfriends and met a classmate, David Young, and we both enjoyed doing the triathlons as a sport. I guess I was a bit of a loner at university and never got as much out of it as I could have done, although when I graduated in 2004, a Cambridge first-class degree in mathematics was a useful passport for future employment. Like many others in my class at the time, I went to London and joined a bank, in my case Lehman Brothers, a City financial services bank. I did well and in 2006 was promoted to the New

York headquarters on Wall St. I saw both the good and the bad operational side of Lehman's and in particular, the ridiculous way they didn't manage risk. So, it actually came as no surprise to me that in 2008 the bank went bust, but it did surprise me that the Feds weren't prepared to bail it out. I ended up without a job, returned to London and set up my own trading company, 'Ranworth Sole Traders'. I traded my own money, did well and, up to this year, three months ago, was trading, trading, trading and accumulating a lot of money.

'It was the 14th of April this year when maybe my life changed in a not dissimilar way to your Falklands experience. I was walking across Putney Bridge when I saw a man climb over the wall and jump into the Thames. The tide was falling and he immediately disappeared. I rushed to the other side of the bridge and we made brief eye contact. At that moment, as I looked at his face, I sensed from his expression – or was it what his eyes were saying to me? – that he didn't want to die. I can't explain it, but I knew he didn't really want to commit suicide. I dived into the Thames and swam after him as he was being swept downriver. I'm a good strong swimmer, as it is part of my triathlon training, which meant I was able to catch up with and eventually get hold of the man who, by that time, was white with fear and barely breathing. I managed to get both of us to the shore and fortunately others had seen events unfolding and were able to recover both of us from the muddy shoreline. When the trauma was over. I visited him on the same evening in hospital. He was in poor shape and he was just able to say thank you to me but since then I have heard nothing from him. I had to make police statements and there was a small piece in the local paper about my bravery but, apart from that, nothing.

The whole trauma of the affair had a huge effect on me. I'm not sure why and I'm not sure whether it was the rescue itself, the fact that the man never contacted me after the rescue or perhaps, most probably, the look in his eyes, realising that he'd made a mistake and he didn't really want to commit suicide after all. However, like the Falklands for you, my life has changed. I felt I needed to do something other than just make money. I now have more than enough money than I need for the rest of my lifetime. I needed to do something else and so I had to change my life. I closed my trading company, decided to go for a long coastal walking journey and now, here I am in Daymouth drinking wine with a retired Lord Admiral!'

'Interesting,' replied Tom. 'I had you down as escaping from some torrid marriage. This is different. Do you have women problems or are you gay?'

'No to both questions and I am surprised you have asked me!'

'I didn't want to be rude or anything like that. My marriage helped me navigate through difficult periods and, in particular, the Falklands tragedy. Being in the navy, I also saw a lot of homosexual activity. In my time there were barely any females aboard and there was a certain inevitability that some men found satisfaction with other men. All very complex and quite beyond me. I do however understand that a sudden traumatic experience can change the direction of someone's life. It did for me and it looks as though it has for you. So, what is your new direction?'

'I don't know, Admiral, and that is what I hope to discover here. I do know, however, that just making money no longer interests me. I'm very lucky as I've already done that and so, well, let's just wait and see what happens.'

'Fine; let's go inside, open another bottle of wine and discover what Jasmine Sanders my housekeeper has rustled up for us to eat.'

*

The following day, Adam took his early morning beach run, reflected on the previous night's discussion with the Admiral and decided that some positive action was now definitely necessary in order to start a new life.

After having breakfast, he took his boat 'Greta' over to the Daymouth shore and headed for the Smugglers Inn where he found Laura cleaning up after a busy night.

'Hi Laura, I'm on a bit of a mission, any chance you could find time to introduce me to the right people at the lifeboat station? I'd like to join up!'

'Oh Adam, that's a surprise, especially as it isn't even ten o'clock yet! But yes, sure, give me a few minutes and we can see if we can find Ted Sandringham, who we call "the Boss", or the Local Operations Manager, Billy Cavendish. Are you sure you want to do this? You're nearly a complete stranger and all the rest of the crew are locals. We're a very tight-knit bunch and you may well have trouble being accepted.'

'I agree, but I want to prove myself useful to the lifeboat and I'm prepared to work hard and to integrate with the rest of the crew. I want to be a real part of the team.'

Laura and Adam walked over to the lifeboat station and found Billy cleaning the inshore lifeboat's outboard engines.

'Hi Billy,' said Laura, 'I have a potential recruit for the lifeboats. This is Adam Ranworth, he's just bought one of the Eastside cottages next to the ferry landing.'

Billy took a long look. 'Well, Adam, we get a lot of applicants and few make the grade. Firstly, you've got to live within eight minutes of the station so that you can respond in time to an emergency "shout", and although we don't have any crew who live on the other side of the estuary, I guess you might just be able to make it time. I think I saw you a while ago with Ben Lewis? He's one of our crew and he was showing you how to use an outboard boat. Those Eastside cottages have running moorings so I guess it's just possible you could make the eight-minute time limit from over that side.

'Anyway, we treat all applicants in the same way. You'll need to come along to our Wednesday evening training at six and explain to the whole crew why you want to join and what your credentials are. After the meeting, all the crew have the opportunity to say in private to the Boss – that is, the coxswain, Ted Sandringham – or myself, what they think of you. It takes just one black ball and then that's it. You're out. We rely on teamwork and everyone has to work as a team. Our lives and the lives of others rely on this and so it's crucial. After that, there are still lots of hurdles before we can even think of putting you on active service and you'd definitely not be on a real rescue shout for at least six months.'

'Message received and thanks for even considering me. I'm fit, healthy and a strong swimmer. I know I'm not a local and my background's probably very different to the rest of the crew, but I do believe if given the chance I could fit in.'

Laura and Adam chatted with Billy for a little and then left, leaving him to continue cleaning the engines. As they left the lifeboat station, they met Ben Lewis in the street.

'Hi Adam,' said Ben. 'I wanted to have a word with you. Laura, is it OK if Adam and I have a chat?'

'Sure, go ahead, I still have work to do. Adam, I thought you did OK with Billy. I even think he likes you, although from what he said, you might not have thought so!'

Laura went off down the road towards the Smugglers Inn and Ben and Adam found a seat overlooking the estuary.

'Sorry about that,' said Ben. 'But I didn't know how you were fixed with Laura and I wanted to talk to you about Jasmine Sanders.'

Adam said nothing.

'You see, Jasmine's husband Jack used to work at Benson's Boatyard with me. We got on well but about a year ago he changed and started selling drugs. I don't think he took them himself, but it was really strange. I know Jack and Jasmine well as we all went to school together and Jasmine told me that she's now housekeeping for you. They had a lovely family and then things really went badly. Jack was had up for peddling drugs and then his father-in-law goes and dies. I just don't believe he fell into the water by accident when night-fishing.'

Adam looked at Ben. 'Why tell me? Surely you should be talking to the police about this, not me?'

'I am afraid it's not that easy. Our local bobby is Chris Thompson; he's a good chap but something of a gossip and I could lose my job if I say too much. Jobs around here for the locals are few and far between and I just can't afford to lose mine. You see, I think there may be a boatyard connection.'

'OK, you can talk to me but I've no idea how I can help. I only moved here a month ago, hardly know any of the locals and I'm not a policeman or a detective. But yes, Jasmine is helping with housework, although I hardly know the woman.'

'Jack worked on the annual winter overhaul of Ian Carbrook's yacht "High Life" and Jack's father-in-law, Dan, was the gardener for Ian's house, which overlooks Taylor's Cove on your side of the estuary. It's one of the biggest houses in the whole estuary. I think either Jack or Dan got involved with Ian Carbrook and that's how Jack ended up in prison and how Jasmine's dad got killed. You see, Jack won't tell anyone who supplied him with the drugs and I think he was scared to tell because of what might happen to his family.'

'Look,' said Adam, 'this is serious stuff and way beyond me. You've got to go to the police.'

'I can't and Jasmine can't. I could lose my job and Jasmine's afraid for herself, Jack and their children.'

'Ben, let me think about this and I'll get back to you. I've got your mobile number and we can talk maybe in a couple of days' time.'

With that, they parted and Adam went back to 'Greta' with his head full of lifeboats and estuary skulduggery.

*

During the afternoon, on answering the doorbell, Adam was faced with Jasmine and her two children, Jamie and Sally.

'Hello Adam, Ben Lewis has just been on the phone to me and I thought I ought to come and see you. I hope you don't mind but I've brought the children too as I couldn't leave them alone at the house.'

After she had organised the children in a corner of the living room and brought out some toys from the pram for them to play with, Adam and Jasmine sat at the table out of listening range but in sight of the children.

'Ben shouldn't have talked to you about his theories and I don't believe he's right. I do apologise and hope you'll allow me to carry on working for you.'

There was a pause as Adam mulled over a response. 'Jasmine, if Ben feels there's substance to what he's said then he must go to the police. I've only just moved to Daymouth and whilst I want to make the estuary part of my life, this is far too serious for me to get involved with.'

'I do understand, Adam, and that's why Ben was out of order to raise these concerns with you. Please do let me continue to work for you; I know Jack was a fool but all I want now is my family back in one piece.'

*

After Jasmine and her children had left, Adam felt he needed a stiff drink and poured himself a whisky. He sat in a comfortable chair and thought about the events of the day. The lifeboat project excited him and he realised he would need to do some homework on that, hopefully with Laura's help. The Ben drugs issue was more troubling and he thought further discussion with Jasmine was needed; he couldn't leave things in limbo as they were at the moment. Clearly, life in Daymouth wasn't going to be simple, but to some extent he was looking for new challenges and at least two had arrived in the last twenty-four hours. At that point, the doorbell rang yet again.

'Good afternoon. My name is James Holberton and I'm the Chairman of the Eastside Parish Council. Your neighbour, Admiral Tom, who I believe you know, suggested you may be able to help us. Would it be possible to have a few words and also invite you to supper?'

'Do come in and tell me how you think I might be able to help.'

Adam offered Councillor Holberton a drink and they sat around the main table.

'Admiral Tom said that you've recently bought this cottage and intend to live here. That's very good news as unfortunately most houses that change hands now become second homes where we only see the owners for a few weeks and then either the place is left empty or let out as a holiday home. The Eastside Parish Council is formed from a small group of residents and I have the dubious honour of being Chairman. We are in fact near neighbours to you; we live in the white house "Estuary View" along the road, overlooking the Eastside beach.

'Our normal council business is usually very mundane, but important for the community here; however, something big is brewing that could alter the whole estuary and certainly Eastside. Draft plans have been submitted to form a large sustainable 'Marlo Eco Park' on this side of the estuary. Basically, it seems to be a heavily disguised holiday park under the cover of an environmentally sustainable ecosystem. The Admiral thought you'd be a useful addition to the Parish Council in ensuring that the right result emerges. The issue has already divided my own family. On the one hand, I'm deeply concerned about the damage it would do to an Area of Outstanding Beauty (AONB), whereas both my wife Grace and my daughter Sarah, who lives with us, feel it will provide much needed employment and life to an area where regular jobs are so difficult to find. I was hoping I could tempt you to supper either tomorrow or the following night in order to meet my family and also hear the opposing views?'

'Yes, tomorrow will be fine,' said Adam, 'and I'd certainly like to meet my new neighbours. I'm however sure that I'm the wrong person to join your Parish Council, I have only just moved here.'

*

Adam arrived the following evening at the imposing shoreside home 'Estuary View', which was a large 1930s, immaculately maintained house with a wonderful view overlooking the estuary towards Estuary Point. He rang the doorbell and was met by an attractive woman who at first sight looked as though she was in her late twenties.

'Hi, I'm Sarah, welcome to Estuary View. We're all looking forward to meeting you. Having new neighbours in Eastside is quite an event and from what my father's told us, you're something of a mystery man. My mother, Grace, is supervising the supper, she's looking forward to meeting you too.'

Sarah led Adam into the main reception room, which, in the evening sunlight, had a stunning panoramic view of the beach in front of the house with the estuary beyond and Estuary Point in the background. James Holberton was standing by the window.

'Adam, very nice to see you and thanks for coming. I should make it clear from the very start that my full title is Sir James Holberton, but I really do insist that I am just called James in Eastside. My knighthood came some time ago for political services and I now really do want to be known only as James. Do sit down; my wife Grace will join us shortly, she's organising supper.'

Sarah, James and Adam chatted over a glass of wine and after a few minutes, Grace Holberton made a glamorous entry.

'So, this is Adam Ranworth, our mystery man! So nice to meet you and what wonderful news to hear that you plan to stay, even through our long and lonely winters. You've probably got the idea already, most local properties that now change hands are either bought as holiday lets or second homes where we rarely see the owners.'

'And this is my wife, the beautiful Grace,' said James. 'She's the person that makes Eastside the social hub of the universe, or should I say Devon? Grace looks after me, Sarah and the house. She cooks like an angel and organises wonderful summer parties on the beach.'

'James; do stop it!' said Grace. 'Adam; what we all really want to know is about you. At the moment you're our mystery man. Admiral Tom was very discreet and all we have learnt so far from the Daymouth grapevine is that you want to join the lifeboat crew. How brave!'

'Well, I'm not sure what to say. Born in Norwich, went to Cambridge, worked in Lehman's bank, which went bust, set up my own trading company in London, closed that down, went for a coastal path walk and here I am having bought a waterside cottage along the road from here.'

'But what are you going to do here? Why Eastside?'

'That, Grace, is a very direct question and at the moment I don't have a clear answer. Perhaps it might be easier for you to tell me what you do in this neck of the woods?'

'Enough!' interjected James. 'I am sure we'll all get to know each other very well in the coming months and hopefully this evening we can talk over one of Grace's wonderful suppers. Let's all have a drink.'

The four of them then sat down and chatted amicably until Jasmine Sanders, Adam's home help, popped her head around the door. 'I've put the starters on the table in the dining room and supper is now ready, Lady Holberton.'

'Thank you, Jasmine,' replied Grace. 'Shall we all go in?'

Adam was surprised to see Jasmine, but then remembered that she had told him that she did help out sometimes with supper parties locally.

James and Grace were seated at each end of the dining table, which left Sarah and Adam sitting opposite each other. Jasmine had disappeared into the kitchen and the party of four started on the smoked salmon starter.

'We're so lucky living here in Devon,' said Grace. 'Our fish supply is wonderful. The salmon comes from a local smoker in Princewater and we can get lobster and crab from the Daymouth fish quay, although you do need to know the locals. Much of the shellfish caught here goes off to Europe and also China of all places!'

The conversation continued amicably with both James and Grace competing to make some sort of point. Sarah had been quiet and Adam attempted to draw her into the conversation.

'Sarah, I suspect that you're quite a few years younger than me but perhaps you can tell me what you do here over the winter. I get the impression that the summer looks after itself with the water, beaches and late evening sunshine like today, but the winter must be different?'

Sarah looked at Adam and smiled. 'Yes, you're right, it can be remote, but I was born and bred in this house and have loved every day of the year, summer or winter, here. I teach at the local primary school at Tordon and that keeps me busy, certainly in the winter months. I'm also a keen sailor and race the family yawl in the spring, summer and autumn; my friend Anthea crews me and we are the only all-female team in the yawl fleet. The Daymouth yawl is a local boat and a lot of fun but also needs maintenance work, which has to be done in the winter.'

'That sounds interesting, perhaps you could take me out sailing sometime? I've never sailed before and it looks as if I am going to settle and be happy here, so I shall need to learn to sail.'

'Sure,' replied Sarah, unsure whether Adam was asking for just a sailing lesson or something more.

'Adam, I am very confident we can find lots of ways to amuse you through the winter months.' said Grace. 'Do you play bridge as we have a local winter group here?'

'Yes and no. I do know how to play bridge but my card game of choice is poker.'

'Oh, how exciting, we'll certainly have to draw you into our bridge parties. Do you play poker for real money?'

'Very rarely,' replied Adam. 'I am actually quite good at it and maybe I could have made a living out of card gambling, but instead I choose to do my gambling on commodities, stocks and shares.'

At this point, Jasmine came into the room, collected the starter plates and then brought in a main course of fish pie.

'I do hope you like fish, Adam. We tend to live off local fish here for most of the year,' said Grace. 'This is my own speciality fish pie; thank you Jasmine, for preparing it so well.'

Adam glanced at Jasmine as she left the room and they briefly made eye contact.

'Whilst we are enjoying our pie, I'd like to bring up one of the reasons I invited Adam to supper,' said James. 'The village is faced with a major issue that is sure to divide the community if it is allowed to progress.

'Eastside is in an Area of Outstanding Natural Beauty, called for short an AONB, but two of our Parish Councillors have ganged up together and submitted a preliminary plan for a Marlo Eco Park. Marlo is a farm region within the parish less than half a mile from this house, where the proposed hundred-acre site, which is currently farmland, comes down to the shore of the estuary. Councillor Bert Appleyard owns the farm and the proposed £30m-plus finance is being provided by Councillor Ian Carbrook. He sold his business some five years ago and now lives in one of the large Taylor's Cove houses at the mouth of the estuary. Their concept is to build some thirty luxury eco holiday villas on the hilly farmland, with each villa having about half an acre of private surrounding land. Wind turbines at the top of the hill and a solar-panel farm would power the whole complex. The exclusive eco park would have a clubhouse bar and restaurant and provide optional private dining in each of the villas. There would be tennis courts, zip wires and woodland trails to keep the customers amused and waterside canoes, paddleboards, electric powerboats and sailing would be available from the private beach access. The whole thing is being spun as a self-sustaining, all-year eco holiday destination with minimal carbon footprint.'

'And Sarah and I are all for it!' exclaimed Grace. 'James thinks it is a nightmare but Sarah and I know Eastside has to change and move with the times, otherwise it will just become a retirement home for the well off. Take for example Jasmine in the kitchen here. She finds it really hard to get work on this peninsula and ends up doing small jobs like preparing our supper tonight. There is so little work for young people that they are forced out of the area. We must create work if we want to keep young families.'

'Yes,' said Sarah, 'and we need a bit of life around here. An eco park would create jobs and life around here. At the moment there's nothing, absolutely nothing.'

Adam was somewhat shell-shocked by the sudden onslaught of passion from all members of the Holberton family and felt as though he was being asked to be a referee in a family feud.

'I am sure there are many pros and cons about the proposal and I for one am certainly not able to draw any instant conclusions. Perhaps, James, you could email me a copy of the proposal and we all could then discuss it.'

Adam hoped this would diffuse the conversation, but Grace wanted to continue.

'James is a stubborn old mule. He's living in the past and wants, like many people around here, to keep it that way. Eastside can barely keep a shop going and as Sarah will tell you, the local Tordon primary school is struggling to stay open. Daymouth isn't too bad, at least there's a bit of life there, but Adam, I am sorry to say that you have chosen to end up in a beautiful but dead spot. Why on earth did you choose Eastside?'

'Grace, I'm not sure yet why exactly I choose to live here, but I take your point, although at the moment I'm very happy here. Yes, it's beautiful. Yes, it's quiet and I'm enjoying that. Yes, the countryside and beaches are fantastic and I'm enjoying that too. And yes, I have found the locals on both sides of the shore pleasant and engaging. In London, I lived in an apartment block where I knew no one and that seemed to be the way everyone wanted it. It is different here.'

Grace gave Adam a hard and exasperated look and then suddenly burst into a glamorous smile. 'Adam, I can see we will have to teach you a few things in the next few months!'

This seemed to mark something of a truce and the rest of the evening passed off in a congenial way. It was gone 11pm before Adam finally left the house and as he walked the short distance to his cottage, he mused on recent events. The decision to trial for the lifeboat was a strong positive, the issue of Jasmine's family involvement with drugs was a definite worry, and now the Marlo Eco Park with the name Ian Carbrook coming up in both drugs and this development was a real concern. From the evening's visit, Adam couldn't really work out the Holberton family at all. James seemed to be an amiable 'old school' sort of person and both Grace and Sarah, a bit unknown. Grace was fiery, of independent mind as well as being glamorous, whilst Sarah had what could be described as having hidden natural beauty.

*

Adam arrived at the lifeboat station at the same time as Laura and she gave him some quick advice.

'Just be yourself and good luck! Remember you only get one chance at being accepted for training.'

They both went into the room together and were met by Ted Sandringham, the coxswain.

'Ah hello, Adam; let me introduce you to the crew. We've a few members missing but most of us are here. I presume Laura or Ben Lewis, who I believe you have also met before, have told you the form. We normally give you five minutes maximum to tell us about you and then we have open house where any of the crew can ask questions. We'll let you know afterwards of the decision. I am afraid our Local Operations Manager Billy Cavendish is away today and he needs to be involved too, so it may be a couple of days before you hear anything.'

Adam gave a short summary of his life, making it clear that he currently didn't know much about boats but he was very fit and competed in triathlons in which, of course, swimming was a requirement. He also talked briefly about the Putney attempted suicide rescue and how that had changed his outlook on his lifestyle and how it was a major factor in him deciding to live in Eastside.

Ted Sandringham stood up and said, 'Thanks, Adam; I made that four minutes and thirty seconds, so well done at keeping to time. Let's have some questions from the floor.'

'Hello, my name is Tina Harding and I'm one of the local doctors here in Daymouth as well as being a member of the crew. I think all current crew members also have other jobs and from what you've told us, you don't seem to have or need one. Do you think this could be a problem for all of us if you were to join up?'

'That's a very tricky question to be asked first! Tina, I honestly don't know… perhaps some of the lifeboat crew may also be your own patients and I'm sure you have found a way of combining your professional medical life with the successful integration into being a member of the lifeboat crew. I hope I shall be able to do an equally good job. Yes, I realise I almost certainly have a very different background to probably everyone in this room; however, I have a strong desire to be part of the RNLI team, integrate fully with Daymouth life and help contribute in the best ways that I can to the RNLI and the town.'

'So, what skills can you add to us?' said Jimmy Lethbridge, who was a local marine engineer.

'One positive is that I'm very fit. I wouldn't have been able to rescue the chap from the Thames if I hadn't been an extremely strong swimmer; from what I've already seen, I suspect the Thames tide is even stronger than here in the estuary. I'm also pretty good at maths and computing. I presume electronic equipment plays an ever-increasing role in all your operations and so I hope I would be able to use that skill to help. I want to be part of your team. I have to admit that, for the last ten years, I've been working mostly by myself as a City trader; however, that is something I need to change and is one of the reasons for wanting to work with the crew and contribute in the best way that I can.'

There were several more questions and, after about half an hour, Ted brought the interview to a close and thanked Adam for attending. Adam then went to the Smugglers Inn for a couple of pints of beer and, after about an hour, was joined by Laura.

'Well done,' said Laura. 'You did OK, maybe a couple of slip-ups but I think they liked you. If you are accepted though it's going to be tough for you to integrate; it will definitely take time.'

CHAPTER 3

Adam had a restless night wondering whether he would be accepted as a trainee member of the RNLI crew. He hadn't been interviewed for many years and now realised he'd been quite nervous during the meeting. Becoming a lifeboat crew member now seemed to be a very important part of his new life.

In the morning, after an early beach jog and breakfast, Jasmine arrived at the cottage to both do the housework and also have a meeting with Adam.

'Let's talk,' said Adam. 'Our lives seem to be getting more complicated by the day.'

They went outside to the terrace that overlooked the estuary and sat around the patio table.

'I guess summer's really arrived. Look at the queue already waiting on the Daymouth side for the ferry. I suppose you're used to this every summer?'

'Yes,' said Jasmine. 'July and August are the months when the whole estuary comes alive. Without it we just wouldn't survive the winter months. Look, Adam, I am so sorry to drag you into all of my domestic mess. I was really surprised to see you at the Holbertons' the other night and Ben Lewis was out of order to tell you about how he thinks Ian Carbrook is involved with Jack and drugs.'

'Jasmine, I'm learning pretty quickly that life here has its own complications and inequalities. I must admit that I have never been quite so close to them as in my first few weeks here; however, I'll try and understand as best I can and, if possible, help. In terms of Jack, I feel I must take some sort of action. Ben raised issues about this chap Carbrook and then within a day I'm hearing that the same man is involved in a controversial £30m project. You don't need to be a rocket scientist to suspect that the Marlo Eco Park project could be a money-laundering exercise if he was the conduit for Jack's drug selling and jail sentence.'

Adam told Jasmine that he would talk to Ben Lewis again and maybe the police. He also suggested that she ask if Jack would be prepared to talk to him if he visited Dartmoor Prison.

In the afternoon, Adam decided a walk was in order to help clear his thoughts; however, as he was passing Estuary View, he was confronted by both Grace and Sarah Holberton.

'Hello Adam,' said Grace. 'We were clearing up after lunch and saw you coming along the road from the kitchen window. We'd both like a word, but for quite different reasons! Have you got time to talk?'

'Yes of course, how can I help?'

Grace clearly wanted to get in first and said, 'My usual bridge partner has gone off for the summer and I've just had an invitation to a summer evening game of bridge with Ian and Susie Carbrook. Would you be prepared to partner me? It's this coming Saturday at seven o'clock. It would be wonderful if you'd come. We could get to know each other and it would also give you the opportunity to meet the Carbrooks. Ian's the chap my husband talked about who's proposing to develop the Marlo Eco Park and it would be a chance to sound him out.'

Adam had to do some quick thinking as to whether it was both a good idea to go with Grace and also, meet up with Ian Carbrook.

'Doesn't your husband James play bridge?' enquired Adam.

'Oh, good gracious, no; he hates bridge and anyway he's going to a gathering on Saturday at his London Club and will be staying in London overnight.'

'Well, OK,' said Adam, 'maybe this once. I'm not really a bridge fan, but if this helps you out, fine.'

'Excellent! I'll come to your cottage at let's say 6.45 on Saturday and we can walk together to the Carbrooks'. I'll let them know I've found a partner. Now, Sarah, it's your turn to have a go!'

'Anthea, my yawl crew, has just gone and broken her leg, which means she won't be able to crew for me in the Yacht Club regatta week, which is in a fortnight's time. I was wondering whether you'd be prepared to sail with me for the week? At dinner, you did express an interest in learning to sail and this might be a chance. We'd need to do a bit of practice beforehand but with you living so near and our yawl 'Golden Eagle' moored close by, I thought it might work out. It's a bit of a long shot, but it would be great if you could.'

'Two invites in two minutes from two different ladies! Yes, if you think you can get me up to speed in time in teaching me how to crew, it would be a pleasure and thank you for the invitation.'

'That's settled then,' said Grace. 'You can play cards with me and play boats with Sarah!'

*

On the following day after his early morning beach jog and breakfast, Adam went across to Daymouth and met up with Laura at the Smugglers Inn.

'Hi Laura, have you any lifeboat news?'

'If you mean your crew application, no. However, there was a shout last night when an incoming yacht got into trouble at the entrance of the estuary on the bar. She was a French boat and they didn't realise that near the estuary bar at low tide, the channel's very narrow, so they drifted onto the sandy bar and got stuck. I was on the all-weather boat, the ALB, and we managed to tow them off without a problem, although I only got to bed at about 2am this morning and so I'm not in great shape today.'

'Well done,' said Adam, 'but sorry you were short of sleep. I think I'll go and see if Ted's about and try and discover if I'm in or out. I'm really finding the not knowing quite stressful.'

When he got to the lifeboat station, he found Ted in the office area writing.

'Hi Ted, is this a good time to have a chat or should I come back later?'

'Maybe later, perhaps in an hour's time. I'm in the middle of writing the report on last night's incident and it's important I keep concentrating in order to get things right and in the proper order.'

Adam made an exit and went for a stroll along Main St.

'Hello there,' said a voice coming out of the chemist's shop. 'I haven't seen you for a while.'

'Beryl, nice to see you again. Sorry, I've been over on Eastside side for the last few days apart from coming for an interview to join the lifeboat crew.'

'Oh yes, I know all about that, I told you when we first met at the top of Ferry Steps that I was the Daymouth gossip and so there's not too much that goes unnoticed by me on this side of the estuary.'

'Well, perhaps you could tell me whether I am in or out of the crew.'

'That, Adam, is for the coxswain to tell you, not me! Anyway, I hear you're going to crew Sarah Holberton in the yawl for the Yacht Club regatta. I hope your life isn't going to be too complicated. Laura from the Smugglers Inn, Jasmine Sanders as your housekeeper and now Sarah Holberton; and don't forget Sarah's mother. Grace may be a few years older than you but she fancies her chances with younger men.'

'Beryl, I just don't know where you get all your gossip. I shall have to be more careful what I say or don't say in the future. You seem to be something of Daymouth's very own Agatha Christie. Talking of murder and intrigue, do you know how I can contact the local policeman here?'

'Try the harbour office just along the road. I saw our local PC Plod, Chris Thompson, go in there about half an hour ago.'

Adam smiled at Beryl, said goodbye and headed off to the harbour office.

*

'Hello, constable, please may I have a private word with you?'

'Yes, of course you can. All the locals here call me Chris and if I'm not mistaken, you're Adam Ranworth who recently moved into one of the Eastside waterfront cottages. How can I help?'

'I'm a bit surprised you know who I am; however, with every day that passes here I seem to be surprised by something. I suppose you know what I'm here to talk about?'

'Well, probably not your application to join the lifeboat team, so then it may well be about Jack Sanders; I think his wife Jasmine's your housekeeper.'

'Yes, you're right about Jack, but Jasmine wasn't keen that I should talk to you. I think she's afraid that Jack or her family will get into deeper water than they are at the moment if the affair gets raised again with the police.'

'OK, so it was probably Ben Lewis then. He's convinced that Ian Carbrook is involved, and the death of Jasmine's father Dan is linked. He's told all of Daymouth except me and the police and if he came to me, I would tell him that he's wrong. Jack is, of course, an idiot as he wouldn't tell us who supplied him with drugs, but we're 95% sure his supply came from a county line syndicate operating from London with an outlet in Princewater. We've been trying to track them down for some time, but they're clever, ruthless and slippery. We looked closely at Jasmine's father's death and couldn't find any evidence of foul play or link it to drugs. Ian Carbrook was a very successful businessman and since he's been in the area he's been heavily involved in good works and Parish Council business at Eastside. I think he's even proposing to provide major finance for a development project on the Eastside side, although I don't know any details. If you like, I can give you the phone number of the Plymouth detective that took charge of the case. Paul Barclay's a good chap and I'm sure he'd be happy to discuss it if you've genuine concerns or information.'

'Thanks,' said Adam. 'I'm most grateful for your comments and suggestions. You seem to be several steps ahead of me at every point and now I feel embarrassed having raised the issue at all; but yes, I would like the contact number and maybe when I've learnt a bit more, I could contact him.'

Adam left the harbour office and headed back to the lifeboat station hoping that Ted would now be free to talk.

'Yes, it's OK to talk now,' said Ted. 'I've just finished my report on last night's shout. I suggest we go and sit in the comfy chairs by the window.'

When both were seated, Ted looked directly at Adam and said, 'I'm afraid you've given me quite a problem. We've a couple of crew members who have reservations as to whether you would fit into our team, or should I say family. I personally think family is a better description of the way we operate here. Daymouth is a bit special; we've a tradition of using local people and we have, for decades, been a tight-knit group of people and think of ourselves very much as a family. In fact, in some cases the bond between the lifeboat crew is greater than the crew's own family ties. The lifeboat crew family bond is one of our great strengths and as coxswain I can't afford to lose that quality.

'Having said all that, I personally liked, particularly, what you had to say about computer skills, and I do believe your skill base could be very useful to us. You were right to say that electronics and computer technology plays an ever-increasing role in our operation and that's an area where we currently aren't strong. So, as those who had reservations about you didn't feel strongly enough to totally blackball you, I'm going to take a risk and say yes, we'll take you on probation, but we will have to take a long and hard look at you before committing any further. I sense you know yourself that you'll have to earn the faith and trust of the rest of the crew and so it will really be up to you to earn your place here.'

Adam's mouth was dry and he was aware that he'd been extremely nervous about what he might have been told. 'Thank you, Ted. I really did think you were going to say no. What a relief. I must say I didn't realise just how much I wanted to do this until I thought I was being rejected. I don't quite know what to say, except thank you again for giving me the chance.'

Ted got up from the chair. 'Now that the formalities are over, let's have a cup of coffee and I'll give you something that will become a very important part of your life here.'

They spent the next half hour with Ted explaining the basics of operation and discussing the way in which 'exercises' were carried out each Wednesday evening and sometimes on Sundays. Ted also gave Adam the all-important pager and explained, 'You need to keep this with you 24/7. If you hear the pager go off, you then have to respond immediately with a message whether you are on for the shout. If you are on, then you drop everything and head straight for the station. I or Billy will then know who's coming and we can decide whether we need the inshore lifeboat, the ILB, and or the all-weather lifeboat, the ALB, and who the crew will be. At this probation stage you'll be just an observer; however, right from the start you must act as though you're fully prepared to do whatever job you're given. We use mobile phones for non-urgent messages, but it's the pager response that is the crucial, time-critical action.'

Adam tried to absorb all the information Ted had given and after thanking him yet again for accepting him, he went off to the Smugglers Inn in the hope of a drink and seeing Laura.

'Well done, Adam,' said Laura who was behind the bar. 'Have a pint on the house. You know I wasn't sure that you would have been accepted, which is why I didn't say anything.

I guess Ted talked about the family bit to you and that's very important to all of us. We sometimes put our lives on the line for others and ourselves and so it's really important we trust one another. I'm very happy to have you in our family and it's a real chance to get to know you, not just across the Smugglers Inn bar!'

*

On returning to the Eastside shore, Adam's mobile fired off and it was Sarah.

'Hello Adam, there's a nice breeze today, would you like to come out for a practice sail in 'Golden Eagle' this afternoon? We could meet up at the boat around two o'clock. She's on the mooring off the house; you could come in your boat and I'll use my paddleboard to get there.'

'OK, why not! By the way, I've just been accepted for probation on the lifeboat and so if my pager goes off, I'll have to go immediately to the lifeboat station!'

'Ha-ha, aren't you the keen one!' exclaimed Sarah.

Adam and Sarah arrived at the 'Golden Eagle' mooring at the same time. The sun was out and a warm sea breeze was blowing down the estuary. Sarah was on her paddleboard wearing a swimsuit with a small rucksack on her back and was looking both very able and attractive.

'You certainly look the part,' said Adam. 'Do you have any sailing gear? I didn't know quite what to wear and now I'm feeling a bit overdressed.'

'You're fine,' replied Sarah. 'I've life jackets in the boat and a whole range of stuff in the boat that you can use if you wish. The important thing is to enjoy and get a feel for sailing.'

The rest of the afternoon involved Adam moving up a very steep learning curve in relation to wind direction and the function of the key parts of the yawl. Sarah was an excellent teacher and soon had Adam able to master the jib, sailing both upwind and downwind. The sunny force-two wind was a perfect introduction to sailing and he was a fast learner.

'You really are a natural at this game,' said Sarah. 'I'm very impressed how quickly you've got the hang of balancing the boat and working the jib. I never expected you to be able to do this so quickly. Oh, watch out, we're in trouble!'

A momentary lapse of concentration by Sarah at the helm had resulted in her not noticing a mooring buoy and it had got caught around the rudder; the yawl had come to a sudden halt and was being swept around by the tide.

'Watch your head. The boom's coming over!' And, with that, there was a sudden crash as the boom slammed across the boat, barely missing both Adam's and Sarah's heads in the process.

It took them some time to sort the tangle of the mooring buoy out and they became the centre of attention of a group of holidaymakers on the beach who were following events. 'That's one problem with Daymouth,' said Sarah. 'If you make a mistake on the water, everyone will know about it within minutes.'

The rest of the afternoon's sailing went without further incident and Adam was warming to the company of Sarah and her undoubted sailing skills. It did feel a bit as though he was back in the classroom being told what to do; however, they were both enjoying each other's company and the glorious weather.

When they got back to the mooring, Sarah pulled out a

couple of beer cans from her rucksack and they sat in the boat with a drink.

'That was fun, Sarah, many thanks; I enjoyed it and learnt a lot.'

'A pleasure for me, too. You were an excellent pupil and a very fast learner. You even survived our little incident with a cool and undamaged head! If nothing else, I think you'll be good on the lifeboat; that requires a cool nerve and attitude. You know I'm quite jealous of you being on the boat. At one stage, I thought about it too, but decided because I'm teaching at Tordon it's too far away to be able to respond to any pager alert. Our next step is to do a practice sailing race before the regatta. Are you up for that? There's a club race tomorrow at two o'clock. Shall we have a try?'

'Yes definitely, but I must be back ashore in time to partner your mother at bridge in the evening!'

*

The Saturday afternoon practice race went well, although Adam found it all a bit hectic with other boats milling about. The wind had been similar to his earlier sail in the week with Sarah and they were pleased with their performance of seventh out of twelve boats in their class.

Adam was changed and ready by a quarter to seven when his doorbell rang and he was faced with Grace who was wearing a long flowing summer dress with plenty of bling. 'Hi Adam, are you ready for a night out in Eastside!'

'I guess so; but please be gentle with me. I've a few bruises; not I hasten to say from Sarah, but your yawl. 'Golden Eagle' does seem to have a tendency to bite as you move around the boat.'

'Yes, I know, that was one reason why I gave up sailing yawls years ago. Terrible boats and of course all those ropes get in the way too.'

As soon as Adam had closed the cottage door, she grabbed his arm, hooked her own arm onto his and steered them along the road towards Taylor's Cove.

'You'll enjoy the Carbrooks. They are, or should I say *were*, good friends of ours. I fear Ian and my husband may have fallen out over the plans for the Marlo Eco Park, but Susie's sweet. James is in London so we should have a very jolly evening. Now, what bidding convention do you follow in bridge?'

'Acol bidding is the only one I know, is that OK?'

'Yes, perfect, that's the one we use around here too. Now I have to tell you that I'm not an ace player. I do it more for the social fun, so please don't expect miracles.'

Adam and Grace arrived at Taylor's Cove and were met by Ian and Susie Carbrook who were in the garden. 'Welcome to Sunny View,' said Ian. 'It's good to see you, Grace, and this presumably this is your toy boy, Adam!'

'Ian you are awful,' replied Grace. 'Adam and I are just good friends and you must be nice to him; he is, as you know, a new resident to Eastside and you may need his support in the future in that Marlo Eco Park scheme of yours.'

'Look,' said Susie, 'we're here to have a nice evening playing bridge and definitely no local politics. Grace, lovely to see you, and Adam, to meet you too. It's also a lovely evening and so we've set everything up by the pool.'

The four made their way to the large swimming pool that was at the front of the house overlooking the golden sands of Sunny Corner beach, where Adam often went for a morning swim.

Susie looked at Adam and said, 'I think I've seen you jogging and swimming from the beach and you may be wondering why we have a pool; well, I'm slightly handicapped in one leg after a ski accident a few years ago, so Ian had the pool especially made for me. We don't use it in the winter but it's a lot warmer than the estuary and certainly the sea. You're most welcome to come and use it if you like when the water gets really cold.'

'That's very kind of you. I'm a keen triathlon competitor and swimming is one of the three sports, so I'm used to cold-water swimming; in fact, I quite enjoy it. But thanks anyway and I may take you up on it.'

Drinks were circulated and the group walked around the pool and garden.

'Susie, you do have such a beautiful house and garden in a fantastic setting and on an evening such as this it looks like paradise.'

'Yes, you're right, Grace, but you have a lovely house too, so I guess we're all very lucky. Adam, how about you? Are you happy at Eastside Cottages?'

'The location is fine and my neighbours Admiral Tom and the Holbertons have been very welcoming. I am also excited to have just heard that I've been accepted on a probation period for the lifeboat. It's early days yet and I am beginning to discover quite a lot of things about the estuary and its inhabitants.'

Adam glanced at Ian Carbrook but could not detect any response to his comment.

'Good luck to you,' said Ian Carbrook. 'We moved down here from East London some five years ago when I sold up my company. What a contrast; I'd worked my socks off building up a European Logistics Company and after I sold that, we moved here. A huge difference and what a joy. We also have a place in Antigua to cover the UK cold months and an apartment in Menton near Monaco. We did a lot of business on the Mediterranean coast and when the money started to come in, I got a taste for the odd flutter at the casino in Monaco. Do you by any chance play poker as well as bridge?'

'I do play poker, but in the past, only for pleasure or very small stakes. I find it quite a fascinating game where my maths background can be very helpful. I have to admit I'm very much better at poker than bridge; however, I can enjoy the social side of bridge more than poker.'

'Excellent,' said Ian. 'I'll remember that for the future and I'll introduce you to some friends; however, tonight we shall play a civilised game of bridge with Susie and Grace. Susie doesn't do poker or approve of me doing it; however, it does take us to Antigua and the South of France, which she greatly enjoys.'

After refilling their wine glasses, the foursome moved to the bridge table and began playing. It soon became clear that the pairings were quite well matched. Ian and Susie had played a lot together and their bidding seemed to be well synchronised. Grace and Adam's bidding was more unpredictable and Adam's skill made up for Grace's mistakes in both bidding and the laying down of cards. They played for nearly two hours with the Carbrooks emerging as close winners.

'That was fun,' declared Grace. 'And Adam, you were an angel. You played so well and covered up my mistakes. We make a great team!'

After further rounds of drinks, Adam and Grace left to go to home with everyone in a cheerful mood.

'We look forward to seeing you both again soon,' said Ian.

'And Adam, perhaps we can have a chat about the Marlo Eco Park project and poker.'

It was dark when Adam and Grace reached Eastside Cottage and Adam said to Grace. 'Would you like me to walk you home?'

'Adam, I thought you'd invite me in for coffee.'

He paused, and then responded. 'I don't think that would be a good idea, do you?'

'Oh well, it was a good try, and no, I think I can manage to get back to Estuary View on my own. Thanks for being such a good bridge player and let's hope we can meet again and play more games in the future!'

CHAPTER 4

Jasmine had talked to her husband Jack during one of her visits to Dartmoor Prison and he was totally against Adam coming to see him. It was only after Jasmine threatened not to visit him at Dartmoor again that he very reluctantly relented.

The car journey to Dartmoor Prison took Adam around the town of Ashburton before he reached the moor itself. It was midday in the summer and the scenery was particularly beautiful, although the copious number of summer holidaymakers made his drive towards Princetown slow. Even in summer, the small town next to the prison struggled to look attractive and the first sight of the prison building was very ominous.

The signage for visitors was good and Jasmine had primed him as to what he should expect. She had said that Jack would be more miserable than usual as she usually visited him weekly and he was taking up this particular week's visiting time.

On arrival, he had to empty all his pockets and the only possession he was allowed to take in was a book that he had brought for Jack as a present.

'Jack Sanders is second on the left,' said the prison officer. 'He's expecting you.'

Adam sat down opposite Jack and put the book on the table that separated them.

'Hello, Jack. I'm Adam Ranworth and I'm now living in Eastside Cottages. Jasmine has agreed to continue as housekeeper for the cottage and I've recently met both your children Jamie and Sally. As a newcomer to Daymouth, I seem to have been drawn into local affairs in a way that I've never experienced before and both Jasmine and Ben Lewis have talked to me about you.'

'I'm sure they have,' replied Jack. 'Look: I'm doing my time and I hope to be out of here in another eight months or so. I told Jasmine you wouldn't be able to help and I really don't want to talk about the affair. In fact, I said stay away and it's only because I don't want to cause further trouble with Jasmine that I agreed to see you.'

'I fully understand, Jack, and I'm not sure why I'm here either, but Jasmine thought you might be able to help me out in relation to an Ian Carbrook who lives on the Eastside shore, and also something Ben Lewis said to me.'

Jack looked straight at Adam and their eyes fully engaged with each other for the first time.

'Before we talk about that, can we get something straight? I'm locked up here and we both know Jasmine is a very attractive woman. I get very jealous of any male around my Jasmine and being in here, it's very easy for the mind to think up lots of terrible things. You have to tell me that there's nothing going on between the two of you.'

'Jack, there is absolutely nothing going on between us. I admit I felt sorry for your family situation and as you probably know I've arranged a monthly allowance for her and all the family. I want to help if I can but there's absolutely no ulterior motive. I've already learnt that Eastside and Daymouth are very small places and that everybody knows nearly everybody else's movements. Please trust me; all I want to do is help, although I'm not sure that I can even do that.'

Jack took a hard look at Adam and eventually gave a faint smile. He then said in a softer voice, 'Jasmine and the kids are the only things that keep me going in this hellhole, so I really do hope you're telling me the truth. You will help look after her while I'm in here, won't you?'

'Yes, Jack, I'll try my best, but at the moment I don't know what to do for the best. Let me explain. I bought a small boat from Ben Lewis and he's convinced that Ian Carbrook is in some way tied up with your father-in-law Dan's death that night when he was fishing off Eastside beach. Dan was Ian Carbrook's gardener and Ben believes there is a drug connection somewhere. He's frightened to go to the police for fear of losing his job and he's tried to persuade me to get involved. Jasmine doesn't believe there is a connection and nor does the local police officer, Chris Thompson. In addition, I've now met Ian socially and he seems a nice enough chap, although he's evidently proposing a £30m Marlo Eco Park at Eastside, which I suppose could be tied up with some sort of money laundering. So, I'm left in the middle of a puzzle that I really don't want to get involved with, but I feel a duty at least to talk to you.'

'I haven't heard anything about the Eco Park project,' said Jack, 'but Jasmine keeps going on about Ben Lewis's theory of a link between Dan's death and drugs. I just want to get out of this place. I made a huge mistake and I and my family are paying the price for me being an idiot. I was lured into something I should never have got involved with and found myself dealing with people from another world. Scary, ruthless and quite horrible. All I want to do is protect myself and my family from them now and in the future and that means I'm saying nothing. I know if I do, we shall all pay a heavy price. There're a lot of drugs in this place, and even you being here today will attract attention. There are people here with connections to the outside who'll pass on information to those contacts and I've got to be careful. I must protect myself and my family, which is why I've not told the police, Jasmine or anyone else how I got involved and who supplied the drugs. I'm in this shit hole because of that, but I know if I did talk, there would be very nasty consequences.'

'OK, I understand what you are saying and it didn't occur to me that even coming here might cause trouble. Can you say anything about Ian Carbrook, good or bad?'

'No, not really. Dan worked for him as a gardener for the last few years and he didn't seem to have any problems with him. He was grateful for the work, even though it wasn't particularly well paid; getting all-year work at Eastside or Daymouth is really difficult. Yes, in the summer months, like now, it's easy, but in the winter, no. The real problem is that there aren't real prospects for young or even middle-aged people like Dan. When I get out of here, I'm not sure if Benson's will have me back. I'm a good skilled boat builder, but even that doesn't count for much now. The estuary's filling up fast with rubber ribs, which are now mostly imported. There used to be work on the farms but that's steadily dried up too. It's a very beautiful area but living as a local, on local wages, is tough; nearly as tough as being in this shit hole.'

Adam tried to raise Jack's spirits but found the going very difficult, particularly as he realised the vast gap between his own wealthy position and that of Jack and his family. At the end of the meeting, he passed on the book, *Maritime History of the West Country*, which he had bought for him, and they parted with a reassuring handshake.

'You will look after Jasmine while I am away, won't you?' said Jack.

'Yes, I'll try and do my best,' replied Adam as Jack was led away by an officer back towards the cells.

*

After Adam had returned from Dartmoor, Admiral Tom invited him in for a drink on his cottage patio overlooking the estuary.

As soon as Adam had sat down, Admiral Tom asked Adam how he had got on at Dartmoor.

'How did you know that I was going to Dartmoor Prison today?'

'Simple,' said Tom. 'Jasmine told me and I've invited her for a drink this evening as well.'

At which point, the doorbell rang and Jasmine joined the party.

'So, Adam, how did you find Jack?' asked the Admiral.

'Hang on a second,' said Adam. 'Jasmine, are you happy for me to talk about this in front of the Admiral?'

'Oh yes, of course. The Admiral has been a rock through all of this and without him, I would probably have crumbled. He's one of the few people here who actually supports me. The Holbertons have been kind, too, but I feel the Admiral actually understands the nightmare Jack and I are going through.'

'Well, OK, but I'm afraid there isn't really much to say; you warned me Jack was very low and right from the start he was concerned that I was having an affair with you. I assured him I wasn't, but I guess when you're in prison you probably worry a lot about that sort of thing. He really didn't want to talk about any drug issues. He was frightened that if he did, both he and his family could be in serious danger. He's really scared of the people that lured him into selling drugs and I believe his concern is entirely justified. I've never been involved in anything like this, but I've no doubt Jack knows what he's talking about. He knows there are real dangers both inside and outside prison from these sorts of people.'

'Oh dear,' said the Admiral. 'This doesn't sound good. Jasmine, you must carry on supporting Jack. Adam, do you have any ideas?'

'None whatsoever, I am afraid. He didn't say anything about Ian Carbrook except that Jasmine's father worked as a gardener for him and that Ben Lewis does the winter maintenance on his yacht, "High Life". He didn't hint that Carbrook had a connection with drugs and all he wanted to do was keep his head down and get out of Dartmoor Prison in eight months' time.'

'Right, let's sit down here and enjoy the summer evening sunshine,' said the Admiral. 'Life's too short to stew on problems that we can't solve here and now, so I'm going to open another bottle of wine and we'll just enjoy the evening.'

'I can't stay long, Mum's looking after the children, but yes that would be lovely to enjoy some different company in such a nice setting.'

As the Admiral went into his cottage to fetch the wine, Adam looked across at Jasmine and then realised why Jack was so concerned about her. She was indeed very beautiful. She'd made an effort to look her best and for the first time since he'd met her, she had a serene beauty and calmness about her that he hadn't seen before.

*

The following day was a buzz of activity for Adam as he had his first RNLI pager call and managed to reach the lifeboat station within the eight-minute limit.

'Nothing special, Adam, but as it's a nice day and I thought you ought to have your first trip on the all-weather boat, the ALB,' said Ted. 'We've had a report of a drifting boat off Wreckers Cove with nobody apparently on board, so it should be a pleasant jolly and you can watch what's going on.'

Ted picked a crew of seven people out of the group of twelve that had responded to the shout, including both Laura and Ben Lewis. Dr Tina Harding was also in the team and Adam remembered that she'd given him a bit of a hard time at the inaugural interview.

He was told to stay out of the way and note what the rest of the crew were doing as the team went through a very structured start-up procedure. Suitably attired in RNLI yellow and orange gear, he felt both a part of the team but at the same time, a bit of a spare part.

It took about five minutes for them to leave the jetty and then they were quickly into the estuary. Because the shout wasn't an emergency, Ted kept the boat to the six knot estuary limit; however, as soon as he was out into the open water, he opened the throttle of the engine and the boat was travelling at an impressive twenty-four knots. At this speed, the ALB created an equally impressive wake and all eyes around the estuary would be admiring the sight of the lifeboat showing its true colours. The engine noise was very impressive too and Laura came on deck to talk to Adam.

'So how do you feel? Not seasick, I hope.'

'At the moment I'm fine and doing what I've been told to do by keeping out of the way. How long do you think it will be before we get to the boat?'

'At this speed I would say fifteen minutes max to Wreckers Cove. It's a beautiful day and the sea state's good. Ted does like to have a bit of a blast in conditions like this, and why not? This is the fun part of the job.'

When the lifeboat arrived near Wreckers Cove, the drifting boat was quickly spotted and they came close to an eight-metre high-powered twin outboard open rib with no one on it.

'Look at that!' declared Tina Harding. 'One hundred thousand pounds' worth of boat just floating around. I bet someone didn't tie it up properly last night and it drifted out with the tide. I'm surprised no one saw it; I think it's Dan Pitcher's boat, all that bling and loudspeakers are a giveaway.'

The estuary sticker on the side of the rib had a code number, and radio contact with the shore quickly established that the boat did belong to the Pitcher family. The boat was brought alongside the ALB and the decision was made to tow it back to Daymouth. Ben was assigned to ride in the boat and Ted decided that Adam could keep him company.

The journey back to Daymouth continued at a very sedate pace with Ben and Adam sitting comfortably in the plush seats of the rib.

'This is the life,' said Ben. 'Pure luxury and nothing to do but enjoy the tow in the sunshine.'

'Yes indeed, but can we have a few words about Jack Sanders? I saw him yesterday in Dartmoor under very different circumstances to us now and I found the whole experience both unsettling and a worry.' Adam then explained to Ben about his conversation with Jack and how he had found him totally unwilling to talk about drugs, or any Ian Carbrook involvement.

'Ben, maybe you could give me some background on what you know about Jack and why you think Carbrook could be involved.'

'I've known Jack and Jasmine for a long time; we went to school together. Jack and I were both lucky to get work at Benson's as apprentices and although the pay isn't very good, it is at least all-year employment. Jack married Jasmine and they were fortunate to get one of the Eastside so-called affordable homes. As soon as they started a family, I know money got very tight as they had a mortgage to pay off and Jack was always worrying about Jasmine because he knew she was very attractive and intelligent. I know the marriage went through a few rocky periods; Jack used to talk a bit about it at work. He felt inferior and not able to provide a more comfortable life for the family. Jasmine earned some money from housekeeping and cooking work, but there still wasn't enough money to make ends meet. He wanted the best for her and the kids, but he couldn't really afford it.

'A few months before he got nicked for selling drugs, I saw quite a change in him and Mr Benson had to have him up for some shoddy work. It was a shock to everybody as the drug bit just seemed to come out of the blue. Then he wouldn't tell anyone where he got the drugs from. Jasmine and I just couldn't get any sense out of him, although I suppose it does make some sense now that you tell me he's saying nothing because he's afraid of the consequences if he grasses on the suppliers.

'After that, Jasmine's father Dan goes and dies whilst night-fishing. I just don't buy it that it was an accident. Dan worked as a gardener for Carbrook, who may well have been the supply source or have known who supplied Jack with the drugs. I just don't believe in coincidences like that and when I was cleaning out Carbrook's yacht last year, I found a packet of white powder under one of the cushion-covers. I left it where it was and didn't tell anyone, but at the time I wondered if he was into drugs.'

'Hang on, Ben, it's one thing to find a packet of powder in Ian's boat and quite another to believe he masterminded the supply of drugs to Jack and the murder of Jasmine's father.'

'Put that way, I agree; but I knew Jack very well and I could sense he knew Carbrook was tied up with Dan's death, but for some reason wouldn't talk about it.'

'OK, Ben, let's leave it at that for a bit. Thank you for giving me some background and now, as we make our way back, how about showing me how to do some of the knots that I need to learn?'

By the time the lifeboat and towed rib had reached the estuary, Adam had learnt how to tie a number of nautical knots including the all-important bowline. The rib was tied up alongside the lifeboat at the jetty and the decision was made to make Dan Pitcher come to the lifeboat station to retrieve it and, as Tina Harding had said, 'Grovel and give an explanation for what was presumably very poor mooring practice.'

When Adam was changing out of his lifeboat gear, Tina came up to him. 'Adam, I understand you're crewing Sarah in the Holbertons' yawl during the regatta. Sarah and I usually have good races against each other. My partner Tim is my crew and it would be good to meet up sometime. It's a pity Anthea has broken her leg; she and Sarah were a great combination. Have you sailed much in the past?'

'Not at all,' replied Adam. 'Complete learner and I've only done a couple practice sessions with Sarah. She is however a great teacher so I do hope I'll be OK.'

'Well, good luck,' said Tina ruefully. 'The competition's pretty hot and watch out for collisions with inexperienced crews.'

Adam wasn't quite sure how to take the last comment and just smiled back at Tina.

*

On returning to the cottage, Adam saw that he had a text message to phone his ex-Cambridge friend David Young.

'Hi David, how can I help?'

'Thanks for calling back. It's August and I've just realised that I haven't done anything about having a holiday this year. We had this big merger project going on in London and I've lost track of time and my senses. Well, the job's now done and I was wondering if I could come and stay for a bit.'

'That would be great, David, one thing though: I've agreed to sail in a regatta in a week's time and so will be tied up with that then. You're very welcome to come down whenever you like, but during that week I'll be pretty busy.'

'No problem. I'm happy to play it either way. I can come before or after the regatta, whichever works best for you.'

'OK, come as soon as you want to, it'll be great to have you down and you can catch up with all the gossip that goes on down here; I could do with a bit of friendly advice.'

'Great! I'll be there in about three days' time. I have to

say that I thought it would be OK with you and I've already bought a couple of kayaks that I'll bring along. We can get some of that triathlon stuff going again and include a bit of kayaking.'

'I look forward to that. Great to hear from you and I'll get the beers in.'

After the call, Adam pondered on how pleased he was at the thought of having the company of an old friend to talk to. Daymouth had been an interesting experience; however, the process of getting to know such a diverse and very different new group of people in such a short time had proved to be unexpectedly challenging.

Within minutes of finishing the phone call, there was a ring at the door.

'It's only me' said Sarah with a big smile. 'I was hoping we could have a final practice sail tomorrow before the regatta as it could be a bit windy and we haven't really sailed in a breeze yet.'

'Yes fine, I've nothing planned; that is, of course, if I don't have another shout like today!'

'I saw the lifeboat go out this morning; were you on board?'

'Indeed I was, and it was an interesting experience. A big rib owned by a chap called Dan Pitcher had drifted out overnight towards Hope Cove and we went and towed it in. Ted thought it would be a good trip for me to gain some experience on the ALB. I didn't do anything other than keep Ben Lewis company in the rib when it was towed back.'

'Ben's a nice chap. He is, or should I say was, a good friend of Jasmine and Jack Sanders.'

'I think he still is. I went to Dartmoor Prison a couple of days ago to talk to Jack and I talked about that with Ben on the boat back to the estuary. We talked about Ian Carbrook as well; Ben thinks he might be involved in the drugs mess that Jack got himself in.'

'Oh, you have been dragged into local gossip, haven't you? I'm sorry, but I've little sympathy for Jack. He has a lovely wife and family, so why blow it on some drugs caper? And talking about gossip, Dan Pitcher is Daymouth's very own rich boy prat and he is an absolute arsehole! Let's meet up at ten o'clock tomorrow morning to go sailing.'

*

Sarah woke up the following morning to see driving rain with a full gale blowing down the estuary and she decided today was not a good time to go sailing yawls. Instead, she thought it might be an opportunity to introduce Adam to Bert Appleyard, the local farmer who, with Ian Carbrook, was proposing to develop the Marlo Eco Park. She was keen that Adam joined the 'pro' group for the project rather than her father, and other Eastside residents, who were very anti. Yesterday's mention by Adam of Ben Lewis's theory that Carbrook might be tied up with drugs had worried Sarah into thinking that Ian's involvement in the Marlo Eco Park could be thought of as being for ulterior motives, which would turn people away from a project that she believed was the right way to go.

'Hello Adam,' said Sarah on her phone. 'Today looks a write-off for sailing, but would you like to come with me to meet Bert Appleyard? He's the farmer involved with the Marlo Eco Project. When I was at college, I worked for him during the summer vacations and got to know him quite well. He's a real loner and so since then I've visited him quite regularly.

He's a rough diamond but you might find it interesting to talk to him.'

'OK, that's fine, Sarah. I had already decided to give my morning run a miss because of the rain. Do we drive, cycle or walk there?'

'Let's walk; it gives us a chance to have a chat first and get wet at the same time.'

Sarah and Adam met up at ten and started walking along the rainswept road towards Bert Appleyard's farm.

'He's a funny sort of bloke,' said Sarah. 'Something of a recluse and very much his own man. His wife left him about ten years ago when she went off with a travelling farm feed sales merchant from Barnstaple and he's never been quite the same since then. He drinks a lot and just lives in isolation. They had two children who've moved up country and neither of them are interested in farming. Their only interest seems to be, how much is the farm worth and when is their father going to sell up? I'm one of the only people who've taken any interest in Bert's welfare and I've visited him regularly since his wife left. Bert's on the Parish Council and I think that's because he's tried several times to sell plots of land on the farm for building holiday houses but hasn't managed to get planning permission. The whole of Eastside is an AONB, Area of Outstanding Natural Beauty, and so getting permission for a new-build is nearly impossible. He thought being on the local council might help him to get permission but that hasn't worked so far. However, times are changing and with the arrival of Ian Carbrook, who came up with this mega plan for the Marlo Eco Park, Bert's farmland would be ideal, especially as some of it has water frontage. Carbrook seems to have plenty of money and although he talks of a £30m development, according to Bert, he's prepared to put in a lot more.'

After a five-minute walk, Sarah and Adam arrived at the farm and Sarah confidently walked straight into the ramshackle farmhouse kitchen.

'Hello Bert, how are you today? I've brought one of our new neighbours to see you. Adam's now living next door to the Admiral in one of the Eastside cottages and he's being drawn into the Marlo Eco Park project.'

'Sarah, I'm not feeling great today. It's pissing with rain. I can't do anything outside and the contractor was meant to come and cut the wheat field. So no, it's not a good day and I've already had to take to the whisky.'

'That's a pity, Bert. Perhaps I could make you and us a cup of tea?'

'If you insist, but I'll have mine with whisky too.'

Bert had ignored Adam but he tried his luck making conversation. 'Mr Appleyard, I hear you have a big project with Ian Carbrook and I'm interested to know about it. The project seems to have divided Eastside in terms of those that are for and those against.'

'You're fucking right there, and excuse my language, but I'm a farmer. All I want to do is sell the place at a decent price. I can't make any money from farming here and I don't think anybody else can. The bastards won't let me build the odd house on the property and so when Ian came along with this scheme to build eco villas, I jumped at the opportunity. He's got the money and I've got the land. In fact, I now think it's a bloody good idea. If something isn't done, this whole bloody area will end up as rest homes for wealthy retired people. There's little work for the youngsters and the place is dead in winter. It used to drive my wife bonkers and look at her now. Gone off to Barnstaple to live with a bloody salesman.'

'Well, do you think you stand any chance with this Eco Park project?' asked Adam.

'I dunno. This chap Carbrook seems to know his stuff and he's been working on the District and County Councillors. He's a clever bugger and, unlike me, he talks the talk that they want to hear. And, unlike me, he's absolutely loaded and that seems to help too. I just wind everybody up and they think I'm from another planet. In fact, I'm not; it's just that I'm a different class of person. Poor, direct and with no fancy airs and graces. They don't understand what real work is all about. They just mix with their own kind and have no idea how real hard-working people have to live.'

Adam was in no mood to challenge any of Bert's outburst and in many respects he had a lot of sympathy for his views. 'So, if you had to give a score out of ten for a successful planning application, what would you give this one?'

'Maybe five, perhaps six. Carbrook has built a team of people around the project. Architects, hospitality consultants, and he's also working hard lobbying the silly buggers that work in planning at the Shire and County Hall. As I said, he's a clever chap and so it might succeed. If I was alone, I'd give it zero. The councillors all around here know me and I wouldn't stand a chance.'

'Here, Adam, have a cup of tea,' said Sarah. 'Bert, here's your tea too and yes, it does have a drop of whisky with it. Let's all sit and watch the rain whilst Bert tells us how we can grow some of the finest wheat in Devon.'

CHAPTER 5

David Young arrived three days later just as Adam was about to go for his morning jog along the beach.

'Adam, great to see you and you do look tanned; this Daymouth air must be doing you a lot of good.'

'David, great to see you too. It must be a few months now since I last saw you and maybe my tan does show. You look quite pale; have you been working too hard?'

'Yes, I have! We've had this big financial project and I was working 24/7, so without you around, I let the exercising slip. I'm now mentally knackered, but hey, this looks fantastic! What a wonderful location. Beautiful weather today and it looks like paradise. Please say I can stay on for a bit? I need to recharge my batteries and at the moment I envy you for making the break from London. I wish I had the courage and resources to do that too.'

'Of course, you can stay as long as you like and at some point, you'll be able to make lifestyle decisions as I did; however, I have to warn you, life in paradise can be a bit more complicated than you might think, and certainly different to what we were used to in London.'

The two of them unloaded the kayaks that David had

brought with him and stowed them on the waterside terrace. David did a rapid change into his shorts and they went for a beach jog that inevitably turned into a beach race. They were always very competitive when exercising together.

When they reached the beach at Sunny Corner, the competition continued in the water as both of them swam out towards Greystone Rocks.

'This is fantastic!' gasped David when they reached the rocks. 'What a place.'

'Yes, it's fun. How about swimming back to the cottage? We can come back later and pick up the running stuff. It's about a mile swim to the cottage and the tide will be with us. A word of warning though: watch out for holidaymaker boats, kayaks and paddleboards, some of them aren't too clever with their navigation skills.'

The swim resulted in a flat-out race between the two of them with a very narrow victory to David.

'Well done,' said Adam, 'you always were the stronger swimmer; but watch out when we get on the bikes!'

They came ashore, showered and sat down in the sunshine on the terrace overlooking the estuary and soaked up the glorious weather and view.

*

As the afternoon went past, Adam suggested they go across to have a look at Daymouth.

'Great idea,' said David. 'I need to meet some of the lovely ladies you've been talking about. Which of them live in Daymouth?'

'I think you're talking about Laura who works at the

Smugglers Inn and is one of the lifeboat crew. Look, David, I know you like the ladies, but I want you to behave. The locals are a close-knit group and I don't want you rocking the boat. I'm trying to live here.'

'Adam, you're beginning to sound just like my mother. I hope you haven't moved down here to set up a monastery.'

They both went down to the beach and Adam hauled in his boat 'Greta' from the running mooring.

'First, I need to teach you some nautical skills on how to operate the outboard and handle the boat. You don't need a licence to drive on the water, but at this time of the year there're so many holidaymakers on ribs, paddleboards and kayaks who may not know what they're doing. On a day like this, it can all be a bit crazy.'

David was a fast learner and after a few trial runs, quickly got the hang of 'Greta'. Adam had to caution him several times for speeding, but within an hour they were both having a lot of fun weaving between swimmers and boats as they explored the busy part of the estuary and also collected the clothes they had left on the beach before going swimming.

'Time to visit Daymouth,' said Adam as he brought 'Greta' up to the quayside. 'Let's go and have a drink at the Smugglers Inn.'

It was the height of summer and, with the regatta coming up, the town was at its busiest. They fought their way through the crowd and eventually got to the bar of the Smugglers Inn.

'Hi Laura, good to see you. Two pints of bitter, please. This is David Young who's staying with me for a bit.'

'Nice to see you, Adam, and hello to David. It's bedlam at the moment. I've never known it so busy. I'm being worked off my feet. I've been at it all day.'

'Hello Laura,' said David. 'Daymouth and Adam are so lucky to have someone like you to serve them drinks! Now I know why he keeps talking about you and why there are so many people at the bar!'

Laura had spent a lot of her life on the other side of the bar dealing with people like David. She took a long look at him and said, 'Thanks for the compliment and I hope you enjoy the drinks. You do look very pale so you must be a visitor from somewhere like Birmingham or London?'

Adam and David took their beer out into the inn garden to seek refuge from Laura and for them to find somewhere to sit.

'Hello Beryl, I'm surprised to see you here in the pub garden. I thought when the tourists were about you hid yourself out of the way! This is David, a friend of mine who has come down from London for a bit.'

'Hello to the both of you,' replied Beryl. 'At last, I have someone to talk to, do come and join me. My goodness, David, you do look pale. Do you spend all your time on the underground in London?'

'No, it's not quite as bad as that, but I'm looking forward to catching up with some sun now that I'm down here.'

'Adam, I do hope you've introduced David to Laura. I had high hopes that you and she would become an item, but you don't seem to have made any sort of move. It's time that girl found someone like you, or maybe David.'

Adam turned to David. 'Beryl is the Daymouth gossip and is a mine of information about everything local, although I didn't know she had potentially paired me up with Laura.'

Beryl continued, 'Look, Adam, I know you have got your hands full with the beautiful Jasmine doing your housework and both Sarah and Grace Holberton chasing after you, not to mention Dr Tina Harding looking on. However, Laura is a match made in heaven for either you or David. I do hope one of you make a move sooner rather than later before someone else who is totally unsuitable comes along and snaps her up. Just look around at all those male holidaymakers on the prowl out there at the moment.'

'But I'm a holidaymaker too,' said David.

'You're different; I can see it in your eyes. Both you and Adam are good guys. I know that.'

There was a momentary silence between the three of them; however, after that, they all had a drink and carried on chatting. The conversation was light-hearted and David quickly felt at home as Beryl and Adam were talking about the town and the coming regatta.

'Oh yes, the regatta's going to be fun!' said Beryl. 'I don't think Adam quite knows what he's let himself in for. He's agreed to stand in and crew for Sarah Holberton in the yawl. Sarah's great rival is Tina Harding and there is no love lost between the two of them. Adam's going to have his hands full on the water coping with that; and then there's the Annual Eastside Regatta Beach Party; Grace Holberton organises that. It's one of the top social events of the year and everyone who is anybody will be there plus a few hangers-on like me. I presume both of you will be going?'

'That's the first I've heard about the beach party,' said Adam. 'Maybe we will be invited?'

*

Jasmine Saunders arrived at Eastside Cottage on the following day and Adam introduced her to David.

'Jasmine, this is David, and he'll be staying here with me for a bit.'

'Hello Jasmine, what a great pleasure to meet you! David didn't say anything about him having such a beautiful housekeeper, you look radiant.'

'David, that's quite enough! Behave yourself. I think the best thing we can do is go for a long bike ride and leave Jasmine to get on with things here.'

They sorted themselves out with cycling gear and started on one of their challenging cycle tours. Adam had now become familiar with the local terrain in Devon and he led them through twisting and hilly back roads until they eventually reached Ashburton on the edge of Dartmoor where he knew a coffee shop.

They sat outside in the garden drinking their coffee.

'Look David, you must stop this chat-up stuff. Jasmine's in a tricky situation and the last thing I, or I believe she wants, is to have you pestering her.'

'Adam, what's got into you? I'm on holiday, the sun's out and both Laura and Jasmine are very attractive. Have you turned into a monk or are you jealous?'

'I'm not a monk and I'm not jealous. I'm trying to make a life down here and I need to be careful. Laura's part of the lifeboat crew and, as I said, Jasmine is in a difficult situation. She's married with two young children. She did housework for the previous owners of the cottage and persuaded me to keep her on. Her husband, Jack, is in Dartmoor Prison at the moment because he got involved in selling drugs. I've visited him there as I got drawn into the possibility that a house owner on Eastside called Ian Carbrook might be involved in some way. It's all very messy and Jack's afraid people like you and me will try and get off with Jasmine while he's in prison. So please at least lay off Jasmine.'

David took a long look at Adam, smiled and said, 'I'll try, but you must admit she does look great and Laura is pretty good too. You are a lucky boy to have them around and as friends.'

After they had finished their coffee, the two of them really tested their fitness against each other by taking a twenty-mile cycle ride around Dartmoor. Both were pushing hard and were being particularly competitive on the challenging climbs that they had to face. A further thirty-mile cycle ride back to Eastside meant that by the time they had returned to the cottage it was fair to say that they were exhausted. Jasmine had finished work and gone home; this left both men time to recover sitting outside in the evening sun overlooking the estuary.

Later that evening, the doorbell rang and Sarah Holberton appeared on the doorstep.

'Hi Adam. I tried to contact you today but you must have been out. It's forecast to be windy tomorrow and I wondered whether we could go for a sail as we haven't practised much in a real breeze. The regatta starts next week and it would be good to get a feel for stronger conditions before then, in case we get any windy days during the regatta.'

'Sure, happy to do that, let me know tomorrow when I should be at the boat. I've a friend David Young staying with me for bit; come through and meet him.

'David, this is Sarah Holberton who lives just along the road and I'm crewing her in the yawl regatta next week.'

'Hello Sarah, what a pleasure to meet you. You look stunning; Adam is such a lucky chap to be surrounded by such beauty and in beautiful surroundings.'

Before Adam had time to say anything, Sarah came in with, 'Nice to meet you too, but you do look a bit pale. Are you ill?'

After a slight pause, David responded. 'Oh, apologies. I did mean what I said, but maybe I didn't say it in quite the right way. And no, I'm not ill, I'm based in London and I've been working very hard over the last few months, so I've not spent time outside for a long while. But now I'm down here, I hope to make up for it; this is a glorious part of the world.'

Sarah smiled, having established her position with David.

Adam then provided some drinks for the three of them and they spent the next hour enjoying getting to know each other and chatting about the upcoming regatta.

Sarah got up from her seat ready to leave. 'I really must go now as my parents are organising the final details for our regatta party, and of course you're both invited. David, you'll be an interesting addition. Someone new, pale-faced and obviously not from this part of the world! There'll be about a hundred people coming and dress is very informal but people do make the effort to look smart. We have a marquee arriving tomorrow to go on the lawn, but if the weather's fine we'll be using Eastside beach in front of the house. Please don't bring presents or a bottle, this is my parents' annual treat to Eastside and Daymouth.'

'That would be great,' replied Adam. 'I'll personally make sure David behaves himself and if he doesn't, he'll be packed off back to London. Let's hope for fine weather!'

*

When Adam awoke on the following day there was a strong wind blowing down the estuary and he'd received a text message from Sarah that they should meet up at the yawl at around 11am in order to catch the midday high tide.

After an early morning beach run, Adam and David had breakfast together; however, whilst Adam was preparing to go sailing, his lifeboat pager fired off.

'Heck. I have to go!' he shouted to David as he ran out of the cottage heading for 'Greta'.

By the time he had crossed the estuary and got to the lifeboat station, Ted was already deciding on the composition of the crew.

'This is a very busy time of year for everybody and I'm going to be short of crew. I've a number of texts to say that people can't make it because they've got to work. We need the ALB for this one as it's a reported fire on a yacht about five miles off. There's a very stiff breeze and it will be pretty rough out there. Adam, I need the support and so you're on board. Do what you're told by me or any of the other crew.'

Adam hadn't expected this and had to collect his thoughts. He quickly texted Sarah to say sailing today was off and then he put on his RNLI heavy weather gear. He had been on four previous training exercises on the ALB, but this was only the second time he had been on a proper shout.

It was a definite emergency and Ted had the boat on full thrust even in the harbour. Within minutes, they were out into open water and the very strong southerly wind was kicking up a big sea. The whole crew was inside the boat and strapped into their seats as they pounded through the waves at about fifteen knots. The noise inside was considerable and conversation between Adam and Ben Lewis, who was sitting beside him, wasn't easy. He leaned over to speak to Adam.

'This is a serious one. Ted said that a yacht caught fire and he thought the crew of three had abandoned the boat. There was only a short Mayday call and then the coastguard control at Falmouth lost all communication. We're short-handed and you'll probably be called into action. I hope you're feeling strong. It could be very difficult. Picking up survivors in this sort of sea's never easy and Ted may need the small daughter rib launched off the ALB stern for recovery.'

At that moment the coxswain came over on the intercom. 'We're approaching the site of the last recorded message from the yacht 'Pegasus'. I need you all to keep a close lookout for either the yacht, which we can't pick up on the radar, or a life raft or individuals in the water. Ben, Jimmy and Adam, get ready to go below and put drysuits on. I may need you to launch the rib or work from the stern platform deck. Tina, get ready for the collection of survivors, they may have burns. At the moment, we're alone on this. The rescue helicopter won't be here for at least another half-hour and the crabber 'Impala' is motoring towards us but won't be here for twenty minutes. Remember, the safety of our own crew is paramount and so no one must take any action without my say-so.'

The whole crew went silent as the ALB smashed directly into the mounting waves with a force-six wind now blowing over the exposed water, out of sight of land.

Thirty seconds later, Ted came back on the intercom. 'OK, Ben, Jimmy and Adam, go down and put your drysuits on. We can't see the boat; it may have sunk. I think survivors must be in the water. In these waves, it's going to be difficult to get anyone on board from over the side of the boat. We'll either need the rib or we'll have to use the stern platform.'

Adam followed Ben and Jimmy Lethbridge, who was the ALB engineer, down below and they all put on drysuits and life jackets whilst being thrown about by the boat movement. In the confined space below, the noise of the hard-working twin engines was colossal and Ben needed to point to Adam indicating that they should move to another section of the boat.

'It's a bit quieter here,' said Ben. 'If Ted tells us to, we lower the transom and that provides a waterline platform to work from. Then we can launch the daughter rib over the platform into the water. It can be really tricky in these conditions. If we go afloat in the rib, it will be Jimmy and myself in the boat. You'll need to stay on the platform. Whatever happens, you do what Ted or I tell you.'

The intercom came alive again. 'We are now at the Mayday location and there's no sign of the yacht; it might have sunk. The plan is to carry out a local box search. All above deck, take observation positions and those at the stern prepare, but do not open the transom, and get the rib for launching, we may need it.'

There was both authority and urgency in the voice of the coxswain. Ted had been a member of the lifeboat crew for many years and coxswain for five. This shout involved high seas, a possible sinking and the real danger of losing lives. He had experienced a yacht fire incident in the previous year and a separate sinking three years ago. The current situation was potentially as difficult as they come, but he knew every incident had the potential to be life-threatening.

Within two minutes, there was a shout from the navigator, Jon Payne, on the intercom.

'Life raft sighting on the starboard bow.'

Immediately, the coxswain came back. 'I'll position us to weather of the life raft with the stern facing the raft, then we can lower the transom and get the rib out to make the recovery. It's far too rough to recover from the side. Ben, prepare to lower the transom when I give the order and get ready for you and Jimmy to take the rib to the life raft. You'll need to make sure there's a line between the rib and the boat; but watch out that it doesn't get caught up in anything like the prop of the outboard.'

Jon Payne came in on the intercom. 'I can see two people on the life raft; they've seen us and seem to be OK. They've both got life jackets on.'

'Good,' responded Ted as he started manoeuvring to windward of the life raft. 'I thought the Mayday said there were three people on the boat?' After a short pause he came back on the speakers. 'OK, I'm in position. Ben, open up the transom, but be careful, the waves are massive.'

Adam had never seen the opening of the transom before and to witness this in the prevailing conditions was awesome and scary. The transom opened like a door on enormous hinges and formed a horizontal platform that exposed the sea literally at sea level. As the boat pitched in the waves, the platform rose and fell, with seawater coming up the lower part of the platform when the stern was in the trough of a wave.

'Blimey, this is scary,' said Adam.

'Quick, connect yourself to a lifeline,' countered Ben. 'I forgot you haven't done this before.'

Adam connected himself to a lifeline and looked out of the open transom at the turbulent sea. By positioning the ALB head to wind, the boat offered some shelter at the stern of the boat and the movement of the boat was nearly only fore and aft, rather than from side to side. The panoramic view of the sea was mesmerising, but suddenly he registered an orange image in the corner of his eye and then recognised it as a near-submerged person.

'There's someone in the water near the stern!' shouted Adam.

Ben immediately pressed the speaker button to communicate with the coxswain.

'Ted, we have a person in the water near to the stern of the ALB. Male, looks absolutely knackered, but I think he's alive. What action do we take?'

There was a short pause and the coxswain then came back.

'Priority is the casualty in the water, we can pick up the life raft people later. Who is the strongest swimmer down there?'

Ben looked around and saw Adam nod. 'I think I must be,' said Adam.

Ted remembered the Putney Bridge story Adam had told at his interview and immediately replied, 'Get a lifebuoy and line onto Adam and send him to swim out to the casualty. Haul him in when contact is made. Tina and Jon, I want you down on the platform immediately to help out. Ben, you need to advise me on positioning the casualty. I can see the person on the stern camera, but it isn't easy to judge distance.'

Jimmy fixed a line to a lifebuoy and put the buoy over the head of Adam. There was no time to think and within seconds Adam was jumping into the water and paddle-swimming towards the orange shape of a person that appeared at the peak of each wave and then disappeared in each trough.

By navigating using the stern camera and with guidance from Ben, Ted was able to hold the stern of the big lifeboat about thirty feet from the casualty and it took Adam about two minutes to reach the man. As he got closer, he was able to see that he was in poor shape and then he saw his eyes.

'Oh no, not another!' Adam said to himself. He had a flashback to seeing the look in the eyes of the man that had jumped from Putney Bridge. 'Not again, not again!' he muttered as he closed in towards the exhausted man.

The man was barely conscious, but his life jacket was keeping his head above water. Adam was able to connect onto him, signal to the ALB and the two of them were then pulled towards the ALB platform.

'Now comes the difficult bit,' said Ben on the platform. 'I need Jimmy, Jon and Tina all to be ready to catch Adam and the casualty when we get them to the boat. Jimmy and Jon: you take the casualty, and Tina and I will take Adam. They both need to come aboard at the same time. Chief, are you happy with that?'

'Yes, but be careful; they mustn't go under the boat.'

Adam had now been in the water for about five minutes and he was becoming tired. He was also getting worried as to how both he and the casualty were going to be brought back onto the platform. As they were being hauled in towards the stern of the ALB, the closer they got, the more frightening the proposition appeared to be.

When they were within ten feet of the ALB, Ben positioned a plastic chute over the edge of the platform and Adam and the casualty were pulled onto the chute and dragged up it onto the platform.

It all happened in seconds and the next thing he remembered, he was lying on the wet stern platform, looking into the eyes of Tina Harding, with her saying, 'You look OK to me. I need to attend the casualty.'

Tina had to work quickly and hard on the casualty as he had taken in a very large amount of seawater. She skilfully attended to him and, using the speakerphone, said to Ted, 'We need to get this chap to hospital as quickly as possible, he has taken in a lot of water. Is there any chance of a helicopter?'

'OK. I'll get onto that and work out the best option. Ben, we need to pick up the two in the life raft. I think the best thing here is for me to get to the windward side of the raft and then slowly drop down until you can throw a line aboard. We don't want or need anyone in the water. When the line is attached, you can haul them in and haul the whole raft up the chute. Do you agree?'

'Yes, that should be OK. Adam looks shot and Tina is caring for the casualty. We should however be OK with Jimmy, Jon and myself.'

'You'll have to be. I need everyone else up here.'

The life raft recovery in fact went well and the two crewmen were safely brought on board. Both were in reasonable condition and extremely relieved to see the third man lying on the platform floor.

'Clear the platform and get that transom closed,' called Ted on the intercom. 'We need to get back to the estuary and calmer water where we can make a helicopter transfer. It's now on its way and should be here in about fifteen minutes.'

The casualty was carried into the survivors' cabin where Tina gave him a strong sedative and wrapped him in a thermal blanket.

One of the other survivors started to shake uncontrollably through shock rather than cold. The third survivor seemed to be coherent but then began to cry with emotion.

'The boat's gone, but thank you so much for saving us,' he sobbed. 'We thought we'd lost Jack too, but here he is. Is he going to be OK?'

'We'll do our best,' said Tina. 'He's taken in a lot of water and his lungs are full of the stuff. We'll do what we can.'

Ted and the navigator, Jon, together with the helicopter pilot, worked out the best course of action for getting the casualty to hospital and decided that an airlift to the helicopter in the shelter of the estuary and then a direct flight to the hospital at Plymouth was by far the best and safest option. This involved a rendezvous off Taylor's Cove and a winch up from the lifeboat. The crews of both lifeboat and helicopter had practised this many times and, providing the casualty was able to cope with the lift, it was preferable and faster than a land transfer and ambulance to hospital.

The lift went well and as soon as the critical casualty was in the helicopter, it sped off towards the Plymouth hospital. The ALB returned to the Daymouth quay and the remaining two survivors landed and were sent off in the waiting ambulance to the local hospital for check-ups. The ALB crew sorted the boat and then went back to the lifeboat station.

'Well done, everyone,' said Ted. 'That was quite something. I think we all deserve a cup of tea. Normally, I'd say let's go and have a real drink at the Smugglers Inn, but the place is heaving and we wouldn't get a minute's peace there. I think we need a bit of calm here together. Everything happened so fast, it's difficult to take it all in at once.'

The crew sat around drinking their tea without saying much and it was only when Laura arrived in the room that spirits were raised. She had rushed over from working at the inn. 'The news is all over the town. People were listening in over the radio and so everyone knows that a yacht went down and you've saved three lives. Brilliant and congratulations, is everybody OK and is the boat OK?'

'Yes,' said Ted. 'We're all in one piece and everyone did their job properly. We were lucky to identify one casualty in the water and two others in a life raft. Picking up the life raft was straightforward but the single casualty was challenging. He's not in good shape but by now he'll be in Plymouth Derriford Hospital and having the best treatment he could have. The crew were great and I couldn't have asked for more. I'm sure we'll learn from the whole experience, but right now I think we all probably need a bit of space to recover and remember, please try and avoid the press. The whole business will eventually come out in the proper channels.'

Laura went over to Adam and asked. 'Adam are you OK? You look a bit shocked.'

Tina was within hearing range and answered, 'Yes, he'll be fine. He was a hero and went in the water to bring in the casualty. It was very brave and I'm sure we are all proud of him. If the chap survives, he may well owe his life to Adam.'

Adam looked at Tina and then Laura before saying, 'Thanks both, at the moment I don't know whether I'm all right or not. I saw the same look in the chap's eyes that I saw from the bloke that I pulled out of the Thames. It's very scary and I need a bit of time to take stock.'

*

David was waiting for Adam's return to the cottage as he had witnessed both the helicopter lift-off at Taylor's Cove and the lifeboat return to the Daymouth quay. When Adam opened the cottage door, David saw the look on his face and he immediately went up and embraced him. 'I've seen that look before; when that chap jumped off Putney Bridge and you saved him.'

'Yes,' replied Adam, 'it's something like that, maybe not quite as bad, but at the moment I feel absolutely drained. Like Putney, it all happened so fast.'

'Do you want to talk about it? I've had that Admiral chap next door asking whether you were on the rescue and both Jasmine and Sarah have phoned. It seems as though everyone's aware of a rescue operation and wants to know about it.'

'Let me go upstairs and have a couple of hours' rest and try and sort myself out. We can talk about it this evening.'

Adam went upstairs and got straight into bed. He closed his eyes and within minutes was asleep. He then slept for over two hours and on waking up, heard voices from downstairs.

As he came downstairs he saw David, the Admiral, Sarah and Jasmine looking at him.

David said, 'Sorry about this, Adam, but everybody was worried about you and, well, they all turned up at different times. We opened some wine and, well, we just ended up chatting.'

'It's OK. I've had a good sleep and feel a lot better. Thank you, everyone, for coming round.'

'We were all worried about you and, I have to admit, wanted to know about the rescue,' said Admiral Tom. 'There's been a lot on the local news about it and even the national BBC lunchtime news had a piece about a yacht sinking off Daymouth. This sort of thing doesn't happen very often and it's in the middle of the holiday season too.'

'Yes, and then everyone saw the helicopter casualty lift and so we all knew it must have been serious,' said Sarah. 'It was really windy too and I heard you were on the ALB because they were short-handed. Tina contacted me and said you were very brave and did a great job. For her to say something like that is very unusual. Over in Daymouth they call her the "Ice Queen".'

The Admiral poured Adam a large glass of wine and Adam then sat down with the group around the table and recounted the story. As he did so, he began to feel much better for being able to share his experiences with others. He had reached the point in the story where the ALB had returned Daymouth when he had a call on his mobile. He saw that the call was from the coxswain, and he took the call on the speaker phone.

'Hi, Adam, I'm phoning to say thank you for everything you did; however, I have some sad news. Derriford Hospital have just phoned to say that the casualty you rescued has just died. His lungs were just full of water and they were unable to save him. I'm really sorry to bring the news, but thought you should know.' Everyone in the room had heard the call and there was silence.

'Thanks, Ted, for letting me know, I'm with friends and am going to ring off now.'

Adam put down the phone, looked around at everyone in the room and began to cry.

CHAPTER 6

The following morning, there was glorious sunshine with a gentle breeze but the emotional roller-coaster experience of the previous day was still very much with Adam, and David as well.

'How about a morning run?' said David, as they were having coffee outside on the terrace.

'Not today,' replied Adam. 'I just don't feel up to it at the moment and I've had a text from Ted asking me to meet him at ten this morning to sort out the reporting of yesterday's shout. David, I'm really glad you're here, I've got to talk this one through with friends. Last time, with the Putney Bridge business, I bottled it up and I'm now thinking that wasn't the right thing to do.'

Adam took 'Greta' across the estuary and met up with Ted, Ben and Tina at the lifeboat station.

'Sorry about this, but because the casualty died after the shout it means a lot more paperwork. There will, of course, be a Maritime and Coastguard accident investigation and the usual RNLI stuff. The Devon coroner will be involved as well. You all did a great job and, as Tina was on board and is a fully qualified doctor, the reporting of the casualties will be that much easier.

'The press are going bonkers at the moment and I've had to bring the RNLI press officer in to handle them. Richard Thoms will be here later to cover the situation, and in the meantime, I'd be grateful if you say as little as possible to anyone. I know this might be difficult in a place like Daymouth, particularly at this time of year when there are so many people about.'

The group then gave brief verbal accounts of their experiences and Ted asked them to go away and write up their respective reports whilst it was fresh in their minds. The meeting was very sombre; Ted finished by saying:

'I'm proud of you all; we worked as a team and from what I can see, we did everything we could to save this chap's life. His next of kin haven't been officially informed yet, but I understand the three on the boat were from Southampton and were heading for the Scilly Isles. From the look of them they were in their early forties maybe with families and children. The one concern I have about the shout was that we were very tight on crew numbers and Adam, although on probation, was involved in the rescue. If someone was looking to find fault, they could say that he shouldn't have been allowed to be directly involved in the recovery of the casualty. The press or an investigation may pick this up, so please be careful what you say in your reports and say as little as possible to other people.'

Tina responded, 'Adam was good. He did exactly what he was asked to do, and yes, he's fit and a very strong swimmer. He was the right person to do the job.'

When the meeting had finished, Adam left with Ben Lewis and they sat down outside on a waterfront seat looking out over the estuary.

'Ben, thanks for your support yesterday, you were great,' said Adam. 'We seem to be drawn to the same problems. Jack and Jasmine, the Carbrook drug issue, Dan Pitcher and his drifting super rib, and now this; a real tragedy and I for one thought we had done some good saving this chap.'

'Yes, I thought so too. I've had one rescue before where we had to recover a dead swimmer, but this one's tough. You think that you've done some good and then discover you haven't; it's hard to take.'

Ben went off and Adam called in to see if Laura was about at the Smugglers Inn. 'Sorry, she's not here today, it's one of her very few days off,' said Charlie Foster, the manager. 'You may catch her at her home, it's on Torr St, over the road and up the hill a bit. She's number 6a.'

Adam was undecided whether to go and see if she was in and he started to return to Eastside, walking towards the quay and his boat 'Greta'. Then he paused, backtracked, and found himself ringing the doorbell of number 6a.

'Oh, hi Adam, what a pleasant surprise! I thought you were my mail order delivery. Do come in.'

Adam felt very embarrassed being in Laura's flat, as he realised that he'd only been with her before either at the inn or on lifeboat business.

'Come and have a drink with me outside,' she said. 'There's no charge, we're not at the pub now! The patio is microscopic but it does have a good view of the estuary.'

They went outside, Laura brought a couple of beers, and they sat down at a small round table.

'Great to see you, Adam. How can I help?'

Adam was lost for words as he himself didn't know why he had come.

'I'm not sure that you can help, Laura, I don't know myself why I'm here. The guy we rescued yesterday has died in the hospital and I guess I just wanted to talk to someone and… well I like you a lot, but maybe never said that to your face.'

'Oh, you are sweet, Adam.' There was a pause and she continued. 'Look, I'm really sorry about the casualty and… I like you too and maybe we can be good friends, maybe even more than good friends; but remember, I'm a very independent person. I love people and that's why I work at the pub and why I'm part of the lifeboat team; but I enjoy my independence too. I was orphaned as a child and I've no parents, no family. I'm on my own and I have to say, at the moment, I'm happy to stay that way.'

'You really are special,' said Adam. 'Beryl was right saying that you were an angel and thank you for saying what you've just said. I was lost for words and you were, what can I say, brilliant. I may have known in the past how to make money, but I'm really hopeless with people. I lost my parents when I was thirteen and since then I've had to fend for myself as well. Maybe we have a bit in common; anyway, let's stay friends and see how things develop.'

*

On returning to Eastside Cottage, David was waiting for him. 'I've been worried about you, are you OK?'

'Yes. I'm a lot better now. I had a long chat about the rescue and the poor chap's death with Laura at her flat and she's helped a lot.'

'Oh, has she? I was feeling sorry for you and now you tell me you were with Laura! You've warned me off Jasmine and I at least thought the coast was clear with Laura and maybe even Sarah. But here you are, back from Daymouth and looking a lot more cheerful than when you went. What piece of magic did Laura work on you, or shouldn't I ask?'

'She was just very kind and said the right things after the meeting with the lifeboat coxswain. Ted's worried that, because I was on probation and involved with the rescue, someone might complain and cause trouble.'

'Surely not? You did your bit and there wasn't any more that you could have done. Come outside and have some lunch, the weather's beautiful.'

Adam and David had lunch together and then, as Adam started to go off to write up his report on yesterday's shout, David said. 'Oh, by the way, that Admiral chap next door has invited us to supper tonight and I've agreed to take Jasmine and her children on the water in 'Greta' to watch you and Sarah sailing next week in the regatta. She was very excited about that and is looking forward to it.'

'David, I know I can't stop you, but please be careful with Jasmine. She is married. Her husband Jack seems to be a nice guy, even though he is locked up in jail at the moment.'

Adam spent the next two hours reliving and writing down his experiences of the rescue and felt a huge relief when he'd finished. The action of writing had cleared his mind, as had the meeting with Laura.

In the evening, he and David went next door and were welcomed by the Admiral, who was already clearly well advanced in his alcohol intake.

'Ah, the two musketeers! Come and join me. Have a drink. I've opened a couple of fine bottles of red wine which must be finished tonight. Jasmine prepared supper, before she went.'

Although there was a significant age difference between Adam and David and the Admiral, it became clear that the three of them were comfortable in each other's company. The Admiral didn't press Adam for details of the rescue operation and seemed more interested in how he and David had become friends.

David explained, 'We were at the same college in Cambridge, both read mathematics and both shared the same sports, ending up with triathlons. We then went into the City and kept in touch. Adam went off to make zillions of pounds trading and I've done OK with acquisitions and mergers. Now, here we are together again, with Adam trying to start a new life and me searching for a suntan and romance.'

'Yes, you do look very pale,' said the Admiral. 'When I first saw you, I thought you'd come down here to convalesce. Anyway, it's good that Adam has another chap down here. I'm far too old to be a proper friend and it's at a time like this that he might need someone like you to talk to. When I was in the navy, one of the most useful parts of the day was when the officers had supper together sitting round a table on board the ship. We had a few drinks and were able to compare notes and discuss issues that had come up during the day.'

The meal Jasmine had prepared was excellent and discussion moved onto the forthcoming regatta week that was due to start in two days' time.

'This will be my fifth year at Eastside,' recalled the Admiral. 'That means I've seen four Daymouth regattas and they were all memorable weeks. The place comes alive with sailing boats racing in the mornings and the afternoons. The estuary's at its busiest and if the weather's fine, it's a wonderful sight. And yes, don't forget the Holbertons' beach party on Wednesday evening. The social event of the year. I presume you two have been invited?'

'Yes, we have,' replied Adam. 'Sarah invited us and you may know that I've agreed to crew Sarah in their yawl, 'Golden Eagle', because her usual crew, Anthea, has broken her leg. Now I gather that David has offered to take Jasmine and her children in 'Greta' to follow the racing on the water.'

'Excellent! Jasmine needs something to look forward to and I'm sure David will be good company. Does he know all about this Eastside Marlo Eco Park project? Has he met the two men proposing the park, Bert Appleyard and Ian Carbrook, and does he know about split in the Holberton family, with Sarah and Grace pro, leaving James very against?'

'No, I haven't talked about the eco park project and no, he hasn't yet met the Carbrooks, Appleyard or the Holbertons, except for Sarah, and yes, I'm sure the eco park may be a hot subject of conversation at the party.'

'This all sounds great fun,' said David, who had now caught up with the Admiral in alcohol consumption. 'I can see I've a lot to learn and enjoy next week!'

*

The first day of the regatta opened with clear blue skies and a light wind. David helped Jasmine and her children, Jamie and Sally, onto Adam's boat 'Greta' and they were soon cruising happily around the estuary with the many other spectator boats on the water. They came alongside the 'Golden Eagle' while it was still on its mooring.

David called out, 'Hi, you two, are you ready for the race? I've looked at the programme and you're the first start of the afternoon. I hope you know the course!'

Sarah looked across at David and smiled, saying, 'Yes;

we're fine, all set and ready for the fray. It's a beautiful day and light winds are just what we need so that we can get used to racing together. As to the race course, it won't be displayed at the start line until ten minutes before the race.'

Adam noted that Jasmine was looking particularly attractive in her top and shorts and called across to David.

'Please look after your crew and my boat and keep out of our way! This racing is serious stuff; there'll be twenty yawls on the start line and I don't want you interfering with our progress.'

'Yes, captain!' responded David. 'Message received loud and clear.'

The 'Golden Eagle' left its moorings and sailed into the starting area. A hooter sounded, signalling that it was five minutes before the start and Sarah briefed Adam on her plan.

'The wind's very light and the first race mark is a long way towards Princewater. The tide will be taking us in that direction and so we need to make sure that we're not being swept over the line before the start. If we are, we'll have to go back and start again. I need you to keep a look out for other boats; remember, if we're on starboard tack, we've got right of way, but on port tack, we must keep clear.'

Adam could feel the tension mount as the clock counted down to the start. He was responsible for the timing and counted down the final seconds, 'Five, four, three, two, one, go!'

'Oh bother! Not a great start,' muttered Sarah. 'Bloody "Phantom" and "Kestrel" are blocking our wind.'

The yawl 'Phantom' was helmed by Tina Harding and crewed by her husband Jim. 'Kestrel' was owned by Lord Robert Harvey with his wife Lady Jenny as crew and Steve

Mansell as helm. Steve was a top professional helm brought in to steer the boat, as Lord Robert was himself a hopeless sailor but a ferociously competitive man, needing the boat and his wife to win trophies at all costs.

Sarah immediately said, 'We must take a tack and get some clear air, Adam. Ready about, and tack now.'

Sarah worked her way between the other yawls and by the time they had come to the first race mark, they were about seventh in the fleet of twenty.

'Not bad, for a first proper race,' she said. 'Look at Steve Mansell, he's already what seems like miles in the lead. We've got Tina just behind us and that's good! I don't know why Tina and I are so competitive with each other, but we always seem to end up having private battles.'

The race went on for the next hour; Sarah and Adam slipped down the fleet a bit and Tina got up to third at the finishing line with Sarah and Adam ending up in the middle of a crowded fleet.

'Well, we can't win them all,' said Sarah as they sailed towards their mooring. 'Not a bad result for our first race. Halfway in this fleet is a pretty good first score for the series of five races. Pity Tina seemed to find some wind to move up to third and it's absolutely no surprise to see 'Kestrel' win. That chap Steve Mansell is a world-class match racer and bloody Lord Robert Harvey ought to be banned from the club for bringing in a professional ringer to helm the boat just so Lady Jenny can be first across the line for the regatta.'

As Sarah brought 'Golden Eagle' to the mooring, David arrived with 'Greta'. Jasmine and her children seemed to be having a wonderful time and there was lots of laughter from the boat. David shouted across to Sarah and Adam, 'Well, was that a good or bad result? We couldn't really work out what was going on but we had a lovely time on the water and the kids really enjoyed it.' Jasmine looked radiant, adding, 'Yes, well done, you two. I think you were tenth across the line and surely that's a good result?'

Adam was mentally exhausted after having to concentrate so much during the race and added, 'I was working so hard during the race trying not to make too many mistakes that I lost track of where we were. It looks as though you all had a good time in "Greta". David: I do hope you behaved yourself.'

*

The following day was very different to the earlier glorious sunshine. A very stiff wind was blowing and there were lashings of rain.

'Will we race today?' asked Adam when Sarah arrived at the cottage.

'Not sure,' she replied. 'We sail in rain, but if the wind's too strong, the racing may be postponed or abandoned for the day.'

David chipped in, 'Well, I'm going to take Jasmine and the kids to Princewater and we're all going to the cinema. We agreed yesterday if the weather was poor that's what we'd do.'

Adam gave David a stern look and uttered, 'For goodness' sake, David, please don't make my life more complicated than it is already.'

'No worries, Adam. You just go and enjoy yourself with Sarah on the water, in the wind and rain, and I'll look after Jasmine and the kids. They deserve a bit of fun and it's the least I can do for them.'

Adam was annoyed with David about taking Jasmine to Princewater and he felt pretty grumpy as he and Sarah went out in 'Greta' to the yawl to rig the boat in the pouring rain and howling wind.

'Adam, this could be really tough. It's definitely weather where we must have our lifejackets on and it'll be totally different to yesterday. We haven't sailed in very strong wind before and everything's going to be new to you. Safety comes first, survival comes second, and any sort of reasonable result will be a bonus. If we get caught in a gust of wind, just let the sail ropes go. We need to balance the boat when going downwind and if you see the bow go down, come aft very fast, otherwise we shall nosedive and capsize. Once a yawl capsizes, they're very difficult to recover. Apart from all that, let's just see how we get on. We're both fit and strong and so if we can keep out of trouble, we could do OK.'

The race started in driving rain with a force-five wind blowing straight down the estuary. Not all the boats chose to race and Sarah tried to raise Adam's spirits by saying that if they just got round the course, they would be getting useful points for their overall score.

With rain and spray everywhere, Sarah shouted to Adam, 'The first mark is near Greystone Rocks and with the wind against tide, it's going to be tough. Normally I'd short-tack up the shore, but with this wind and our lack of practice, I think we'll be better off using the whole width of the estuary.'

Sarah held back at the start and they cautiously tacked their way to the first mark, rounding it towards the back of the fleet. 'Now the fun begins as we go downwind,' yelled Sarah. 'Watch out for other boats and hold tight! Oh look… 'Kestrel' is capsizing! Steve and Jenny will be in the water! No; they're recovering, but they'll be full of water. That's their race done. Watch out, Adam… gust coming!'

A huge gust of wind hit their boat and 'Golden Eagle' took off in a cloud of spray. 'Blimey,' gasped Adam as the boat screamed down the estuary, barely under control. Sarah was in fact an expert sailor and managed to keep enough control to keep the boat upright. Looking behind them, Adam saw that there were at least three other yawls as well as Lord Harvey's in trouble. 'It's carnage; should we retire?' shouted Adam.

'No way!' yelled Sarah. 'Let's go for it!'

The rest of the race was a battle of nerves, bravado and physical strength. Adam witnessed just how tough Sarah was. Although quite small, she was immensely strong both in courage and physical strength. Her helming skills were outstanding and she even managed to find time to teach Adam how to operate the boat in the extreme conditions.

They finally crossed the line in fourth, one place ahead of 'Phantom'.

'Fantastic!' shouted Sarah. 'We've beaten Tina, and in these conditions, too! Adam you were fantastic; I could give you a kiss!'

The rain was still lashing down when they reached the mooring and they quickly unrigged and took 'Greta' back to shore. As they walked into the cottage, they found David, Jasmine and her children playing a game of hide and seek in the living room.

David looked up and said, 'Ah the wet mariners return! How did you get on?'

'We were fourth and had an incredibly memorable sail,' said Adam. 'How about you? Did you all enjoy your jaunt to Princewater?'

*

The highlights for the third day of the regatta were the sailing and also the prospect of the Holberton party. The sun was out and the wind had come back to a gentle breeze. In the yawl race, Sarah and Adam finished in the middle of the fleet, a few places behind Tina and Jim Harding, with Steve Mansell and Lady Jenny returning to their winning ways after the soaking and retirement they had endured from the previous day's racing. The weather stayed fine for the evening and preparations were in full swing for the Holbertons to have their party on the beach using the garden marquee for food and the band.

In the early evening, David and Adam were sitting on the terrace of Eastside Cottage when David turned to Adam saying, 'I've promised to give Jasmine a hand at the beach bar this evening so I'm going up to the party now. When are you planning to come up, and are you bringing any lovely ladies with you?'

'David, I'm not, as you say, "bringing any lovely ladies with me". I'll ask the Admiral if he'd like to join me and we'll probably get there in an hour or so. Please, please do not get too involved with Jasmine. I know she's very attractive but Jack will not be amused if he gets to hear that you're playing around with her. Eastside's a very small place and I hope to live here, certainly for a bit.'

David said nothing, smiled and then left. When he arrived at the beach, Jasmine was already busy at the beach bar dispensing drinks to the early arrivals. Guests from Daymouth had to work out the challenge of getting across the estuary to the Eastside beach and a number of launches and rubber ribs were moored offshore with Sarah busy bringing people to the beach using the family small boat.

'What fun,' said David as he came up to Jasmine at the bar giving her a quick kiss on the cheek. 'It's great your mum has taken the children for the night. This looks like a proper grown-ups' party. Mine's a beer please!'

'Hi David, where's Adam?' said Sarah as she brought a group of Daymouth guests up the beach to the bar.'

'Oh, he's sulking in the cottage and said he'd be up in an hour or so.'

At that moment, Sarah's parents came down from the house to join the party. Grace was dressed in the only way she knew for this sort of occasion: lots of bling. James was more measured, his extravagance being a Panama hat.

'David,' said Sarah. 'These are my parents, Grace and James. I don't think you've met them before.'

'Delighted to meet you and welcome to our party,' said Grace. 'Both Jasmine and Sarah have already told us about you and it's good to have new faces at the party each year.'

There was a further surge of new arrivals when two large boats arrived, mooring off the beach using their own ribs to bring people ashore. Ted had brought the main ALB lifeboat complete with crew. The Holbertons were strong supporters of the RNLI and it was their way of showing appreciation to invite all the lifeboat crew and their partners to the party. The second boat was Lord Harvey's motor yacht 'Invicta'. He was founder of the London-based Harvey Hedge Fund and they had a holiday home in Daymouth. His wife Jenny was the keen sailor and the reason that Robert Harvey had enlisted Steve Mansell to helm the Harvey yawl 'Kestrel'.

Adam arrived with the Admiral and they collected a drink from the bar where David was happily helping Jasmine. The Admiral drifted off to talk to Beryl, who had also come across on the lifeboat, and Adam was taken aside by the lifeboat coxswain, Ted.

'Thanks for your report, Adam, it was very useful. I've just seen Charlie Holder over there, he's the local reporter for the *South Devon News*. He's here with his photographer. They may not know who you are but try to avoid them. Our press man Richard Thoms isn't here tonight and any lifeboat communication is better coming from him.' Ted paused and then asked. 'Are you all right?'

'Yes, I am OK,' said Adam. 'Thanks for asking. I'm crewing in the regatta with Sarah in their yawl and that's helped me take my mind off the rescue. Yesterday I also learnt that yawls can be very exciting, or should I say scary, in a strong wind.'

'Glad you're back out on the water. Laura told me on the boat coming over that you were a bit shaken up. We need to get you back on the lifeboat soon. I have to say, you've definitely got what it takes to be a member of the crew; all the others have said so too. I think as soon as this rescue investigation is over, we should fast-track you as a permanent fixture.'

Ted's comments raised Adam's spirits and he decided it was time to enjoy the party rather than worry about recent events and David's antics with Jasmine. Looking around the beach, he found a group of the lifeboat crew.

'Hi Adam, come and join us,' said Laura. 'What a great party and I'm not behind the bar! Ben's already pushing us to go and get some food in the marquee, are you coming?'

'Thanks Laura, excellent idea.'

Both Ben Lewis and Tina Harding were in the group and as they walked up to the marquee from the beach, Tina introduced Adam to her husband, Jim. 'I guess you've seen each other before. Jim crews for me in "Phantom" and we seem to have spent much of the time crossing paths with you and Sarah in our yawls.

Jim looked across at Adam saying, 'Nice to meet you, Adam, and welcome to the Sarah/Tina water battle zone! Goodness knows why they compete so much with each other on the water in the way they do. When they're on dry land they are quite civilised with each other! I've been watching you and I have to say you look as though you're really sailing well with Sarah. I've been crewing Tina since we got together and it took me ages to get the hang of it. Take yesterday, for example, you and Sarah did incredibly well to just stay upright in that wind.'

The party food was provided by the local Tordon pub and there was a very generous spread for the very large number of guests present. There also seemed to be an endless supply of drinks from both the beach bar and the bar in the marquee.

Ben Lewis was already well advanced with the beer consumption and joking with Ted that, as coxswain of the lifeboat, Ted had to stay off the booze whilst, as a passenger on the boat back to Daymouth, he could get absolutely smashed, and that is what he intended to do.

Ben and Adam ate their buffet food together and after they had finished, Ben said, 'I must go and find Jasmine while I'm on this side of the estuary and before I get too plastered. I might even get a dance with her when they've cleared the food away. Did you know there's a band and dancing? The Tordon Top Hat Band; they're fantastic.'

Ben was about to go in search of Jasmine when he held back and said to Adam, 'I still worry a lot about Jack and I've just seen that Carbrook guy here tonight and that's reminded me again of the whole drug affair.'

Ben went off and Adam drifted towards the beach. The evening light was now beginning to fade and the pathways were lit with an array of coloured lamps creating a Caribbean atmosphere.

'Ah, Adam, I've been looking for you,' said Sarah, who had now changed into an attractive party dress. 'I met David with Jasmine and he said you were sulking. What's that all about? Come and meet the Harveys, they own that bloody great motor yacht "Invicta" moored off the beach. Lord Robert's a total pain, but Jenny's super.'

Sarah and Adam picked up further wine supplies from the beach bar and then joined a group of yawl sailors including the Harveys. Sarah then introduced Adam to Robert Harvey.

'Lord Robert, can I introduce my new crew, Adam Ranworth; he's recently bought one of the Eastside cottages next to the ferry landing. He used to work in the City.'

'Hello,' said Lord Robert. 'I've never heard of you, but of course the City's a very big place. Do you have a boat down here?'

'Only an outboard boat to get me across the estuary and back. Your own boat looks very impressive. Does it have a professional crew?'

'Yes of course! Crew of six. We use it here and in the Med.'

Sarah saw that conversation between Adam and Lord Robert wasn't going particularly well and so she tried to change the subject and brought Lady Jenny, Robert's wife, and Steve Mansell, the professional helm, into the conversation.

Sarah said, 'Adam and I saw "Kestrel" have quite a moment in yesterday's race. You did really well not to capsize; was there any damage?'

'No damage except a bit of pride,' replied Steve. 'Jenny

was very quick and saved the day. The fault was mine and I don't like making mistakes in front of the boss. Lord Robert sponsors some of my professional sailing in the Med, where I'm normally based in Monaco.'

'Monaco sounds exciting. Is there something special about the place?' said Adam.

Lady Jenny interjected: 'They say it's a sunny place for shady people. But maybe that is a bit unfair. Robert keeps our boat "Invicta" down there quite a bit and I have to say the weather on the Côte d'Azur is a lot better than the UK. However, tonight's wonderful. Sarah, your parents are most generous for laying on such a great party.'

'Well, it won't be long before it really begins!' responded Sarah. 'I think I can hear the Top Hat Band warming up.'

The group started moving back towards the music coming from the marquee and Adam asked Sarah where he could find the loo. 'Go behind the marquee, through the vegetable garden and then onto the gravel drive where there are some posh mobile loos.'

He followed Sarah's instructions using the illuminated pathways, as now it was becoming quite dark. As he worked his way behind the marquee, he noticed two embracing figures who were, in fact, kissing. 'Oh no,' he said to himself, 'it's David and Jasmine!'

*

The Top Hat Band were amazing and within minutes of starting their session, nearly everybody was packed into the marquee and dancing or just swaying with the music. It was difficult to see quite who was dancing with who, as everyone was having a great time and getting tangled together. Even Beryl and the Admiral, whilst not dancing, were swaying with the music and enjoying the atmosphere. Grace Holberton was always in the centre of the action but there were plenty of other people of all ages determined to enjoy themselves too.

Sarah grabbed Adam. 'Come on, it's time for you to get those dancing shoes going.'

Dancing wasn't his speciality; however, Adam was quickly sucked into the melee of people and ended up prancing around with nearly all the women he knew and some of the men too.

He caught various glimpses of Jasmine trying to dance with Ben, although by this stage of proceedings, Ben's alcohol consumption was causing him to have great difficulty coordinating his movements. Later, he saw Jasmine dancing with David. She looked radiant and the both of them seemed blissfully happy.

The band went on to way past midnight and the drinks continued to flow. Exhausted by all the dancing, Adam went to the beach and sat down enjoying the distant sound of music and the tranquillity of being alone by the water. He'd been there for just a few minutes when he saw Laura coming along the beach.

'Can I join you?' she said.

'Yes of course you can. I was thinking of you too.'

'That's nice, Adam. You were really sweet when you came to my cottage a few days ago and I do understand how that rescue must have affected you. I am afraid it can be a downside to being on the lifeboat crew, but maybe you were aware of that anyway after saving the life of the man that jumped off Putney Bridge.'

She paused and then said. 'Look; I have to make a quick choice. Either I go back to Daymouth with Ted in the lifeboat or I come back to your cottage here and spend whatever is left of the night with you. What would you like me to do?'

Adam was taken by surprise, but realised he had to make a quick choice. 'Well, that's a wonderful invitation that I must accept. Laura, I'm a bit mixed up at the moment. You are right, the death of the casualty we recovered has got to me. I wouldn't have had the courage or sense to ask you back, particularly as I have now had quite a lot to drink. But yes, please do come.'

*

Adam woke up the following morning with Laura lying by his side in bed. She said, 'Good morning, Adam. That was great, I think we both needed that and it was a lot of fun. But now, I see I am late for work, and so we must get up and get me across the estuary pretty sharpish.'

Adam looked at Laura. 'On the first day that I stepped into Daymouth, Beryl said you were an angel. She was right and now I know you're a great lover too.'

They dressed and went downstairs and were very surprised to see David and Jasmine sitting around the table drinking coffee.

'Ah, we thought we heard stirrings in the night,' said David. 'Jasmine and I are just having some breakfast before she pops off to collect her children and then she'll go back to the Holbertons' to help clear up. Did you both have a good night? We did.'

CHAPTER 7

As Adam took Laura back across the estuary, the water surface was glassy smooth and there was not a breath of wind.

'I don't think you'll be sailing today,' said Laura. 'I looked at the forecast yesterday and it showed no wind at all for today. That means sailing will be off and the pub will be packed out with sailors and hangers-on with nothing to do but drink. Good for business but bad for my workload, particularly after last night. Oh look, there is Lord Harvey's boat still moored off Eastside beach. Doesn't it look pretentious in this beautiful estuary?'

Adam steered 'Greta' around the super yacht and had to agree with Laura's sentiments: the boat looked totally out of place.

'Yes, you're right, Laura. Maybe it would be OK in the Mediterranean but not here. I know Sarah's very unhappy with Lord Robert for bringing in a professional sailor to helm their yawl so that it and his lordship's wife Jenny can win the races.'

'I guess that's Daymouth for you. A playground for the very rich and sometimes a tough place to work for the not so rich; but I do love it here. Lots of interesting people and the lifeboat as well. And people like you, Adam, to meet and get to know! By the way, I did enjoy last night but let's keep things simple. For the moment, a one-night stand. I really don't want to complicate either my life or yours at this stage. Maybe later, who knows?'

Adam dropped Laura off at the Daymouth quay and they parted with a smile and a brief kiss on the check. He then motored back across the estuary to his mooring where he was met by Sarah, who was walking along the beach.

'Ah, the wanderer returns!' declared Sarah. 'I've just been to the cottage and David said you'd popped over to Daymouth. I think I can guess what you were up to as I couldn't find you anywhere towards the end of the party; however… I have news. Racing has been cancelled for the day the forecast is confidently predicting no wind. So, Robert and Jenny Harvey have invited us all to tea on board "Invicta" this afternoon. I know Lord Robert's a pain but Jenny's lovely, so it would be good if both you and David would like to join us on board what is definitely the largest boat in the estuary. It even makes the ALB lifeboat look small.'

'OK, that's fine by me. Have you told David?'

'Yes, and he's happy to come. I did say that Jasmine wouldn't be going as she will be spending all day clearing up after the party. I presume you saw that they were very much an item last night and she was at your cottage this morning.'

'I'm afraid I've little control over David's love life and I guess that goes for me too. Sarah, I do hope we're still OK with each other?'

'Adam, you must live your own life and make your own decisions. I know Laura well and she's one of my friends. I'm beginning to know you and have discovered you're a great crew. Let's hope we can keep sailing together as well as we have been up till now.'

*

Adam and David arrived at the Harvey super yacht in 'Greta' and headed towards the stern platform where two of the 'Invicta' crew had been assigned to deal with the arriving guest ribs, launches and small boats.

'Thanks,' said Adam to the smartly dressed crew as he and David stepped on board.

'Pleasure, sir,' he replied. 'We'll put your boat with some of the others on moorings and collect them for you when you want to leave.'

Adam and David climbed up to the main deck.

'Blimey; I have never seen anything like this before,' said David. 'So, this is what you get if you win the Euro Lottery or run a very successful hedge fund! Loads of money!'

'Something like that,' replied Adam. 'But we should be on our best behaviour, we are after all guests of the Harveys and friends of the Holbertons. In Daymouth, it's a very small world.'

Sarah was already aboard and intercepted them before they joined the main group.

'Now, you two, behave yourselves. You're both very lucky to be invited this afternoon and neither Laura nor Jasmine are here to distract either of you!'

It was clear to both men that Sarah was in a somewhat feisty mood. David immediately tried to lower the temperature.

'Sarah, your parents' party was wonderful last night and you were the perfect hostess. Maybe Adam and I wandered off-piste a bit but what a generous gesture from all your family; thank you very much.'

'Bollocks to you,' said Sarah. 'Let's go and meet the crowd!'

There were between twenty and thirty guests, most of whom were yawl sailors. Sarah steered Adam and David towards a group that included Tina Harding and Tim her partner, who were in conversation with Steve, the professional helm for the Harvey yawl.

'Hello, Adam,' said Tina. 'I presume this is your friend David. Didn't I see him last night with Jasmine Sanders? Presumably you know her husband is in prison.'

'Yes, that's absolutely right,' replied David. 'Jasmine and I are friends and I hope I'm bringing a bit of enjoyment to her and her children at such a tough time. Am I right in thinking you are Dr Tina Harding, one of the local GPs and also the helm of "Phantom", which has regular tussles on the water with "Golden Eagle"?'

'Enough!' cried Sarah. 'This is meant to be a civilised tea party and we should all be on our best behaviour.'

After the traditional English tea served with Devon scones, champagne followed and it was not long before conversations became quite animated. Ian and Susie Carbrook were also guests and Adam introduced them to David.

'Nice to meet you, David,' said Ian Carbrook. 'It's good that Adam has a young friend to keep him company here, those of us on the Eastside are all getting on a bit. Of course, in the summer, a lot of things are happening about the place like now, but in the winter, it's a different story. Have you heard about my plan to build Marlo Eco Park? It's an attempt to provide year-round employment for locals and help provide a more balanced economy around here.'

'Yes,' replied David. 'Adam did say something about the eco park and how it had split the residents of Eastside in terms of approval or horror. Do you think it will be a good financial investment?'

'Good question, David, and no, I don't. I made my money transporting fruit from the Med across France and then to London. I made a lot of money and can now afford to be a bit generous. Maybe in the long term, the eco park will prove to be a good investment, but certainly not in the short term.'

Adam had followed the conversation and thought about Ian Carbrook's possible involvement in the supply of Princewater drugs and Jack Sanders' imprisonment in Dartmoor jail. He thought to himself, *Drugs to London from the Med, and could Marlo Eco Park be a money laundering opportunity?*

The conversation moved on and Sarah's parents joined the group.

Grace said, 'Adam, so nice to see you, and David too, and hello Ian and Susie; I do hope you all enjoyed our party last night. We were so lucky with the weather.'

David immediately chipped in, 'Grace, it was fantastic and I was only just saying to Sarah how wonderful your family were to organise such a splendid and fun occasion.'

'Flattery will get you everywhere and thank you; you must give me your phone number! I know we're all having a wonderful time at the moment, Robert and Jenny are super hosts, however, our own beach party is now over and with Ian and Susie here, we need to think of the future and those long autumn evenings. I have a plan, and I'm hoping Adam, and maybe even you too, David, might be interested in getting involved? Last night, I was discussing with Ian and Susie how we were going to survive the autumn! Being here with all the excitement of the regatta and parties like this is wonderful. However, come September, we need a plan B. Ian and Susie are happy to go along with my idea, but we do need at least one extra person to be involved too.'

Before David or Adam could interject, Grace continued, 'As you know, Susie and I love our game of bridge. Ian's OK with it but James won't play the game, particularly with me! We're planning to go to Monaco this autumn for a week and I was wondering, Adam, if you'd come too to be a fourth bridge player? You could bring anyone else you'd like if you thought you needed some younger company; maybe David or someone else? It will be school time, so Sarah will be teaching and can't come.'

Adam paused for thought and then replied, 'Thanks for the invitation, Grace, but at the moment I just can't make a snap decision like that, I'll get back to you later. Surely all this Marlo Eco Park business will be coming up in the autumn and I thought nearly all of you were on different opposing sides?'

'That's one of the whole points about going!' said Grace. 'I thought it would be a good idea to go off together even if we did have different views and use it as a way to at least to stay friends. There'd be one rule: no discussion of Marlo! The estuary's far too small a place to have enemies. At the end of the day, we're all in this together, whether Marlo happens or not.'

'Well, maybe, let me think about it.'

The champagne continued to flow as Adam and David moved from group to group and it was early evening before they met up with their hosts.

'Many thanks for your invitation on board,' said Adam. 'This is my friend David and he's down from London for a break from work. We have to say, your boat is magnificent and nothing like anything we've seen or been on before.'

'Well, you clearly haven't been to the Med much before and particularly Monaco,' replied Lord Robert. 'They're two a penny there and some are very much larger than this. Daymouth estuary is a bit small for this sort of boat and "Invicta" will be going back to the Med quite soon. The UK doesn't really provide great facilities for boats like this and of course the weather just cannot be relied on either.'

Both Adam and David were not sure how to respond and it was Lady Jenny who helped out.

'I think I heard from Grace that you two may be going to Monaco for an autumn break. That would be lovely. Grace and James are such fun. We also met the Carbrooks at the party last night and they seemed very pleasant; I understand they are going too. We have an apartment in Monaco and Robert keeps the boat down there most of the time. Both James and Robert enjoy a game of poker at the casino, although I believe they both detest playing bridge. What's your game, Adam? Poker or bridge?'

'I can do both but haven't specialised in either. There is a strong mathematical element in each and that interests me, but before to coming to Daymouth, I was a trader in the City, and that was quite mathematical too. Now that I'm here I've got interested in being a member of the lifeboat team and, well, just discovering about Daymouth and recently learning how to crew in yawls with Sarah.'

'Yes,' replied Jenny. 'My helm Steve's noticed you sailing with Sarah and commented to me how well you and she seemed to be getting on with the boat. He's a world-class helm, so I guess you should be flattered.'

Lord Robert seemed to be annoyed that he was being squeezed out of the conversation by his wife and came in with a blast. 'So, Adam, you think mathematics is important! Look, here I am on the biggest super yacht that Daymouth can take, having run a hedge fund for the last twenty years. Have I used mathematics to get there? No way. It has been all gut feeling and, yes, I have to say, being ruthless. If you want to get on in life, you have to be ruthless.'

At this point, David took up the challenge Lord Robert had put down. The champagne had obviously been coursing around everybody's blood and passions was rising.

'I don't really agree, Lord Robert. Both Adam and I studied maths at university. Adam has used it in trading commodities and I've used it for acquisitions and mergers. Whilst maths is not everything in life, far from it, it does provide a framework to help in establishing whether financial transactions are viable and not loss-making.'

'Absolute tosh!' yelled Lord Robert, who was now clearly very drunk and red-faced. 'Look, I make my money not by mathematics but by identifying a weak company. I then short them, and I presume you know what that means. I borrow shares on a targeted company and then immediately sell them off and wait for the stock price to fall. I then later rebuy shares in the same company and return them to the borrower and usually make a very fat profit. If I am really ruthless, I drive the price down until the company goes bust then I have to repay nothing! At this very moment, I'm driving Plymouth Super Boats into liquidation by successive shorting.'

You bastard, thought David, however he refrained from saying that aloud and responded, 'Surely that will put many people in Plymouth out of work? I thought Plymouth Super Boats was one of the city's main employers?'

'Well, they shouldn't be working for a firm with such crappy management. As I said, you have to be ruthless in business to be really successful like me; maths has nothing to do with it.'

At this point, Adam came into the conversation. 'David, I think it's time that we should be getting back on land. Thank you very much for the hospitality and good luck tomorrow Jenny for the last day of the regatta. Come on, David we need to find "Greta".'

With that, they made a swift exit, passing Sarah on the way to whom Adam said, 'Hi Sarah we're off before there is a nuclear explosion!'

*

As they put 'Greta' onto the running mooring in front of Eastside Cottages, Admiral Tom leant over the sea wall of his cottage and hailed them. 'You two, would you like to come and have a drink? I am still recovering from the Holbertons' party last night and, in the past, I've found the best thing to do for that sort of thing is have another drink!'

Adam looked at David and said, 'Maybe that's not a bad idea; I think we also need to come down from the party and our visit to "Invicta".' He shouted up to Tom, 'Yes, that would be good. We'll come round in a couple of minutes.'

The three men were soon sitting on Admiral Tom's terrace that overlooking the estuary, all with glasses of Scotch in hand.

'I do find a good glass of whisky helps clear the head,' said Tom. 'Presumably you've been drinking on board "Invicta"; I saw you and others leaving the yacht. Was it a good do, like the Holbertons' party last night?'

'Yes and no, Tom,' replied Adam. 'Unfortunately, I think Lord Harvey had drunk a bit too much champagne. He blasted off at us that, in order to be successful, you had to be ruthless and he then bragged about how his hedge fund was currently shorting a major Plymouth company and pushing them into bankruptcy. Not the sort of thing you want to hear at a so-called civilised Daymouth tea party.'

'Oh dear, I'm not totally surprised to hear that about Lord Robert. His wife Lady Jenny is charming, but Robert is quite the reverse. I don't really understand why he has to behave in that way. To some extent, yes, there are times when you have to be a bit ruthless. Adam, you've heard my Falklands story. After that, I sharpened up and had to match the ruthlessness of some of my naval colleagues in order to end up as an Admiral. But in doing that, I hope I always managed to be civilised. It sounds as if Robert went over the top. Anyway, what about you two and your love life? I know in the past I've said to Adam that I wouldn't interfere with his life, but I couldn't help noticing that you, David, were very close to Jasmine last night, and this morning I think I saw Adam taking Laura back across the estuary.'

David and Adam looked at each other and smiled, with Adam taking the initiative to speak first. 'Tom, yes you are right, but don't get us wrong. On my part, Laura and I are good friends and I hope it will stay that way and certainly both Laura and I know Daymouth and Eastside are very small places where everyone sooner or later gets to know everything that's going on. So yes, we're good friends and nothing more.'

'This is beginning to sound like a Catholic confessional,' said David. 'From my side I'm very aware that many people have their eyes on the beautiful Jasmine and are intrigued to know how she's coping with Jack in jail. She and I are both aware of this too and I won't step over the line. We and her kids are having a great time and I believe, Tom, you too have a soft spot for her. Don't worry, I'll look after her.'

There was a pause and then Tom spoke. 'Thanks lads, I do think you're two good chaps and I'd have been happy to have you as officers on any of my ships. Yes, I do have a very soft spot for Jasmine. I thought the Sanders family were in a good place before Jack got involved in this drugs business. The kids are lovely too and Jasmine really cares for them. I have to say that I like Laura as well. Beryl's told me all about her and I've seen the way she can cheer up the whole of Smugglers Inn on a bleak winter day. And while we're all in our confessional, I also have to add Sarah to the list. She and the Holbertons are basically very nice people and I admire what they are doing for Eastside, although I do worry about this Marlo Eco Park project rocking the boat.'

'Oh, that came up too at our tea and champagne party,' said David. 'Grace is trying to organise with the Carbrooks an autumn Eastside group to play bridge in Monaco and she wants either Adam or myself to come along to make up the fourth player. It also appears James doesn't like bridge but is happy to have a casino poker flutter like Lord Robert Harvey when he is in Monaco.'

'But David, surely that would be a nightmare,' said Tom. 'The Holbertons are split on their support for the eco park and Ian Carbrook is the prime mover for the whole project.'

Adam joined into the conversation. 'Yes, Grace is aware of the problems and gives it as a reason for everyone going in order to maintain Eastside harmony. I'm not convinced that would work, but I may go as it is a chance to get to know Ian Carbrook a bit better and also see the mass of super yachts that Lord Harvey was going on about. Carbrook did allude to being in haulage of fruit from the Med to London and evidently, he's prepared to put a lot of money into this eco park whilst admitting it won't be a money maker, certainly in the short term. The jury still seems to be out in my own mind as to whether he's involved in any drugs issue and the reason Jack is in jail.'

The Admiral went indoors and brought out a large bottle of red wine. 'Let's put everything behind us for a while, have a few more drinks and discuss the prospects for tomorrow's last day of the regatta. Will the no-good Harvey yawl triumph over "Golden Eagle", or perhaps will our local doctor Dr Tina and her husband Tim emerge as the regatta trophy winners?'

*

Both Adam and David were somewhat worse for wear on the following morning as the previous day's cocktail of champagne followed by whisky, then red wine and finally, late into the evening, brandy, had taken a heavy toll. The morning coffee was most welcome but neither of them felt like going for their regular morning run.

They were, however, suddenly woken out of the doziness when Adam's lifeboat pager started to ring.

'Heck! I'm on a shout,' exclaimed Adam. 'I must go, as they may be short of people, now we're in the peak of the holiday season.'

Adam rushed down to his boat and crossed the estuary in super quick time. He moored on the Daymouth quay and then ran to the lifeboat station. Ted was already there explaining to a group of the crew that the shout involved a yacht in the shipping lane that had been making an overnight passage from France to Plymouth and had been in collision with a container ship. The yacht was evidently damaged but the container ship seemed unaware of the collision and had continued on its journey. A fishing boat was some ten miles away and making towards it, but there was a danger of the yacht sinking.

'I need a good team and we're a bit short because of the time of year,' said Ted. 'Engineer, navigator Jon, Ben Lewis, Laura, Jimmy Lethbridge, and I think Billy.'

Ted looked at Adam and pondered for a moment before saying, 'Sorry Adam, not this time. We still have the previous incident enquiry with the fatality active and I just can't afford to have you involved in another shout until that one is cleared.'

Adam felt a mixture of disappointment and relief. He knew he was probably still over any sensible alcohol limit and he also then realised if he went on the shout, he wouldn't be back in time to crew Sarah in the final regatta yawl race.

He helped prepare the lifeboat and watched it leave at speed in a cloud of spray. On his way back to the quay, he met Tina running down Main St towards the lifeboat station.

'Am I too late?' she said. 'I was dealing with a patient at the surgery. Has the boat gone?'

'Yes, it's a damaged yacht in the shipping lane. There was no mention of casualties. I think they were short-handed, but Ted said I should stay ashore because of the enquiry into the fatality on the last shout.'

'That does make sense, Adam, but I guess we're both disappointed not to be on the boat. We do however have the chance to sail on the yawls this afternoon. Now that we're here, alone together, this is an opportunity for me to say something.

'I want to say to you that the rivalry between Sarah and me is purely due to both our competitive spirits, nothing more. But I will let you into a secret. And don't you dare tell my partner Tim or anyone else for that matter that I've said this. You already appear to be a better yawl racing crew than Tim will ever be!'

'Thanks Tina, that's a very nice and supportive thing to say. It's greatly appreciated, particularly at this moment. Since I came to Daymouth, my life seems to have been turned upside down. It's as though I've been in a washing machine and I am not sure if the wash is starting, in the middle or coming to end.'

Tina turned and went back to her surgery and Adam returned across the estuary in 'Greta', unsure whether he was sober, still drunk or just confused.

*

The lifeboat shout and brief talk with Tina Harding had stirred Adam out of his lethargy and hangover.

'So, David, what are your plans today? I'll be off soon to get the yawl with Sarah in preparation for the final race. The wind seems to be coming in nicely and so we should certainly race today.'

'Well, I've been thinking things over and decided I better cool off a bit with Jasmine. I was going to take her and the kids on the boat to watch the racing today, but I now think the best thing to do is stay away from her and the children for little while. People are obviously noticing and I don't want gossip to get back to Jack in prison. If I was in his position, I would be devastated.'

*

There was a good breeze blowing in slightly overcast conditions when twenty yawls came out for the final yawl race of the regatta.

'Let's try and keep it steady,' said Sarah to Adam. 'Steve and Jenny have to win in "Kestrel" if they want to win overall and we all know that's the most important thing as far as Lord Robert is concerned. I don't think either we in "Golden Eagle" or Tina and Tim in "Phantom" can win overall, but at the moment we are both close on points and Tina will definitely not be keen for us to be ahead of her in the final results.'

'Sarah, I'll do my best, but remember, I did have an awful lot to drink last night.'

'And whose fault do you think that was? You and David managed to wind Lord Robert up yesterday and neither of you behaved very well at our party.'

'OK, apologies. I really will try and do my best.'

There was a pause and then Sarah added, 'Apologies from me too. We all seem to be a bit jumpy at the moment. Let's try and concentrate and do our best.'

As soon as the race got underway, it was clear that that the Harvey yawl was again sailing in a league of its own. Steve Mansell made the perfect start and was leading the other nineteen yawls by at least a minute at the first mark with Sarah and Tina locked in a mid-fleet battle for most of the race. At the finish, Steve and Lady Jenny were convincing winners, thereby securing the week's overall winner trophy. Sarah and

Adam beat Tina and Tim by one place and, without doing the sums, it was not clear how this affected their overall regatta position.

'Another close one,' said Sarah. 'I just don't understand why Tina and I always seem to end up so close to each other. Anyway, well done, Adam, you crewed very well and any triumph over Tina is a very good result for me. You were a great crew even if you were a bit subdued today.'

As they approached the mooring for 'Golden Eagle', David arrived paddling one of the kayaks he had brought down from London. 'Well done, you two, at least you beat Tina even if you couldn't catch Steve and Jenny. That guy is amazing.'

'Thanks, David,' said Sarah. 'Where are Jasmine and the children? We've got used to seeing them after each race.'

'I thought maybe I should lay low for a bit in that department.'

*

The regatta prize-giving was held at the Yacht Club in the evening and there was warm applause for Steve and Lady Jenny when they went up to receive the yawl regatta trophy. Lord Robert had elected to stay away as he was still sulking over his drunken conversations at the 'Invicta' party and declared to anyone who would listen that he was too busy with work to come ashore and celebrate his wife's triumph.

Although Sarah and Adam had beaten Tim and Tina in the final race, the Harding team ended up one place in front when all the races were taken into account for the overall results, with Tina and Tim fifth and Sarah and Adam sixth out of the twenty yawls that had been racing.

After the prize-giving, Sarah, Adam, Tina and Tim sat around drinking together on the club house terrace in a relaxed atmosphere.

'That was good racing today,' said Tina. 'I really enjoyed that and it was lucky both Adam and I didn't go on this morning's lifeboat shout otherwise we wouldn't have had a sail. I saw Ben Lewis earlier this evening and he said the shout was all a bit of a non-event as the yacht was barely scratched and could make its own way back to Plymouth. Sarah, I have to say you seem to have upped your game for this regatta, well done. Did your crew have anything to do with that?'

CHAPTER 8

After the regatta had finished, activity in the estuary started to reduce, with the super yacht 'Invicta' and other cruisers departing. David was keen to stay on for a while and suggested to Adam that they use the kayaks to explore the upper reaches of the estuary. 'It's fantastic weather today. The sun's out and the forecast's good; surely we should take advantage of that and do something a bit adventurous?'

OK! Let's do it now, this instant!' agreed Adam. 'I'll do a packed lunch and you can get the kayaks sorted. We can start by exploring East Creek where the proposed Marlo Eco Park comes down to the water and then go onto North Creek, which is further up the estuary and towards Princewater. The tide's rising so we should have enough water to navigate the creeks for the rest of the day.'

They were soon on the water; David had been using his kayak the previous week but it took some time before Adam gained full control of his own craft and could match David's paddling speed. There was very little wind and, with the sun shining, the conditions were excellent for being on the water, wearing just shorts and tee shirts.

'Hey, this is fun,' said Adam. 'I've no sails or ropes to worry about, we're so close to the water and yes, it's great exercise, particularly for the arm muscles. Let's have a pact: no racing today. Endurance, yes, but this doesn't need to turn into a competition.'

David looked across at Adam as they paddled past the beach in front of the Holbertons' house. 'OK, we can try, but quite honestly, I've never known a time on a sporting occasion when we haven't ended up racing each other.'

By following the beach on the Eastside of the estuary it was not long before they reached the East Creek and Marlo Farm beach.

'This is the beach area that Ian Carbrook and Bert Appleyard want to develop as part of their eco park,' said Adam. 'I have to say at the moment it looks very beautiful and unspoilt. Maybe changing it with a commercial development isn't such a good idea?'

'You might be right, Adam, but I'm all for progressive change and with Brexit coming up, the country has got to learn to stand on its own feet. Jasmine and Sarah are all for the eco park project and they should know. They've lived here all their lives and are aware of just how tough it is to get a job. Hey… talking of ladies, that looks like a damsel in distress over there on that island, she's waving at us!'

'You're right,' said Adam. 'Let's paddle over to see what she wants.'

Adam and David canoed towards the island until they were within hearing range.

'Are you OK?' shouted David. 'Do you need help?'

'I'm OK, but yes, I could do with some assistance. I walked over the mud when the tide was low, and now I can't get back to the beach until it goes out again this afternoon.'

David glanced across at Adam and smiled. 'We do have a damsel in distress and she looks quite pretty from here!' Turning to the woman, he shouted, 'No problem, we're on our way!'

They beached the canoes and walked up to where the woman was standing.

'Thank you for coming over. I'm Paula Chase and I'm part of the AONB, Area of Natural Beauty team who are investigating the Marlo beach in relation to a planning application. I came with a chap called Justin Turner who's over there somewhere on the mainland. Justin's a representative of the Marlo Eco Park proposal. I walked over here in shallow water, the island's part of the overall planning proposal, and I wanted to check on its ecosystem. Justin was a wimp and didn't want to get his feet or suit wet, so I left him at the beach. I left my rucksack and mobile phone with him too, so I've no communications here. It's great that you were canoeing and saw me. I wasn't expecting anyone to be around and clearly Justin's gone off somewhere out of range. With the rising tide, when I started to make my way back across the water, it was getting a bit scary, so I decided it was safer to stay put until the tide goes out.'

'Don't you worry, Paula, we can sort this out for you. I'm David and this is Adam we're kayak novices but only too willing to help damsels in distress! Our kayaks are single seaters and can only take one person, so let me suggest Adam stays here with you and I kayak across to the beach, find Justin and bring your bag and phone back. That way, at least you'll then have communication until the tide goes out enough for you to walk across.'

'That's very kind. Yes, that would be great. I'm happy to spend a few hours here and see if I can find any eel grass and seahorses along the shore.'

David paddled off towards the beach whilst Paula and Adam found a place to sit.

'It's really quite embarrassing for me to get caught out like this,' said Paula. 'I'm used to foreshore work and should have realised that I could get cut off. Anyway, it's not the end of the world and I can make good use of at least a couple of hours exploring the foreshore before the tide peaks and then starts to fall again.'

'I'm curious that you said you were with someone from Marlo Eco Park. Surely as a representative of the AONB team, you would be on opposing sides of the application?'

'Well yes, you're right, but the Marlo team are being very clever and the top brass suggested that we work together to assess the eco issues involved. You see, Marlo are pushing the eco aspects of the proposal as a way of getting planning permission in an area of genuine outstanding natural beauty. It could be thought of as a clever ploy, which is certainly what my boss Councillor Humphreys thinks. I'm not quite so sure. The prat, Justin Turner, who's a land agent for Marlo and who doesn't want to get his feet wet, certainly can only see the commercial side of the proposal. However, Ian Carbrook, who's the money man behind the proposal, is much cleverer than that and although I could be wrong, he genuinely seems to want to blend commercial, social and eco interests into one package.'

'That's interesting,' mused Adam. 'But where does this eel grass and seahorse business come into it?'

'Oh, that's a bit of an eco thing that gets some people around Daymouth very excited. Eel grass can grow around here and it's a favoured site for beautiful, small seahorses to breed. They're unusual little creatures and if there are any of them near the island, or the Marlo beach, that could mean water access being prohibited and the end of the project.'

'If that's the case, I'm not really sure whether I hope you find some or not!' replied Adam.

*

Meanwhile, David had canoed to the main Marlo beach and sighted the suited land agent, Justin Turner.

'Hi Justin! I'm David and I've come from the island. Paula is marooned there for a bit as the tide has come up and she's got to wait for the tide to fall before getting back. She told me you were on the beach and you had her mobile phone and bag. I've offered to take them over to her.'

'Silly bitch. She wanted me to go across too, but I wasn't prepared to do that and, well, look, I'm not dressed for that sort of thing. The bag and phone are in my car. Do you want to walk over with me to collect them? Then I'm off. I'm not going to wait around for her.'

As they walked to the car, David asked Justin about the eco park proposal. 'This is a great opportunity for Bert Appleyard to make some money. I'm his land agent and we have tried other stuff before with no success. This Carbrook chap's got the money and plenty of it, so providing the bloody eco warriors don't cock it up, Bert and I should do very well.'

'I suppose I was asking whether the proposal was a good idea for the whole area,' said David.

'Dunno about that. That's not my problem. Look, here's the bag and mobile for you to take over to Miss Eco Warrior.'

David returned to the island and gave Paula her bag and mobile.

'Not sure that I got on too well with your colleague Justin; he didn't seem to be my type of person. I hope you've got your own car over there; he said he wasn't waiting for you.'

'Yes, I do, I wasn't getting on with Justin either. All he seemed interested in was the money side of the proposal. Anyway, many thanks. I can phone my boss Councillor Humphreys and now go in search of seahorses.'

'Can I make a suggestion?' said David. 'Why don't we all sit here and have an early lunch with the sandwiches and other bits Adam has in his canoe. Then Paula can get us up to speed on those seahorses; they sound intriguing.'

Adam collected the lunch that he'd prepared for two and shared it out for the three of them. Paula then enjoyed explaining some of the key eco issues for the Daymouth estuary including the beautiful, but tiny seahorses and the troublesome Pacific Oysters. She added, 'Quite honestly, I don't see the problem with the oyster issue, but diehard eco people say Pacific Oysters are an "invading species" and endangering our own indigenous oysters. As far as I am concerned, they both taste pretty good, but some people can't bear to eat any of them at all. And then, there's the famous red algae that sometimes appears in the estuary. This algae is given the impossibly complex name *Dinoflagellates*, which sounds scary and very technical. Again, it's not clear whether this "red sea" is good or bad, but it certainly is something the eco people can worry about.'

'It all sounds a bit technical to me,' said Adam. 'But how could the Marlo project affect all of this?'

'For me, the big issue is whether Marlo would set a precedent for more development in the Daymouth estuary. From what I have seen of their proposal, on its own, it looks good. There's been a lot of thought put into it and maybe surprisingly for someone who works for the AONB team, I see the benefits; however, if it marks the thin end of a wedge, with many more popping up in the estuary, it could become both an ecological and commercial disaster.'

'Well said,' responded David. 'You know, I really think we should get to know each other a bit more, let's exchange mobile numbers, I'm currently staying with David at Eastside Cottage next to the Daymouth ferry landing.'

Adam gave a resigned look to David but Paula responded, 'That's very kind of you, but I think my fiancé wouldn't approve of that.'

'Oh well, not to worry, it was worth a try and anyway I do genuinely agree with your views.'

It seemed the right moment to leave Paula to search for seahorses and Adam and David set off in their kayaks with friendly goodbye waves.

*

It was getting hot in the midday sun as Adam and David paddled out of East Creek and then along the estuary towards North Creek.

'This is a really beautiful and quiet part of the estuary,' said Adam. 'Fantastically peaceful and out of range for all but the most intrepid holidaymakers. Look… there's a huge bird above. Maybe a buzzard or it could even be an osprey.'

'Well, don't ask me what kind of bird it is,' replied David. 'The only thing I can say is it's not a London pigeon or one of those bloody seagulls that seem to be everywhere in Daymouth. But yes, you're right, it's an incredibly peaceful and beautiful location, particularly on such a blue-sky day as this.'

The two of them paddled on for about an hour and then reached the point where the main estuary continued to the town of Princewater and a tributary forked towards North Creek.

'This is where we turn right along North Creek. Be careful, David, there are some shallow bits in the main channel, but there are also some beautiful unspoilt sandy beaches on either side. We're very unlikely to see any other boats or people along here.'

As they paddled along North Creek, the quiet serenity of the area was broken by a group of youths shouting from the shore.

'Ooh you; piss off, this is our place.'

David and Adam canoed towards the centre of the creek in the hope of avoiding the group of three youths and a girl; however, within seconds, they were being bombarded by stones that were being thrown by the youths and landing with splashes of water around their canoes.

'Blimey, this is dangerous,' yelled David. 'That one nearly hit me. Ouch, that one did hit me and my hand is bleeding. We need to get out of here!'

Both Adam and David paddled furiously further along the creek to get out of range as they heard the group on the shoreline beach continue shouting and swearing at them.

'They must be either pissed out of their minds or high on drugs to behave like that,' said David as they got out of stone throwing range. 'The bastards, they need to be taught a lesson and you and I need to do something about this. Look, they have drawn blood on my left hand.'

Adam and David paddled on in silence until a bend in the creek took them out of sight from the stone-throwing group.

'Right; I'm going ashore to sort this lot out and you're coming with me.'

They looked at each other and Adam could see the determined look on David's face; he also had come up with a thought of his own that had his mind working hard.

They beached the canoes and inspected David's bloodied arm.

'Looks bad, but in all fairness, it's only a graze,' said Adam. 'Do we call the police? I think they must have been on drugs to be that far gone and behave in that way. Perhaps they could lead the police to the source of the local drug supplier and maybe the supplier that Jack Sanders in Dartmoor is afraid to identify?'

'Maybe,' replied David without conviction. 'But those bastards do need to be taught a lesson now. They'll be long gone by the time the police might arrive. You and I are going to sort this out here and now.'

The two of them set off on foot following the contour of the creek until they reached the beach area where the youths in swimming costumes were sitting next to the water.

'They haven't seen us yet,' said David. 'Let's stay behind the embankment and first of all find out how they got here.'

David and Adam crept around behind the embankment and discovered four bicycles. David let all the tyres down and threw the single bike pump that was on one of the bikes into a hedge. They then crept up to the top of the bank and saw the youths' clothes strewn around a tree near the top of the embankment. David inched his way to the clothes and rifled through the pockets, discovering three sheath knives and four mobile phones. He silently passed the mobile phones to Adam and then hid the knives in a nearby bush.

The youths were now sitting in the sun listening to loud music from a radio and looking mindlessly out onto the water.

David, followed by Adam, walked down from the embankment and came within metres of them before they realised that they had company.

'Who the fuck are you and what do you want?' growled one of the youths as he spun round and attempted to stand up.

'We are the canoeists you have just thrown stones at and we have come so you can apologise to us,' said David.

'Fuck off,' said the one now standing. 'Jonny, get the knives and we'll teach these blokes a lesson.' Jonny, who was one of the two other boys on the ground, started to move to get up, but was clearly unsteady on his feet and not sure what was going on. 'OK, Dean,' he replied.

David looked straight at Dean and said, 'We've got your knives and all your mobile phones. I know there are four of you and two of us; but I can assure you that we're in a lot better state than any of you. Now, how about an apology?'

At that moment, Dean made a lunge at David, which David easily countered and he quickly had him in an armlock and squealing with pain on the ground.

'Try that again and my friend here will throw all your phones in the water.'

Dean continued to groan whilst held in David's armlock and Jonny slumped back onto the beach. The third youth and girl remained with glazed and helpless expressions sitting on the beach.

'Now, how about that apology from you all. It's pretty clear you are out of your minds on some sort of drugs,' said David, as he further tightened his armlock on Dean.

Dean paused and tried to assess the situation but his mind was astray and the armlock very painful. Eventually, he muttered, 'OK, I apologise. It was only a bit of fun and we weren't doing any harm. We need our mobiles back; we must have them.'

Adam saw an opportunity to extract some information from the group.

'OK, if you all apologise, I may not throw your mobiles in the water. But, before that, we need to know who your local drug supplier is. We don't want to buy drugs, but we do want to know who is supplying this stuff to young people like you in this area.'

Dean immediately responded, 'We can't tell you that! Our supplier's secret and we'd be in really big trouble if we told you.'

'You're already in big trouble. Possession of offensive weapons, violent and dangerous behaviour. Even if you haven't already got a police record, you will have after this. And don't forget, no cooperation, no mobile phones.'

Dean was clearly the gang leader and all eyes were on him. There was a long pause and then he eventually replied, 'OK, but promise that it wasn't us that told you. Princewater and around here is a very small place and we could be really in the shit if certain people know it was us that grassed them.'

'Go on, let's have it. Places as well,' urged Adam.

'His name's Frank Green. He operates from the Prince Rupert pub at Princewater. We only take soft stuff, but I know he does trade in heavier gear.'

'Thank you,' said Adam. 'I'll leave the mobiles on the beach and you lot, make sure you've cleared off before we canoe back.'

David released Dean from his armlock and Adam threw the mobiles onto the beach, looked at Adam and they both made a quick exit.

Neither said anything until they were some distance from confrontation. 'Not sure if we handled that quite correctly,' said David. 'But you got some information that might be useful and, if nothing else, they'll be learning it's a long way to push their bikes back to Princewater.'

*

Adam and David returned to their kayaks and paddled back, passing the now deserted beach where the yobs had been. Both were consumed by thoughts of the beach altercation and were focused on getting back to Daymouth as quickly as possible.

They brought the kayaks to the Daymouth shore and decided to find the local policeman Chris Thompson and then go and have a drink at the Smugglers Inn.

PC Thompson was in his office and Adam briefed him on their adventure along North Creek. After explaining the story, Adam finished with, 'The key point was that these yobs said their drug supplier was a Frank Green who operated from the Prince Rupert pub at Princewater.'

'Ah, a person known to us,' said PC Thompson. 'Frank Green's tricky. The police at Princewater have had him on their radar for some time, but he's clever and definitely a nasty piece of work. We nearly had him a couple of years ago but a potential witness withdrew from giving evidence at the last minute. The Prince Rupert's interesting, though. I'd have normally thought of that as a respectable pub down by the quay and I am surprised the landlord hasn't picked up on that sort of thing. I'll make a record of this conversation and pass on the information to detective Paul Barclay at Plymouth; he may want to speak to you. I certainly don't like the sound of these kids having knives and it's a pity you didn't get their names, but by the sounds of it, you did teach them a lesson.'

Adam and David left feeling a bit deflated having been criticised for not getting the names of the yobs; however, the sun was still blazing down and they both decided it was time for a beer at the Smugglers Inn.

The Inn was crowded with visitors; however, as they went out into the garden they saw Laura and Sarah Holberton at a table enjoying a good chat.

'Come and join us!' called Laura. 'We were only just talking about you two. It's my day off and Sarah's been bringing me up to date on Eastside gossip and of course that means you two.'

David and Adam joined them at the table and Adam recounted their day's adventure in both East and North Creek.

'Well, you have had an exciting day, haven't you?' said Sarah. 'I'm interested you went on a rescue mission for Paula Chase, too, as I was only just telling Laura about her and how she may be on an opposing side to me. Ian Carbrook contacted me today and asked if I would be prepared to speak at the October planning meeting for the eco park. Evidently, each opposing side of the application is allowed a five-minute slot at the meeting where a designated person can make the case for or against the application. Ian thought that having a youngish local female might help their case for the application and I've agreed to do it. I have met Paula Chase on a number of occasions before, as she's visited my school at Tordon and talked to the children about her AONB work. She's a really nice person and certainly does know her stuff about seahorses, red algae and those dreaded *Dinoflagellates*. She may be chosen to speak against the application, or come to think about it, it might be her boss, Councillor Humphreys. So isn't it a small world in Daymouth? David, I do hope you didn't try and flirt with Paula; her fiancé's the captain of the Tordon Rugby club.'

David said nothing and attempted to steer the conversation to events in North Creek. 'And how about this chap Frank Green? Have either of you two heard about him before?'

'No, David, I haven't,' said Sarah. 'But I can see from the expression on your face that you did fancy Paula. You know, David, I don't think that any female under the age of forty is safe with you around and maybe I should extend that to older women too.'

'Sarah,' said David. 'You're being too harsh; and in case you're fretting about Jasmine, I can assure you, I'm only trying to be friendly to her and her children and I've realised that people have been noticing. I want to stay friends with them but assure you, I do not want to rock the boat, particularly with Jack still in prison.'

'Talking of which,' said Laura, 'your extraction of the name Frank Green from this group of youths, yobs, or whatever you want to call them, is interesting. I've heard the name before and he may be the drug source that Jack wasn't prepared to reveal to the police. His name's come up a few times in conversation here at the inn, but I'm not sure that I could put a face to the name. Well done for telling Chris Thompson all about this, it may be very useful information to the police and it just could help get Jack out of prison.'

At that moment, Ben Lewis came out of the bar with a pint of beer in his hand and came up to the table. 'Just finished work and it's so hot I thought I'd have a pint before going home to my parents' house. Can I join you?'

'Sure,' replied Laura. 'Adam and David were telling us about their kayak adventure today along North Creek where they were bombarded by a marauding mob from Princewater.'

David then explained to Ben that the marauding mob were in fact a group of three youths and a girl. When David mentioned the name Frank Green, Ben immediately butted in. 'Jack and I were in the same class as Frank at Princewater School. We didn't have much to do with him and he was always getting into trouble. His father was always in trouble too, I think for nicking cars and motorbikes. I've seen Frank in Daymouth a couple of times, maybe once here at the inn talking to Dan Pitcher, the prat that owns the drifting rib that we recovered some time ago. Do you think this Frank Green information could help Jack get out of prison?'

'Not sure about that,' said Adam. 'It's early days and from my meeting with Jack at Dartmoor I got the distinct impression he just wanted to do his time and then get out. Even if the police do get Frank Green, I suspect Jack will want to stay out of it.'

'How about Ian Carbrook?' continued Ben. 'I'm sure he is tied up with all this somehow. Does this information put him in the clear?'

'Again, not sure about that,' continued Adam. 'Frank Green could well be Jack's supplier but someone in turn must be Frank Green's source of supply. I guess it is just possible Ian Carbrook's the mastermind behind it all. But Sarah, you've just agreed to speak in support of Carbrook's planning proposal, what's your view?'

'Well, I personally have never thought of Ian and Susie

as drug barons. My parents know them a lot better than I do, and they get on really well with them. Adam, I thought you'd agreed to go with them to Monaco in the autumn? You've now got me worried about all of this. I did agree to speak in support of the Marlo project because I believe it will be good for Daymouth and in particular Eastside. It didn't occur to me that it could in any way be linked to a drugs issue.'

David tried to lighten the conversation. 'Hey, you lot, this is a beautiful summer's day and here we are in a beautiful location, with two beautiful ladies. Why don't I go and get another round of drinks and we enjoy the early evening and quietly watch the sunset over Daymouth?'

CHAPTER 9

The morning after the kayak adventure, Adam and David were having a late breakfast when Admiral Tom knocked on the door of the cottage and came in. 'Hello, you two. I hear you had a bit of excitement yesterday.'

'How on earth do you know about that?' said Adam as he pulled up a chair for Tom to join them at the table.

'Ben Lewis phoned Jasmine last night and she told me about your drug discoveries when she came to work this morning. She's still in my cottage and pretty worried about this chap Frank Green and how it might affect Jack in prison.'

'Oh heck, I hadn't really thought about that,' said David. 'Look, I need to go and see her right now. Tom, is that OK with you? Perhaps you could stay here and talk it through with Adam.' David got up and, without waiting for Tom to reply, went next door.

They sat at the table for some time before the Admiral spoke. 'Things seem to be hotting up, Adam. The regatta and the Holberton party are over and now the whole drugs business is raising its head, and I hear the eco park planning application will be heard at the beginning of next month. I must say that since you arrived at Eastside, life certainly hasn't been dull.

Don't get me wrong, I've very much enjoyed having both you and David next door. We've had some good evenings together and I'd miss you if you left. But to be honest, I am worried for Jasmine. I really do like her and her family and I just don't want things to go wrong for them again.'

'You're right, Tom, and I've been affected by the lifeboat fatality in which I was involved. I had a sleepless night worrying about a whole range of things, not least as to whether I'd made a sensible decision to come here in the first place. You see, I have made new friends, such as yourself, but I've also got sucked into a whole range of other peoples' lives. It's been exciting but a bit scary. Before I came to Daymouth, all I was thinking about was trading. I was successful and it totally occupied my mind. Since I've been here, my involvement in the lives of others has multiplied and the complexity of the whole thing has increased. Maybe I've gone backwards in coming here?'

'Adam, for me, it's Jasmine I'm worried about. You're a bright chap with everything going for you. You still have a lot of life in front of you and there are many good people living in Daymouth. Frank Green and his cronies are clearly rotten apples and you might add Lord Robert Harvey to that list. Remember, we live in an area that most Brits would call paradise and you've got the finances to enjoy a lifestyle of your own choosing. My suggestion to you is just keep going and enjoy the good bits and sort out the challenges.'

Meanwhile, next door, David was trying to console Jasmine. 'I apologise if I've upset you, Jasmine. You know I care for you and your family; I wouldn't want to do anything to worry you.'

'But you have, David. You've discovered the name of this chap Frank Green and then gone and told the police. They'll link it with Jack and visit him in Dartmoor and word will get out there. That means trouble for both Jack, in prison, and maybe me and the kids here. Jack's really frightened of these guys. The prison's full of drugs and the gang's controlling them both on the inside and outside. They're hardcore and vicious. Jack knows he's got to keep his head down and say nothing, otherwise he and us, his family, are in real danger. David, I'm so scared.'

David put his arm around her and held her tightly. 'I'm so sorry, I really didn't think this was going to be a problem to you; in fact, I thought that some good might come out and that the drug dealers would be caught.'

Jasmine started to cry and David's eyes also began to water. 'Jasmine, I can't bear this. You know that I like you a lot, in fact I believe I'm falling in love you, and that somehow seems to make it worse.'

David couldn't believe what he had just said, but he knew he was saying the truth. Both were now in tears and holding each other.

'What a mess,' David said. 'I shouldn't have said what I just said, it only makes matters worse. I'm so sorry for everything.'

'David, I understand. I feel the same way for you too, but I've tried to hold it back. When you came to Eastside, you were so pale I almost laughed, but now it's different. We've had a wonderful time and the kids are so happy with you. Jack's been very difficult and I've tried to put him to the back of my mind. Now this has come up and suddenly I'm in turmoil and it's now no longer a dream; what are we going to do?'

*

By the time the Admiral had got back to his own cottage, both David and Jasmine had talked things over enough for them to appear reasonably normal.

David said, 'Hello, Admiral, good to see you back. We've just had a chat and I ought to get back to Adam and leave Jasmine to get on with her work here. You do know that I'll do everything I can to help her, don't you?'

'Yes, David, I do,' replied the Admiral. 'This Frank Green business seems to have rocked the boat a bit for both of you and you should get back.'

Later, as Adam and David sat around the kitchen table, 'I guess we need to sort a few things out,' said Adam. 'This Frank Green business has brought me up with a jerk and I've just told the Admiral that I'm not sure Daymouth is the right place for me.'

'Adam, your problems are nothing compared to mine. I've just told Jasmine that I am falling in love with her and evidently, she feels the same for me too.'

'I did warn you,' said Adam. 'But I guess that's not important now. What are we going to do?'

'I don't know.'

There was a long silence and then Adam suggested, 'Let's take a walk along the beach and try and clear our heads.'

The two of them set off and walked along the sand towards Sunny Corner. The tide was out and the morning sunshine was building in strength. The exposed sand was a brilliant yellow that contrasted with the clear blue water and sky. Daymouth estuary was looking its best.

'You know, the Admiral is right,' said Adam. 'This is a fantastic place that most people would give their right hand to live in, and here we are confused and unsure.'

David paused. 'Adam, I think I've got to go back to London. I've upset everything here with Jasmine. Before I came, she and her family were toughing it out while Jack was in prison. Now she's confused, I'm confused, and it's all because I haven't discouraged our relationship from the word go. I'm an idiot to have taken it this far and yesterday highlighted what a fool I've been. The only solution I can see is that I leave and let everything cool down. I do hope you and I can stay good friends.'

'Of course we should stay friends, but let's try and sort out whether it's a good idea for you to go running back to London.'

The two of them carried on walking to Sunny Corner, each lost in their own thoughts. They stayed at the cove for a couple of minutes just looking out to sea and then continued walking along the cliff path that followed the rocky shore, both trying to make some sense of their jumbled minds. After about half an hour, they reached a small inlet and went and sat on a small stony beach.

Eventually, Adam spoke. 'David, we go back a long time and we've shared a lot together. This isn't the time to part company. We're in this together and shouldn't walk away from the situation. I chose to live here, I'm not sure why, but the place has already got into me. I'm not going to leave, not yet anyway. As for you, well, you've also become part of Daymouth and there's something strong between you and Jasmine. It's not clear how it's all going to pan out, but surely you shouldn't totally desert her. I agree maybe in the short term the best thing is for you to go back to London. But you need to be here if necessary and only time will tell whether anything develops further. So don't walk totally away from her; I've seen how happy the two of you can be.'

There was a long pause as Adam himself digested what he'd just said whilst David thought through those words and his own thoughts.

It was David who broke the silence. 'OK, you're right. I'm not going to run away. I'll talk it through with Jasmine. I'll give her all my contact details and then in a couple of days I'll go back to London. She can contact me there if she wants, or needs, me and I'll stay in regular touch with you. I want to support you too, but at the moment I think I'm better off away from here. Let's hope you can help resolve the issue of the drugs and support the right team, whoever that might be, in this eco park planning application. Let's see this through together.'

'Thanks mate,' said Adam. 'That means a lot to me and I was thinking along the same lines. You know, I think we're growing up as a consequence of all this. We're both over thirty, but as they say, better late than never.'

*

On returning to the cottage, David went in search of Jasmine to talk about what he was proposing to do and Adam got on the phone to Chris Thompson, the policeman in Daymouth.

'Hello, Chris this is Adam Ranworth on Eastside. I hope you don't mind me calling you, Chris, but all the locals seem to.'

'Not at all, how can I help you, Adam?'

Adam then went on to explain how Jasmine was desperately concerned that her husband Jack could be drawn into any police enquiry into Frank Green and that the whole family could be in danger from drug gangs.

'Adam, I submitted my report last night and I've already spoken on the phone to DI Paul Barclay at Plymouth this morning. He said he'd start organising police surveillance on both Green and the Prince Rupert pub. He needs hard police evidence to catch this chap and doesn't want to rely on members of the public that can later be leant on by the gang to not give evidence. I'll remind him about Jack Sanders in Dartmoor, but rest assured we're very aware of the situation there. Involving Jack at this stage in the enquiry wouldn't be helpful to anyone.'

At the end of the phone call, Adam felt relieved but still concerned. His whole focus on life seemed to have changed over a matter of a few hours and his mind was racing as to what he needed to do.

David got back a few hours later saying, 'I've talked with Jasmine and I think she's OK at the moment. It appears that when we went for our walk, the Admiral spent time talking with her, which helped a lot. Anyway, yes, I'm going to go back in a couple of days and we'll see how things pan out.'

'David, I've thought about that too. Before you do go back, I'm going to spend the night in Daymouth so you and Jasmine can have the cottage to yourself for a bit. It's the least I can do and please don't stop me. I want you and Jasmine to enjoy some special time together before you go back to London.'

*

The following morning, Adam decided it would be better if he spent the day away from Eastside. He crossed the estuary in 'Greta', went to the Waterside Hotel and then headed to the Smugglers Inn for lunch. There were only a few people about and Laura was serving behind the bar.

'Hi Laura. I have news and a bit of a proposition to make.'

Adam explained the situation and told her that David would be going back to London the next day. 'It's a really tricky situation, but both agree a cooling off between them is a good idea, particularly with this Frank Green issue developing. I must say I didn't realise just how far it had gone between the two of them.'

Laura replied, 'Oh, Sarah and I worked that out some time ago and that's what we were talking about when you and David last came in here for a drink. In fact, we both agreed that David is a much better fit for Jasmine; but Jack's her husband and the father of their two children. So, now you've given me the news, what about the proposition?'

'Well, I want David and Jasmine to have the chance of some time alone together so I've said they can stay overnight at the cottage before he goes. I feel it's the least I can do and I'm staying on the Daymouth side tonight in order that they can have the place to themselves. I've booked a room at the Waterside Hotel and, well, I wondered if you'd like to join me? If you can get the evening off, we can have supper as well? Of course, it's all entirely up to you and I quite understand if for whatever reason you can't accept.'

'Let me see,' responded Laura. 'Am I available tonight?' There was a pause. 'Yes, no prior bookings. Am I free this evening?' Another pause. 'Maybe, I'll need to check with Charlie, but he owes me loads of evenings and so I think I'll say yes too! Of course, you do realise that the hotel's very high profile and it won't be many minutes before the entire town knows about our fling at the Waterside. But yes, let's do it and have some fun. Have you booked the room in the name of Mr and Mrs Ranworth or Mr Ranworth and possible escort?'

After lunch and drinks with Laura at the Smugglers Inn, Adam left in good humour and made his way to the lifeboat station.

'Hello Adam, good to see you,' said Ted. 'It's about time we got you back on the boat. How about next Wednesday afternoon? We've got a training session planned.'

'Sure, very happy to do that,' replied Adam. 'Have you any news on the yacht shout where the poor chap died?'

Ted explained that the whole process would take weeks if not months to come to a judgement; however, the RNLI were satisfied with his report. He'd recommended that Adam be put forward for a bravery award, but this had been vetoed because he was on probation at the time and technically shouldn't have been actively involved in the shout. There was also the Marine Accident Investigation to be completed as well as the coroner's report. Ted continued, 'We do need people like you on the crew and you've proved that you've got what it takes. We already think of you as one of the family and all the crew want you aboard. You seem in particular to have made a very good impression with Ben Lewis, Tina Harding and Laura Clift, and that's very impressive. Laura and Tina can be very exacting, so you've done well.'

'Thanks for that, Ted. It's good to feel accepted by both you and your crew.'

As Adam came out of the lifeboat station, he literally bumped into Ben Lewis on Main St. 'Oh sorry, Ben, what's the rush?'

'I'm late for my meeting with Ted. I've decided to apply for the RNLI chief engineer job at Daymouth. I'm fed up with Benson's and need a change of life. My wages there are very low and, although I love my parents to bits, it's time I got my own place and some independence.'

'Well, good luck, you sound as though you're thinking positively and I hope you get the job. Go for it!'

Ben disappeared into the lifeboat station only for Adam to then be confronted by Beryl, the Daymouth Gossip.

'Ah Adam, I hear you are in the news again!'

Adam couldn't believe she already knew about him and Laura at the Waterside Hotel; however, this was Daymouth, and he then thought anything was possible.

'I hear you have extracted the name Frank Green from a load of youths in North Creek. You could have saved yourself a lot of time and come to me as I knew Frank's father, Nicker Green, as he was known. Always nicking stuff, mostly cars. Frank was no different and he got in with a really rough lot in Princewater. I've seen him around Daymouth in the last couple of years, hanging around with that chap Dan Pitcher, who seems to have more money than sense.'

Adam felt an immediate wave of relief that Beryl hadn't mentioned the Waterside Hotel, only for Beryl to continue. 'And yes, I just met Laura who was very excited about being taken out to the Waterside Hotel for supper. I wonder who with?'

Horrified that the news had spread so quickly, Adam was already very aware that his invitation to Laura would become public knowledge in Daymouth, and so maybe the sooner people knew, the better. Not, however, wanting to continue the interrogation with Beryl, he changed tack.

'Beryl, I am wondering if you know how the people of Daymouth are viewing this proposed Marlo Eco Park development on Eastside. Surely that will affect Daymouth too?'

'Ah, you are a clever one changing the subject, but yes now the planning application is headline news in the local paper, I've heard lots of very surprising gossip. Do you know, nearly everyone I've spoken to in Daymouth is for the project and that really does surprise me. The local traders are for it and the attraction of significant all-year employment in the area is a definite bonus. I must admit, I expected the conservationist, traditionalist, the environmentalist and many other "ists" that I can't at the moment think of, would be against it. We'll just have to wait and see, as they will certainly show their faces at the planning meeting next month. Will you be going?'

'Not sure, Beryl, but I know I must be going as I've got things to do. Bye for now.'

*

Adam had been lucky to secure the same room at the Waterside Hotel where he spent his first night in Daymouth. Room 302 was spacious and had a balcony that had a commanding and beautiful view of the estuary. He arranged the clothes that had been delivered to him at the hotel on the bed in the way he wanted and waited for the arrival of Laura.

At 7.30 in the evening the receptionist phoned the room and said his guest had arrived. 'Please send her up to room 302,' he replied and then he waited for Laura.

When she walked into the room, she was taken by surprise. 'Hey Adam, what's this about?'

'Just a small present I bought from JayJays. If it's not right, they're happy to change it or change the size. The woman in the shop knows you and guessed your size and the style of something you might like.'

Laid out on the bed was a long, yellow, stylish dress, matching shoes and some jewellery.

'I'm sorry, but the jewellery is pure bling and not the real stuff, but I thought we should try and make this a special occasion rather than just sneaking off to let David and Jasmine have a night together.'

'It all looks fantastic,' exclaimed Laura. 'I've never had anything like this as a present before and I've never even been inside this hotel. The room's brilliant and that view is something special. You are wonderful and thank you so much.'

Laura was very excited and went into the bathroom to put on her new dress and accessories. She had in fact already made a big effort to look smart but this raised everything to a new level.

Eventually she emerged into the main room and Adam was impressed. 'You look great,' he said. 'Well done you, and well done JayJays, they seem to have got it spot on.'

Laura felt a little embarrassed but pirouetted around in her dress with a huge smile on her face. 'You certainly know how to make a girl happy. Thank you so much. I really do feel that I can take both the Waterside Hotel and their posh guests on at their own terms.'

Adam had also brought some smart clothes with him and the two of them made a very impressive couple as they entered the hotel dining room. 'This is fun,' said Laura. 'I can see the headlines in the local paper. "Bar maid of the Smugglers Inn stuns staff and guests at the Waterside Hotel in Daymouth".'

The hotel had a dress code for meals and guests and staff were all smart; however, Laura and Adam had raised the bar several notches with their arrival and pre-meal cocktail drinking. Laura was loving behaving in a way that was totally alien to her normal friendly, chatty and classless way. 'This is like being a film star, and why not just for a few hours?' Adam smiled and was delighted that he could see that she was really happy and enjoying herself.

The meal was delicious and they lived the dream with radiant smiles. Afterwards, they retired to room 302 and completed a very memorable evening and night together.

Meanwhile, on the Eastside of the estuary, Jasmine's mother, Judy, had agreed to an overnight babysit and David was standing at the cottage door when Jasmine arrived. 'Mum's agreed to have the kids for the night and so here I am. David, I do love you and having the use of the cottage is wonderful, but I'm so sad that you're going. I'm afraid that I'll spend the whole time crying.'

The evening and much of the night was indeed spent with both David and Jasmine in a very sombre mood and it was only whilst in bed and in the darkness of the early hours that they felt able to able to express their love for each other in the only way that true lovers can.

After a breakfast of coffee and toast, Jasmine left the cottage with tears in her eyes. Deep down, she knew that David was right to go back to London, but as she walked away from the cottage, she feared that a wonderful opportunity in her life was fast disappearing and would be impossible to recover.

*

Later that morning Adam got back to the Eastside from Daymouth and asked David, 'Well, how did things go between you and Jasmine?'

'OK, I suppose, but it was all rather sad. Adam, I must thank you for allowing us to stay here; it was special and I hope won't be the end of our relationship. How did you get on in Daymouth?'

'Oh fine,' replied Adam. I stayed at the Waterfront Hotel in room 302, the same room that I had for my first visit here.'

There was a pause and then he said, 'Are you sure you're ready to go back to London?'

'Yes, I couldn't bear to go through another Jasmine farewell. I'll get my things together, go and say goodbye to the Admiral and then push off. Would you be kind enough to explain the situation to the Holbertons? I'm not sure that I could face that at the moment.'

David went and saw the Admiral and then collected up his belongings suggesting he leave both of the kayaks at the cottage as he would definitely want to return at some stage. He told Adam that the Admiral had been very understanding and said he would make contact with either of them if he felt Jasmine needed help.

Finally, they gave each other a hug outside the cottage and David said, 'This is it. I'm off. Keep in touch and I'll come down like a rocket if you need any help. I guess you've got to sort yourself out and decide whether you're going to stay, but please help resolve this drugs business before going if that's what you decide to do. Also, good luck with the eco park proposal, that could have a big impact on Daymouth, Eastside and maybe Jasmine too.'

As David drove away, Adam was left in the cottage feeling somewhat lonely. They'd both been through something of a roller coaster few weeks and now everything seemed a bit flat.

*

That evening, Adam went up to the Holbertons' and was met by Sarah as he approached their front door.

'Hi Adam, nice to see you. Jasmine told Grace this morning that David was leaving for London today and so we thought you might like to come for supper with us this evening and now you're here! I was just about to come down and invite you!'

'Thanks, Sarah, that's great. Yes, David's gone and I'm feeling a bit adrift after all the events of the last couple of weeks.'

As they went into the living room, Sarah's parents were sitting looking out of the large window at the sun setting over Daymouth.

'Ah, Adam, lovely to see you,' said Grace. 'Do come and join us watching this glorious sunset before we all have supper. Jasmine's already given me her version of why David has left in such a hurry. Would you like to add anything?'

'Well, I'm not sure what Jasmine said, but I think it would be pretty similar to my own version. David felt he was getting too close to Jasmine and our kayak adventure, which resulted in the discovery of the name Frank Green and then the disclosure to the Daymouth police, scared her. He decided the best thing to do was to go back to London and give time for matters between him and Jasmine to cool off. It's sad to see him go, but hopefully he'll be back sometime soon.'

'Oh, I do hope so,' replied Grace. 'He's like you, such a nice man. Now do come and have a drink, watch the sunset and we can then talk about the future over supper. It's only shepherd's pie but I've made enough for everyone.'

Later, Grace brought in the supper from the kitchen and the four of them sat around the dining table. Sarah initially talked about how pleased she had been to have Adam crewing for her during the regatta and how excited she was to have done so well. Then Grace tried to talk about her Monaco holiday plans, but James intervened saying that the most important future matter was the Marlo Eco Park planning application that was coming up at the end of the month.

'I'm really troubled by this application and have heard for the first time today that my own daughter is going to speak at the meeting in favour of it. I'm feeling isolated. Adam, what is your position on the matter?'

'That's a tricky one, James. A couple of days ago, David and I kayaked along East Creek and we met a woman called Paula Chase from the AONB team. She'd got herself marooned on the Marlo Farm island while checking it out for seahorses. We spent some time with her and surprisingly she seemed to be quite keen on the proposal, although her boss, Councillor Humphreys, was, as you might expect, against it. I'm moving towards supporting the proposal, but I haven't yet seen all the details.'

Grace's face lit up. 'Wonderful, Adam, I feared you might align yourself with my husband, who is still living in the past and dogmatic that it would be a disaster if given planning permission.'

'That's unfair of you, Grace,' muttered James. 'Daymouth and Eastside are Areas of Outstanding Natural Beauty and, let's face it, the reason why we live here. If this type of application is passed it would mark the beginning of the end of all of that. I just don't see why you and Sarah can't realise that will happen.'

Sarah responded, 'Dad, I really don't think you've looked carefully at the application; it's full of good environmental ideas that are way ahead of their time. For example, each of the thirty modular luxury chalets will be in their own half-acre of ground. Cars have to be left at the reception and vehicle movement within the 180-acre park will then be carried out using electric battery golf-style caddy cars allocated to each chalet and staff. Guests will be able to cook for themselves in their chalets or have meals delivered from the central kitchens or eat in style at the main restaurant area. Electric power will be generated using the eco park's own wind turbines and solar panels. It will be top of the range and not like the old-fashioned holiday camps of your generation.'

As they ate their supper, the debate around the table continued for some time until Grace put a stop to it by saying, 'That's quite enough for one evening! The most important question now is: Adam, are you coming to Monaco to have fun after the planning hearing? I need a bridge partner and Ian Carbrook and James would like to introduce you to their poker group. The Harveys, with their super yacht, should also be at there and so I'm sure there will be chances to get on the water and see at first hand how these super rich Monaco people manage to exist in their tax-free super everything principality.'

'Not sure about the Lord Harvey bit,' replied Adam. 'During his regatta party, David and I had a dust-up with his lordship; I suspect he's probably best avoided. Yes, I'm happy to come and discover all that Monaco has to offer. I think I do need to broaden my experience of different locations before deciding to settle down in one place. Sarah, will you be coming too?'

'Very sorry, no. I start teaching at Tordon tomorrow and that runs through until Christmas. There is a short half term but that doesn't fit with the dates when Mum and Dad are going to Monaco. I have however managed to get the day off to do the Marlo planning meeting. Maybe we could have a few more sails in the yawl before the end of season and I would really value your input on Marlo.'

Before Adam could reply, Grace said, 'Well, that's set then. Wonderful, I'll tell the Carbrooks and we can sort out details later. None of us will let this Marlo business interfere with our holiday and Sarah, you could come for a weekend if you wanted.'

The topic of conversation then moved onto Jack and Jasmine Sanders and whether the North Creek discovery of the name Frank Green was of significance.

'Poor Jasmine, the whole thing's a tragedy,' said Grace. 'She's such a lovely person and her children are delightful. Jack seemed a nice enough chap but to get involved with drugs had to be madness. He always seemed to be struggling to finance the family and that was a reason why we gave her work here. I've never heard of this chap Frank Green, but I'm not surprised she's worried.'

'Ben Lewis knew of him,' added Sarah. 'He apparently hung out with Dan Pitcher in Daymouth sometimes. But remember, Ben was convinced that Ian Carbrook was in some way involved in the whole drugs business and you are going on holiday with him.'

'Sarah, that's quite enough! Ian and Susie are lovely people and it's impossible that Ian's involved. Ben's a good chap and I know he was a friend of Jack's, but he has to be wrong on this one and I just don't know where he got the idea from.'

Adam sensed it was time for him to leave and got up to depart. 'Thank you so much for supper tonight and thank you for sharing your thoughts on all the subjects of the moment. I really feel I should be off now and prepare for life again without David. I met Ted Sandringham yesterday and I'll be doing lifeboat exercises with them. I'll have a very careful look at the eco park project application and find out exactly what these precious seahorses are about. They may be a key issue in whether the application gets approved or not.'

Sarah saw him to the door. 'Adam, thank you for supporting me. My parents at times can be very difficult and thank you for being a great crew in the yawl.' She then kissed him on the check and gave him a hug. 'School tomorrow, it seems as though the party is over for this year.'

CHAPTER 10

Before they set off on the all-weather lifeboat training exercise, Ted spoke to the whole crew ashore. 'Thanks everyone for coming. We've a full crew for this session and the weather's looking good but a bit choppy. I plan to go to sea and practise person-overboard recovery using Dead Eric. We'll switch positions a bit later in the afternoon but to start with, this is how the boat is organised. In the wheelhouse with me will be Jon Payne as navigator and Adam as an observer. Adam, technically, is still a probationer and so needs to be away from any direct operations, particularly as the earlier rescue this year is still under review. We also have a new probationer, Tony Collis, on board today and I'd like him to be on deck, again only acting as an observer under the guidance of Ben Lewis and Tina Harding. Jimmy Lethbridge will of course be the engineer; however, some of you may not know that Jimmy will be leaving us shortly as he's been promoted to the RNLI training centre at Poole in Dorset. Their gain and our loss, but anyway, well done, Jimmy. Laura, I'd like you to look after the stern deck with Bruce and manage the plastic overboard person, Dead Eric. Bruce has been with us for many years and although technically retired, he still enjoys coming out and of course he has a fantastic amount of experience. So, unless there are any questions, jump to it and we can get on the water.'

There were no questions, but Ben Lewis went over immediately to Adam. 'Adam, we need to talk. Can we meet up when we come ashore, I may have some important information about the drugs business. I overheard something in the Smugglers Inn last night.'

'Come on, you two,' called Ted. 'We're treating this operation as we would a shout. Chop-chop.'

Adam nodded acknowledgement to Ben and they both responded to Ted's orders and went to their respected duties, preparing the boat for sea.

The wheelhouse of the lifeboat was rather like the Starship Enterprise with many controls, a multitude of coloured lights and different visual screens. 'OK Jon, let's go,' said Ted. 'Keep to under six knots in the estuary and then head due south at about twenty knots for fifteen minutes to get clear of the Daymouth Headland. There could be a fair sea running and the wind's force four southerly; we'll have it on the nose on the outward journey. Adam, you just sit back and enjoy the ride; watch all that's going on inside and outside the boat. Keep your eyes open for anything unusual and don't be afraid to alert me or Jon if you see something unexpected.'

Adam belted up in the specially designed wheelhouse seats and as they sedately left the Daymouth quay he saw his own cottage on the port side. The sun was out with a few people on the beaches but there was not much holiday boat activity as it was getting near to the end of season.

Most of the craft on the water that afternoon consisted of fishing boats together with a few sailing cruisers returning to Daymouth on the rising tide. As they continued along the estuary, Adam noticed a group of outboard ribs moored off Sunny Corner with some of them being used by their occupants for line fishing. Amongst the boats he recognised the Dan Pitcher rib that he had helped to recover on a previous lifeboat trip and wondered what he or his cronies could be up to in that part of the estuary.

When the lifeboat reached the estuary limit buoys, Ted opened up the throttle of the twin diesel engines and Adam was pressed back into his seat as the boat surged forward. The wind had in fact increased to a healthy force five and as the boat reached more exposed water, the waves began to build.

'Are you OK, Adam?' said Ted. 'I know you've been out with us before but this is quite spicy. A full-on southerly into Daymouth is exciting and the exposed parts of the coastal cliffs get a bit of a battering.'

'Yes, I'm fine,' replied Adam, although when he looked in a viewing mirror, he could see he'd gone a bit pale.

Laura called on the intercom. 'Our new boy Tony is feeling seasick. I've given him a pill and Tina's on the case. Are we still going ahead with the Dead Eric overboard drill?'

'Maybe, let's see how we get on. This is good practice and I need to know everyone can cope with seas like this.'

Ted continued to push the lifeboat into the waves. He was in his element and knew the boat could take much greater punishment than it was currently being subjected to.

There was a crackle on the radio and then a pause. 'Daymouth lifeboat, Daymouth lifeboat, this is Falmouth coastguard. Immediate task.'

Jon Payne responded, 'Daymouth lifeboat, receiving.'

'We need your position; we have an emergency.'

Jon gave the coastguard the lifeboat's coordinates and everyone in the wheelhouse listened to the response.

'We have two land-based reports from the Daymouth cliff coastal path of a motor vessel dangerously close to the seaward side of Daymouth Headland. It appears to have no steerage and is about to founder on the rocks in the heavy onshore waves. We can't detect an AIS identification signal for any boat in that area and we've received no Mayday signal. Urgently investigate and report back.'

Ted grabbed his intercom and responded, 'Message received, will investigate immediately and report. Out.'

He switched to the internal intercom. 'OK guys, we have an urgent shout of a motor vessel that could be foundering on the exposed cliff side of Daymouth Headland. The boat is not transmitting an AIS automatic identification system and has not called Mayday. If it is in trouble, this is very strange. We're now responding to the shout. Ben and Laura, go down below and put on drysuits, we may need to launch the daughter rib off the stern deck.'

Within seconds, the lifeboat was surfing at over twenty-five knots in huge waves back towards the possibly endangered vessel.

As they approached the headland, Jon picked up a boat on the radar that was very close to the cliff. 'Course 332 on the port bow. Yes, I now have visual sighting below the cliffs. Looks to me about 15m long, blue hull with a cabin above deck.'

Within another thirty seconds, the whole crew of the lifeboat were able to see the blue-hulled boat being tossed about close to the rocks at the foot of the cliffs.

'OK,' said Ted. 'I've got it now. That doesn't look good. We need to get her name and report back to Falmouth. Is anybody on board?'

'Looks like two men in the cockpit, but it's difficult to see,' said Tina. Yes, it's a motor vessel, the sort of thing that could have come across the Channel; I think that's a French flag on the mast. It's incredibly close to the cliff, maybe even on the rocks.'

Ted radioed back to Falmouth, giving the boat's exact position and edged the lifeboat closer in.

'I can see the transom,' called Tina. 'The boat's name is "Fleur de Landemer" and it's from Cherbourg. Looks in pretty ropey condition and yes, there are two men above deck and they're waving at us. Big waves are breaking over the whole of the boat in the surf.'

'We must act now before she gets smashed up on the shore,' said Ted. 'Laura and Ben, get onto the rear deck and throw them a heaving line and let's hope we can pull them off before it's too late. We haven't enough time to get the crew off the boat here, it's too dangerous.'

Ted positioned the lifeboat so the stern was facing the French boat, which was now side on to the rocks at the cliff base. 'OK; throw the line now.'

Ben expertly threw the heaving line, which had a knotted 'monkey fist' on the end, and the line caught in one of the railings around the 'Fleur de Landemer'. One of the men on the boat grabbed the line and immediately started to pull it in.

'Well done, Ben,' shouted Laura. 'Here's the towing line.'

Ben attached the towing line to the heaving line and indicated to the men on the French boat to haul in the towing line and secure it to the bow of their boat. There was so much wind and wave noise that it was impossible for them to talk to each other, but they seemed to know what they had do.

As soon as the line was secured, Ted eased the lifeboat away from the shore and after allowing for a very generous length of tow rope to be let out, said, 'OK, secure the tow rope and we will see if we can get her off the rocks.' He gently opened up the power of the twin diesels and saw that, as the towline tightened, the French boat was almost effortlessly drawn off the rocks.

'Incredible,' said Adam, 'I wouldn't have believed that was possible. The power of the lifeboat and the way you did that was amazing.'

'We were lucky; another couple of minutes and that boat would have been locked on the rocks and probably would have broken up as we pulled it off. I'm still worried though. It looks to me that the hull's been damaged and she'll be taking on water.'

Ted radioed to the Falmouth coastguard that they had successfully been able to tow the French boat off the rocks, but he thought the hull was probably damaged. Their current position was very exposed to the onshore wind and large breaking waves so they were in the process of towing the boat around the Headland Point and into the more sheltered water of Headland Cove. It would be safer there to get the two men currently on the French boat onto the lifeboat and it should take about fifteen minutes to get round the point, providing the boat didn't sink or capsize in the meantime.

Laura came in on the lifeboat intercom. 'Ted, I really don't understand why they haven't been using their radio. Perhaps they had an electric wipe-out? I presume you can see the boat from where you are? It's pitching a lot and I think it must be taking on water.'

'Yes,' replied Ted, 'I'm not happy, but if we can get it round the point into the shelter, we can get up close and recover the two crew more safely.'

Ted sensed that the towing characteristics of the boat were changing and he thought about reducing speed; however, he made the decision to maintain speed and get to sheltered waters more quickly.

The lifeboat and its tow, 'Fleur de Landemer', pitched their way around the Headland point and when they reached the quieter water of Headland Cove, it was clear that the French boat had a substantial list. 'We need to act fast and get those chaps off the boat,' said Ted. 'I'm coming alongside her.'

The two Frenchmen were hauled onto the lifeboat by Ben and Laura.

'*Merci pour le sauvetage,*' said one of them. '*Nous ne parlons pas anglais mais il faut savoir qu'il y a douze migrants dans la cabine avant. Voici la clé.*'

Laura shouted into the intercom. 'They don't speak English but I think they are saying there are twelve migrants in the forward cabin. One of them gave me a key!'

'Shit,' muttered Ted under his breath and then spoke on the intercom. 'Who speaks French? Jon, report the situation to Falmouth and let's get these people out.'

Adam was out of his seat and saying, 'I'm OK with French. I'll go and talk to them on the aft deck, Ted. What do you want us to do?'

'That boat isn't stable,' replied Ted. 'I've seen something like that before. I think it's going to capsize. We must work fast. Tell Ben to put on the dive gear, he's the only one who's done the training for it. Adam, find out exactly where these migrants are on the boat. Jon, tell Falmouth we need full backup fast.'

As Adam was extracting information from the two now very frightened Frenchmen, there was a shout from the intercom.

'The bloody boat is capsizing,' exclaimed Ted. 'I can see it going. Stay clear everybody, I've got to move the lifeboat away from it.'

There was silence from everyone on the lifeboat as they witnessed the 'Fleur de Landemer' roll over on its side and then, within a few seconds, completely invert, with its damaged hull totally visible.

'Blimey,' gasped Adam and the others looked on in silence. Adam grabbed the intercom. 'Ted, one of the Frenchmen said there are twelve migrants in the front cabin and he gave Laura the key to the cabin. He said they were instructed to leave them locked in until a boat came from Daymouth to collect them when it was dark.'

At that moment, Ben came out of the cabin holding his flippers and goggles, with his dive suit and air canister on his back.

'Yes, I've got the key,' said Laura. 'Is it safe to try and see if we can open the door?'

'No,' responded Ted. 'That boat could sink at any moment. Jon, I need guidance from Falmouth.'

Whilst Jon was contacting Falmouth, Ben was going through the safety checks of the dive equipment he had put on and said to Laura, 'The only way to access the forward cabin is for me to dive and go in from under the boat. It looks as though the damage to the hull is amidships and so it's possible there's an air pocket in the forward section. But how long will the boat stay afloat like it is at the moment?'

'I don't know, Ben,' replied Laura. 'We need to wait for instructions from Ted. This is a scary mess and those poor people on board may already be drowned. The French bastards should never have put the boat on the rocks in the first place and they should certainly have released the migrants from the cabin when they got into trouble. What a mess.'

'We need photos of the boat,' shouted Ted down the

intercom. 'Falmouth want photos so they can assess the condition of the boat. They will not allow any diving recovery until then. We must also put a buoy on the towline and release the buoy and line from the lifeboat to avoid being dragged down if she does sink. I'll circle the boat around the hull. Jon, you take photos and Adam, use our mobile camera so that the images can be relayed directly to Falmouth. We've twenty metres of depth at the moment and I can't see how we can possibly tow the inverted hull further ashore into shallower water. Anyway, I've got to follow instructions from Falmouth. A helicopter's been scrambled but that won't be with us for at least twenty minutes. The coastguard and police are on their way but again that's going to be about twenty minutes. The fishing boat 'Quest' will get here in ten minutes. The rescue's now on channel 16 and so we can expect other boats from Daymouth to be here shortly.'

Ben and Laura sorted a buoy onto the towing line and cast that off. Jon set Adam up with the camera and within two minutes, images of the upturned hull were being transmitted back to Falmouth. The two Frenchmen sat silently in the upper cabin unable to communicate in English and absorbing the significance of the tragedy that was unfolding in front of them.

'OK, Ben, you've got permission to dive, provided both you and I are happy with that,' said Ted on the intercom. 'Ben, what do you think?'

'No problem, Ted, that's what I spent a week training to do at the diving school last year. I don't want a line, as that might get caught. I have the cabin key the Frenchman gave Laura and am ready to go.'

'OK, do it. The sooner the better and be careful. If you meet any problem, return straight away. Do not take unnecessary risks. I want you back here within ten minutes whatever the situation.'

'Hey-ho, here we go,' said Ben to Laura. She gave him a hug and a kiss on the cheek, saying, 'Good luck.'

Ben jumped off the stern of the lifeboat and swam the short distance to the upturned hull. All eyes were on him as he submerged.

There was continual radio comms between the lifeboat and Falmouth and several boats were coming in on channel 16, alerting them to their movements. This was turning into a full-scale emergency with more and more agencies getting involved. Falmouth coastguard reported that the police would arrive on the headland within five minutes and the Daymouth Dive Company had been alerted and should be with them within half an hour.

The minutes ticked by and, much to Ted's relief, the capsized boat appeared to be stable and not visibly sinking any further in the waterline. One of the two French crewmen had turned deadly white and the other had started shaking.

'Come on, Ben. I need to see you. Why isn't he on a line, Laura?' asked Ted on the intercom.

'He wouldn't take one. Said it might get caught in something.'

'He should have taken a line. We only have one dive suit on board. We've no control, he's on his own. Jon, get onto Daymouth Dive and see when they are going to get here.'

After five incredibly long minutes had passed with no sighting of Ben, Daymouth Dive reported on channel 16 that they were coming out of the estuary with two divers ready to go and would be with them in about ten minutes.

'We've got Ben Lewis diving under the boat and haven't

had any sign from him for several minutes,' radioed Ted to the dive boat. 'Hurry, this is not looking good.'

'Laura, how long has Ben got oxygen supply for?'

'His tank was full and that should be good for forty minutes, maybe an hour, so he should be OK on that score,' replied Laura. 'Look: I can see the dive rib coming in the distance.'

Adam's mind was racing. He felt helpless and unable to do anything positive. An instinct was to dive into the water and then do an underwater dive without oxygen; however, he knew that about thirty seconds was his limit and that wouldn't be enough. He went across to the Frenchmen and, speaking in French, asked them to explain the boat layout and possible problems Ben might experience. The response was worrying and Adam relayed them to Ted. 'The French guy says there was a lot of fishing gear in the main cabin as they had to take it all out of the front cabin in order to get the migrants in. He also said there were two women and three children in the group.'

'Oh shit, this is terrible,' muttered Ted. 'We must get alongside and get the Daymouth divers into the boat as soon as possible. Ben should have surfaced by now.'

The dive boat eventually arrived and Ted briefed them of the situation.

'We have one diver, Ben Lewis, who has been down there for twelve minutes and he went in without a line. Since then, we've learnt from the French crew, who don't speak English, that there's a lot of fishing tackle in the main cabin that may have caused Ben problems. He went down with the key that can unlock the forward cabin where there are twelve migrants trapped, and now maybe drowned. Seven men, two women and three children. Since it capsized it does appear to be floating in a stable mode, but of course there is always the danger of sinking. Do you want to get permission to dive from Falmouth?'

'No Ted. We're going down straight away. Ben's a friend of ours. OK, boys, in you go and we'll use attached lines.'

Two divers went into the water and submerged beside the upturned boat.

There was silence on the lifeboat as the seconds and then minutes went by. Eventually, one of the divers emerged, came to the surface and took off his mask.

'Not good. Ben's tangled in the fishing stuff with his mask off; he's drowned. Everyone in the forward cabin we believe has also drowned. Jim's still checking but it's really grim. Ben was one of our mates. It's so unfair; he was such a good bloke.'

Everyone on the lifeboat and the dive boat was stunned and speechless. The second diver emerged and gave a thumbs-down gesture, indicating there were no survivors.

Ted was in tears and unable to speak. Tina picked up the intercom. 'Falmouth coastguard, Falmouth coastguard, this is Daymouth lifeboat. We have a dive report that one of our own crew, Ben Lewis, has drowned whilst inside the upturned boat, and that all twelve migrants in the forward cabin have also drowned.'

*

The recovery of the bodies went deep into the evening and it was gone midnight before the lifeboat returned to Daymouth. A coastal patrol vessel had arrived from Plymouth and that was used to take the bodies to Plymouth harbour. The two French crewmen of the 'Fleur de Landemer' were taken away by the police and the 'Fleur de Landemer' itself remained capsized overnight in Headland Cove with a police patrol boat on station.

The lifeboat crew were devastated by events and barely able to communicate with each other. All were wrapped up in their own emotions trying to come to terms with what had happened. As a doctor, Tina Harding had seen death and grieving more than any of them and she tried to console, in particular, Ted and Laura, who were finding it very difficult to even speak.

As they approached the Daymouth estuary, a rib came out to meet them. The RNLI press officer, Richard Thoms, climbed aboard the lifeboat from the rib, went up to the wheelhouse and addressed the whole crew.

'Obviously, this is devastating news for all of you; it's a terrible tragedy to lose a member of your own crew, who I am sure you all knew well. It's also a tragedy that twelve migrants have also died under these dreadful circumstances. I do need to warn you, however, that this is already national and international news. When you get ashore, there are already a significant number of reporters on the quay with TV satellite van support. They will all be wanting information and storylines and they will make the next few hours even more difficult than they probably are at present. We, that is, the RNLI, would be grateful if you would say as little as possible to the press or TV, asking them to respect your own privacy at such a difficult time. Ted, as coxswain of the lifeboat, they will certainly target you. Do you feel you can cope OK?'

'No,' replied Ted. 'Not at the moment. I just want to get the lifeboat into Daymouth and go and see Ben's parents, Jim and Julia. I know them very well.'

'Ted, you must do that,' said Tina. 'Don't worry, I'll field any of the press and the rest of the crew will take care of the boat. We're in this together and we must support each other. We all did what we thought was right and Ted, you know you have all the crew's support.'

'Thanks Tina, I appreciate that. I must go and see Jim and Julia before I do anything else. I presume they've already been told the news?'

*

Ted ignored the commotion at the quayside and strode off, heading straight to Ben Lewis's parents' home at the top of the town. Tina Harding was brilliant with the press.

'We are all very aware that you are hungry for information about this tragic incident,' she said. 'However, as perhaps you can imagine, this has been a very difficult experience for us all. There has been loss of life, and as a doctor I know only too well the effect that can have on people. Everything is very raw. In addition, I'm also sure that many of you have been involved in reporting other major incidents and will know that the police, and in this case, other agencies, will need to establish information and take statements. So please respect this and do not pester any of the crew. The RNLI will of course inform you of events when they have been given permission to do so.'

The assembled press stepped back from the quay allowing the crew to moor the boat and return to the lifeboat station in silence. Even when they were inside, very few words were said. Adam changed out of his lifeboat kit, slipped out of the back door and crossed back in 'Greta' to his cottage on Eastside. When he got into the cottage, he looked at his mobile to see text messages from Jasmine, Sarah and David, all concerned about what they had heard on the news.

The doorbell rang and Admiral Tom walked in.

'Are you OK, Adam? We were all so worried. We heard someone on the lifeboat crew had drowned and an unspecified number of migrants too.'

'Yes, I'm in one piece, but Ben Lewis, the young lad from Benson's Boatyard, drowned trying to rescue twelve migrants who were locked in a forward compartment of the upturned French boat that had come across the Channel from Cherbourg.'

'Tragic,' said Tom. There was a pause and he then continued. 'You will be in shock. I'm in shock too as it reminds of the Falklands. Thank you for telling me. I think the best thing both of us can do at this late hour is to go and try and get some sleep. Don't hesitate to call me if you think I can help.'

CHAPTER 11

Adam woke up with his mind full of the previous day's events. He believed that he might have been able to save Ben's life if he had questioned the Frenchmen more deeply on the first occasion that he spoke to them. If Ted had known there was fishing gear in the main cockpit, Adam was pretty sure he wouldn't have allowed Ben to dive. *Oh no*, he thought, *I've contributed to his death*.

David Young phoned from London asking whether Adam wanted him to come down to the cottage. 'The national news this morning is full of the Daymouth rescue bid, the drowning of one of the lifeboat crew, as well as twelve migrants. I remembered you'd said you were going on the lifeboat yesterday and, well, I thought it could be you.'

'No, it was Ben Lewis,' said Adam. 'But I now think I might have saved his life if I'd got more information earlier out of two Frenchmen whom we did rescue. They kept the migrants locked up in the boat during our rescue from the shore. How could they have done such a thing? I've been thinking about it all night and I just can't understand why they didn't unlock the forward cabin when everyone on board was in real danger of being washed onto the rocks.'

'Look, Adam, would you like me to come down? You know I want to help and, yes, I would love to come and see Jasmine for a bit.'

'I'm sort of OK and no, don't come down now. I've just remembered that before we left on yesterday's exercise, Ben told me he had some important information he wanted to share with me. We didn't have time to talk about it, but at the time I assumed it was about drugs. Maybe it was, maybe it wasn't and maybe I'll now never know what it was about. But if it was drugs, both Jasmine, and Jack in Dartmoor, could be drawn in and so you're better off staying in London. If I need you, I'll let you know.'

After the phone conversation, Adam began to think more and more about Ben wanting to tell him something before they left on yesterday's exercise. He couldn't remember Ben's exact words, but the more he thought about the short conversation, the more he felt it was important and maybe even relevant to the attempted landing of the migrants.

Adam had another phone call, this time from the Holbertons. Sarah spoke first, but said she had to rush off to teach at Tordon school. Grace continued the conversation saying how the whole family and others were devastated to hear the news, adding that, to their knowledge, this was the first attempted migrant landing Daymouth had ever experienced.

Then Jasmine phoned having heard about Ben's death. 'Adam, this is terrible. My father dies, Jack goes to prison and now Ben's drowned trying to save migrants. The world's falling apart. Is there anything I can do to help?'

'I don't think so,' said Adam. 'I've just spoken to David and he's offered to come down but I said no. I think we need to sit tight for a while and see how things develop. Yesterday,

Ben said he had something important to say to me, but we didn't have time to talk properly. Just stay put and care for your family.'

After the phone call, Adam decided that he wouldn't go round to see the Admiral. Instead, he got into 'Greta' and crossed the estuary. The press and TV with their satellite vans were still in evidence and there was significant police presence.

The lifeboat station was full of unfamiliar faces, most of whom were wearing some kind of uniform. The police, coastguard, Royal Navy and the customs officers were all in there and eventually, Adam found Ted looking exhausted and under pressure. 'Hello Adam. This is all pretty grim, but I'm glad you've come over. The French boat's still afloat with a Royal Navy recovery vessel from Plymouth standing by. The lifeboat needs to go out to cover the recovery, but I've said that none of yesterday's crew should be involved. You'll need to write a report of what happened and you'll be interviewed. Last night I saw Ben's parents, Jim and Julia. As you can imagine, they're absolutely distraught, but I had to do it.'

'You did the right thing, Ted,' replied Adam. 'I don't know them, but I'll go later today. If I don't do it now, I might never go. It'll be hard and they don't know me, but I did know Ben and I do feel a responsibility. I was there. Ben was a good guy doing what he felt was the right thing. He was a hero and someone who very sadly paid the ultimate price.'

Having got directions to the Lewis house, Adam set off before he had time to change his mind.

'Hello Adam, I'm so sorry to hear about last night's lifeboat incident.' It was Beryl pursuing him along Main St. 'Terrible news, I do hope you're OK and it's very sad about Ben. He was a good, hard-working chap.'

'Yes, Beryl you're right, it's dreadful; sorry I can't stop to talk at the moment. I'm on a bit of a mission.'

Adam continued along Main St and climbed the hill to reach the Lewis home. His head was buzzing working out what he was going to say, but as he rang the doorbell, his mind went blank.

'Mr Lewis?' said Adam.

'That's right,' came the reply.

'Mr Lewis, my name's Adam Ranworth and I was one of the crew on the lifeboat yesterday. I want to say to you and your wife how terribly sorry I am. Ben was a hero and you need to know that.'

'Thank you,' said Jim Lewis. 'Come in and say that to Julia. She's beside herself with grief, but your words might help.'

Jim led Adam into the kitchen where Julia was sitting crying.

'This is Adam who was on the lifeboat yesterday. He's come round to say how sorry he is about Ben.'

Julia looked up at Adam in a flood of tears. Adam stood motionless, then he moved forward, knelt down and put his arms round her.

'I am so, so sorry this has happened. Ben was a friend and I want you to know he was a hero too.'

They stayed embraced for some time until Jim broke the silence. 'I think we could all do with a cup of tea.'

Adam then recounted the events as best he could remember, as he felt a compelling need to explain to them the circumstances of what had happened and that Ben had been a true hero. They listened in silence.

'Ted told us about this last night,' explained Jim. 'Thank you for your own words. We'll now have to come to terms with it all. Ben was our only child and he lived with us. We were a real family and, well, at the moment I just can't believe he's drowned. We do appreciate you coming here to talk to us. Ben's mentioned your name a number of times. You're the chap that bought one of Eastside Cottages and you know Jasmine and Jack Sanders who were school friends of Ben. It was only yesterday that Ben said he had something important to tell you.'

Adam was unsure whether to probe any further on the subject as, at that particular time, he too was in an emotional state.

'Did he say what it was about? Before we left the shore, he told me that he had something important to tell me, but we never had the opportunity.'

'I'm afraid not,' said Jim.

There was a long pause that was eventually broken by Julia raising her head and saying, 'He might have made a note of it in his diary. Ben keeps a diary by his bedside where he used to make a record of his weekly wages. I think he sometimes scribbled in bits and pieces of news too. His bedroom is, or do I now mean was, his own space and we didn't go in there. I didn't read his diary and I now never want to, but Jim, you could go and have a look with Adam and see if there's anything written down that might be useful.'

Adam followed Jim up the stairs and opened Ben's bedroom door saying, 'I don't think I've been in this room for over two years.'

He found Ben's diary notebook by the side of his bed and flicked through it, finding the last entry. 'Here we are, the last note he made was "Overheard Frank Green and Dan Pitcher talking in the Smugglers Inn. Frank said there was a big consignment coming in overnight." That's it, I'm afraid, Adam. Does that make any sense to you?'

'It does now,' exclaimed Adam. 'As we went out on our lifeboat exercise yesterday, I saw Dan Pitcher's rib moored in Sunny Corner and wondered what it was doing there. Ben probably thought what he overheard at the Smugglers Inn was all about drugs, but I now suspect it could have been about migrants. It looks very much as though Dan Pitcher and Frank Green were involved with migrant smuggling and the Pitcher rib was going to be used to pick them up when it got dark last night. Of course, the foundering of the 'Fleur de Landemer' put a stop to that. Jim, this is important and the police must be told about the notebook. What do you think? Should I take it to them or leave it and get them to see it here.'

'Adam, my mind is so confused at the moment, you should do what you think best.'

'Maybe it's best if they come and collect it from you here. Can you and your wife cope with that? This could be very important. It could well be crucial evidence in securing arrests for this migrant smuggling and for all I know could also link to drugs. Frank Green's a known drugs dealer in Princewater.'

Leaving the notebook in the bedroom, Jim and Adam went downstairs and explained their finding to Julia. The notebook discovery helped her from just thinking about the loss of her son and she said, 'Do anything that you can to help bring those involved with this terrible tragedy to justice. You must tell the police and they can come here and collect any evidence they want.'

*

Adam went straight back to the lifeboat station where, if anything, there were now even more people than during his first visit. He found Chris Thompson, the local policeman, in the crowd and described what he had discovered.

'Right, Adam, I think you'd better come with me. The migrant drowning has brought Special Branch into the investigation from London and they're with DI Barclay at the moment in my harbour office.'

Adam followed Chris Thompson to his office where Paul Barclay and a group of plain-clothes Special Branch detectives were sitting around a table talking.

'Sorry to butt in,' said Chris, 'but Adam Ranworth, who's a member of the lifeboat crew, has some important information that I think you should know about.'

'This better be good,' said one of the plain-clothes detectives, who was clearly the leader of the group. 'I am now leading this enquiry. My name is Fraser, so get on with it and make it snappy. We've a lot of ground to cover.'

'OK,' replied Adam. 'Is Fraser your first or second name?'

'Don't piss me about, Mr Ranworth. I haven't got the time for that. As far as you are concerned, I'm Fraser.'

Adam explained how Ben Lewis had tried to tell him about something important before they went on yesterday's exercise, but the opportunity to talk didn't come up. At the time, Adam said that he assumed it was about an ongoing drugs issue. On the way out of the estuary, Adam had noticed a moored rib in Sunny Corner owned by a local called Dan Pitcher. Today, Adam had been to see Ben's parents, Jim and Julia Lewis, to express his condolences. They alerted him to a diary notebook that Ben had kept in his bedroom, and Jim Lewis discovered an entry dated two days ago saying that Ben had overheard

Frank Green and Dan Pitcher talking in the Smugglers Inn where Frank had said there was a big consignment coming in overnight. Presumably, Ben thought the consignment was drugs, but it now looked as though it could have been migrants. Adam's conclusion was that Dan Pitcher was probably the conduit for bringing the migrants ashore but the exchange didn't happen, after the French boat had been wrecked on the rocks.

When Adam had finished, Fraser looked at Paul Barclay and Chris Thompson. 'What do you two make of this?'

'Sounds plausible to me,' said Chris. 'Dan Pitcher's a spoilt rich brat who could easily be involved. Frank Green's a local drug dealer who's a nasty piece of work. Paul, am I right in thinking that you already have him under surveillance for drug stuff at the moment?'

'Yes, that's right,' added DI Paul Barclay. 'We've been trying to nail him for some time but potential civilian witnesses are too frightened to give evidence.'

'OK everyone. Firstly, Adam, my apologies for being a bit sharp at the start. This is something very positive that we can act on and so at the moment this information is not to go out of this room. I assume no one else except Mr and Mrs Lewis know about this?'

'Correct,' responded Adam.

Fraser paused in thought and then said, 'I'm not sure quite who you are, Mr Ranworth, but rest assured within half an hour I will have a full background on you. I'm impressed by what you've said and it could be a crucial lead. We shall need a full written statement from you in due course. Paul, I want you, with backup, to go immediately and visit the Lewis's. Recover the diary and search for any other evidence. You need to tell the Lewis's that under no circumstances are they to tell anyone else about the diary and Adam's visit. And Paul, link up with one of my men to update us on this chap Frank Green. We'll concentrate on Pitcher and see if we can get any CCTV coverage from the harbour on yesterday's movements of his rib. Pitcher and Green could well be involved, but they're unlikely to be the key operators and those are the ones I really want to get. We're already questioning the two Frenchmen from the capsized boat and are working on their Cherbourg connection. It's the UK side that I really want. Maybe the migrant and drug trafficking are linked, but that doesn't have to be the case.'

*

The whole of Daymouth seemed to be in a very sombre mood as Adam made his way down Main St. He saw a few people he recognised but managed to avoid them. The TV satellite vans were still on the quay and both holidaymakers and locals were hanging around, curious for further news of the disaster. He knew at some stage he'd have to go back to the lifeboat station but in his present state of mind he'd no appetite to join the thronging mass of officials that were there.

He got into 'Greta' and motored back to the Eastside of the estuary where he was met by Admiral Tom.

'Adam, I've been looking for you. Are you OK?'

'Yes, I think so, let's go inside and have a drink.'

They went into the cottage and he put on the kettle. 'What would you like, Tom? Tea or coffee?'

'A good strong whisky and I suggest you have one too. I know it's barely past midday, but from the look of you, I think you need a proper drink.'

They sat down both with whisky glasses in their hands. 'Tom, I'm afraid there's not much I can say. The police are investigating and I've got strict instructions to say nothing to anybody. I know I can trust you, but I need to obey them to the letter. It's very frustrating; sharing what's happened would be a way of helping me understand what's going on and I would really have valued your thoughts.'

'I understand,' replied the Admiral. 'A lifetime in the Royal Navy did teach me a few things, including keeping secrets. I know the world's moved on since then but there's still a time and place for secrets and this sounds exactly like that.'

Adam prepared a snack lunch for them both and they tried hard to avoid talking about yesterday's drama.

When the doorbell rang, he opened it and saw Jasmine. 'Oh, Adam you are here. Have you any news?'

'Come in, Jasmine, I've had lunch with Tom and told him that the police have said I must say nothing about the whole incident to anyone and I am afraid that includes you.'

'I've just phoned Jim and Julia Lewis and they have said the same thing. What's going on, Adam?'

'Be patient, Jasmine. What I can say is, Special Branch, down from London, are on the case and we just need to let them do their stuff.'

Jasmine burst into tears and clutched Adam. 'I'm so scared; can either of you help me?'

The Admiral came across to them. 'Jasmine, this is not the time to ask Adam questions. Ben Lewis has lost his life and we all need to grieve for him. It seems that the tragedy has revealed other things and we should respect the police in keeping this secret for the present and do not press Adam who has been told to say nothing.'

Jasmine looked at both Tom and Adam. 'My father dies. My husband goes to prison and now this; one of our friends is drowned. Where will it all end?'

*

Later in the afternoon, when Jasmine and Admiral Tom had left, the doorbell rang again and this time it was Sarah and Grace wanting to know how Adam was, and what news there was. Yet again, Adam had to explain that there was an ongoing police investigation and he couldn't say anything.

'You poor dear,' exclaimed Grace. 'How frustrating for both you and us.'

'Mother, please don't be so patronising. It's quite terrible news about Ben and those poor migrants too. We saw one report that said there were twelve of them and women and children were involved. All my children in school today couldn't talk about anything else and they were really frightened.'

'Yes, it's an utter tragedy and I'm sure the whole area's in shock. In fact, the journalists weren't too bad last night when we came ashore but I guess it's inevitable that not only locals but people all around the world want to know what's happening. My problem is that at the moment I'm not allowed to say anything at all.'

'Adam,' said Grace, 'we would love you to come to supper tonight even if you can't say anything about yesterday; we can talk about other things such as the Marlo Eco Park planning application, which is coming up soon and, don't forget, our super trip to Monaco afterwards.'

'That's very kind of you, Grace, but no. I'll stay here and work out what I am going to say in my report of the events.'

*

It was nearly 10pm when the cottage doorbell rang once more.

'Sorry to bother you at this late hour, but we need a chat,' said Special Branch detective Fraser.

'OK, fine,' replied Adam. 'How did you get here?'

'You are a nosy bugger aren't you! We have our ways, including the use of powerful ribs. I've got a man standing by with the rib off your foreshore waiting to take me back to Daymouth when we've finished.' He smiled and walked into the cottage.

'Would you like a drink?' asked Adam.

'Good idea, a whisky if you have it. Yes, I'm on duty, but this is a fact-finding call. I hope you are going to have one too.'

They sat around the kitchen table both drinking whisky and Fraser began. 'We've done our homework on you and surprisingly found quite a lot of stuff relevant to this case. So relevant that I thought you needed to know what we know. You may be a key player in the whole investigation and equally it may turn out your involvement is marginal. However, my gut feeling is that you could be a very important "person of interest" to us and we need you on our side.

'Let me start by telling you what our intelligence knows.

'Unknown to you, you first came up on our database as a potential recruit for MI5 when you were an undergraduate at Cambridge. MI5 is always very interested in top university undergraduate mathematicians to work, for example, at GCHQ; however, at the end of the day you just missed the cut and you weren't approached.

'Next. Companies House data reveals you were spectacularly successful in business and I'm glad to say you appear to have been a good boy and paid your taxes.

'Then this year things start to get a bit more interesting. There's a police report that you fished a chap out of the river Thames at Putney and after that, activity seems to have happened around Daymouth.

'Firstly, you contacted the local police to relay a concern about a drug-related involvement of a Mr Ian Carbrook that Ben Lewis passed onto you. Then we have a record of you going to Dartmoor Prison to visit a Jack Sanders who was in prison for peddling drugs. That was a big surprise to me until I learnt that Jack's wife Jasmine Sanders is your housekeeper.

'The last entry up to now is that not long ago you reported a canoe drug incident near Princewater where you extracted the name Frank Green from a group of yobs.

'So, Adam, you seem to have been drawn into a drugs scene around here. And today, you turn up telling me what could be important information relating to migrant smuggling. We know drug and people trafficking can be linked and of course at Special Branch we're involved in both.

'I'm not sure whether this Ian Carbrook chap is involved, but you've certainly given us enough evidence to take a very close look at both Dan Pitcher and Frank Green. This afternoon we got CCTV images confirming that the Pitcher rib was where you saw it yesterday and that it came back into Daymouth after the French vessel capsized.

'I'm now going to share some confidential information with you. We have enough to pull Pitcher in for questioning and we plan to do that within the next twelve hours. He seems to be a weaker person than Frank Green and so he's our first target for questioning. It's going to be a busy night. Adam, you're a key part in this investigation and we want you on our side, that's why I am bringing you up to speed.'

Adam sipped at is whisky, starting to appreciate the full significance of his actions to the police and taking in the details of the profile that they had amassed on him.

'Well, you certainly seem to have a pretty complete record on me and I'm not sure whether to be impressed or concerned; however, you have made me realise my involvement could be of significance to you and, rather scarily, to other parties too. Do you think I'm in danger?'

'At the moment, no, but it's a fair point and we might have to have someone keep an eye on you. I want you to behave normally and, of course, keep everything I've told you completely confidential. I want you to come over to Daymouth tomorrow and at some stage write a full report including the Ben Lewis, Ian Carbrook, Dan Pitcher and Frank Green background. I know you'll need to write a report on the RNLI incident, but please keep the two reports separate. You're a clever chap, so you'll know what I mean.

'I've said enough for now and I still have a very busy night in front of me, so I'll leave you in peace. You may not see me again for a bit, but rest assured we're on the case. This is serious and it may get tricky. If you notice anything strange or want to get in touch, here is a contact card. You may not get straight through to me but use my name and I'll contact you.'

Fraser got up, shook Adam by the hand and left.

*

The following day started with lashing rain coming in from the sea. The temperature had dropped and with it, the whole mood of the estuary. Summer had turned off, autumn seemed to have been missed out and winter had rushed in. The sunny, idyllic Daymouth estuary was now a cold, wet and a windy place.

Adam was awake early and he used the time to write his RNLI incident report. He followed the instructions of Fraser's previous evening meeting by keeping the details to mainly nautical matters. His night had been very troubled with the continual thoughts of Ben Lewis, his parents and also the tragedy of drowned migrants. This was by far the most traumatic experience of his life and significantly greater even than the Putney or previous sinking yacht incidents. In those cases, he hadn't known the casualties, but in this one he'd known Ben well and also felt partly responsible for his death. Throughout the night, he'd been in turmoil thinking about how he might have saved Ben's life if he'd spoken earlier to the Frenchmen about conditions in the cabin and felt compelled to include this aspect in the report he was writing.

When the report was finished, he set off across the estuary for Daymouth. The weather was so bad, he decided to take the ferry rather than battle with his own boat.

'I haven't seen you for a long time,' said Harry Payne the ferryman. 'What a terrible tragedy. We all knew Ben; he was a good local lad. I know his parents too and they'll be devastated.'

'Yes,' was all Adam could say and they crossed the wet and windy estuary in silence and their own thoughts.

The wind and rain seemed to have driven the TV satellite vans away from the quay, and there was hardly anyone outside on the streets. The lifeboat station was, however, still busy and Adam eventually found Ted.

'I've done my report, Ted, and here it is. How are you feeling? Are you OK?

'Thanks Adam; no, I'm not really OK. This one has got to me. It's like losing a son. Ben was family and I'm not sure that I have what it takes to carry on as coxswain. I'll have to train someone else up before I go, but at the moment I just haven't the heart for it.'

Adam desperately wanted to tell Ted about the Dan Pitcher, Frank Green development in order to take his mind away from the tragic elements of the rescue but he held back, having been instructed to keep it confidential. Instead, he said, 'Ted, I'm struggling too. If I'd told you before Ben dived that the cabin was full of fishing gear, you wouldn't have allowed him to go down. Life is all about very fine margins and you've saved so many other lives. We can get through this if we pull together. You've said so many times that we're team and a family and so we must help each other.'

Ted's eyes were watering over, although he was one of the toughest and bravest people Adam had ever known; at that instant in time he seemed to be one of the most fragile.

'Come on, Ted, you need to get out of this lifeboat station. We've got to face the world sometime. Let me buy you a pint and hope that Laura's behind the bar. She might be able to cheer us up.'

The Smugglers Inn was quiet and Laura was indeed at the bar. 'Ah, Ted and Adam. Great to see you both. All the locals have been staying away. I don't know why. Maybe because they don't know what to say about Ben? The bad weather's also driven both journalists and visitors away, so here I am with hardly anyone to serve apart from you.'

Laura was able to work her magic at raising spirits and it was not long before the three of them were able to open up and talk freely with each other.

'I've never had nightmares,' said Laura. 'But last night was awful. All those people drowning. It was terrible. However, today it seems something of a release. I know it happened. We were all there and now we just have to get on and do the best we can. We must help those that need help and, as far as Daymouth's concerned, that's Ben's parents and maybe the lifeboat crew. None of us will forget this one.'

Her words seemed to break the ice and Ted visibly cheered up. She fetched three hot pasties and together they collectively managed a sense of normality over a bar lunch of pasties and beer.

*

The wind and rain were continuing to lash down as Adam left the pub. He walked purposely along Main St and then up the hill towards the home of the Lewis's.

'Hello, it's me again, Adam Ranworth; can I come in?'

'Of course you can,' said Jim. 'We've just had lunch and I was starting to talk to Julia about Ben's funeral arrangements. She's being very brave, but it's difficult.'

The three of them sat round the kitchen table.

'I've also been thinking about the funeral,' said Adam. 'I'd like to pay all the costs of the funeral and for a wake, a celebration of Ben's life at the Waterside Hotel. Please do accept my offer. It's something I want to do for Ben, for you and for Daymouth. The funeral would be whatever you want it to be and the wake at the Waterside Hotel again would be your choice. I just want to do something for you and Ben and maybe the best way I can do that is provide the finance. I am fortunate to be in a position that paying for this sort of thing isn't a problem, and it's something I really do want to do.'

*

With rain still lashing down, Adam walked away from the Lewis home and he felt pleased that they had accepted his offer. He also sensed that a genuine bond had been established between them all. Jim had told Adam that the cost of the funeral arrangements had in fact already been a worry to them and they were very grateful for his generosity. The bond however seemed to be more than just money. He felt that both Julia and Jim had brought him into their own family and he was feeling a warmth of understanding with them.

When he arrived at the harbour office, he found that there was still a very high level of police activity. Paul Barclay, the detective from Plymouth, explained what was required from him in relation to a statement of events and as he was leaving the office, he met Special Branch Detective Fraser.

'Adam, we meet again! I've some news for you. We've pulled your man Mr Dan Pitcher in last night and he's been singing like a canary. Blames Frank Green for everything and was sweet enough to give us a full written statement of everything he knew including the migrant caper and some drugs distribution. Unfortunately, Dan's father got wind of his son's arrest and a top lawyer is now on his way down from London to defend the poor boy. But we've got what we need with signed statements from him and, at this very minute, we also have Frank Green under arrest at Princetown, which is where I'm off to now. So, Adam, you were right and your little detective work has given us a good start in terms of getting to the bottom of this migrant business and maybe even the drugs supply around here. I certainly don't expect Frank Green to be such a soft touch as Pitcher was. Someone yesterday said Dan Pitcher was a prat and that is exactly what he is. He's small fish, but it's a start. We're now on the trail of some much bigger fish. Remember: everything I've told you is absolutely confidential.'

CHAPTER 12

Three days after the 'Fleur de Landemer' had capsized, the police announced that two Frenchmen as well as Dan Pitcher and Frank Green had been remanded in custody charged with assisting smuggling of migrants. The police gave no further information saying that the investigation into the tragedy was ongoing.

As the days passed, the press and TV moved onto other more topical news stories and Daymouth started to return to something approaching normality.

Jasmine visited her husband Jack in Dartmoor Prison where she discovered he'd already heard about the arrests of Dan Pitcher and Frank Green. He made it clear that he still wasn't prepared to say anything to anyone about his own drug supplier. He just wanted to do his time and then return to his family.

Adam tried to keep a low profile, but he was finding it difficult to remain silent about his involvement in both the migrant and drug issues. Added to which, David Young was contacting him regularly to find out how Jasmine was coping. Finally, Adam agreed that he could come and stay in order to go to Ben Lewis's funeral

*

The funeral took place two weeks after Ben's drowning and by then, autumn had decided to arrive in Daymouth, with the leaves beginning to turn a golden colour and fall to the ground. The estuary was quiet on the day of the funeral with the sun intermittently breaking through the clouds. There wasn't a breath of wind on the water. In the morning, Harry Payne was busy ferrying Eastside residents across to Daymouth for the funeral, but thirty minutes before its start, he moored the ferry, changed his clothes and joined the multitude of locals and others going to the church.

The church was packed with people from both sides of the estuary and the arrival of the hearse containing the coffin marked the beginning of a very emotional service. Jim and Julia Lewis were sitting together in the front row alongside Ted Sandringham and his wife Tessa. The Lewis's had few relatives and the remaining hundreds of people in the church were made up of friends, locals, members of the lifeboat community and those that simply wanted to pay their respects to a brave lifeboat man.

The church went silent as the coffin was brought in and six of the Daymouth lifeboat crew slowly carried the coffin on their shoulders down the central aisle. They positioned it on trestles in front of the dais and Ted Sandringham stood up, came over to the coffin and draped the Daymouth Lifeboat RNLI flag over it. Tears were falling from his face and the whole congregation was caught up by this very emotional and symbolic action.

The vicar went to stand by the coffin and addressed the congregation.

'I had intended that this funeral service would be a celebration of Ben Lewis's life; I know the family well and this is what they would want. However, as I now stand in front of you and see the church fuller than I have ever seen it before, and when I look at the faces of you all, I realise that this is a very, very sad day for Daymouth. I realise that the loss of a member of our lifeboat crew is something that touches everyone in our community. The lifeboat is at the centre of the town and is part of all our lives. Some of you will have known Ben personally, but others will not, and you are here because you know he gave his life to rescue others. Together, we need to share the tragic loss of a young life.'

There was then a prayer followed by a hymn sung by the Daymouth choral society and the church choir.

The vicar got up again and said, 'Today, there are no Daymouth fishing boats out at sea as all the crews are here in the congregation. They have made a special request for a song to be sung and I have asked Rachel Cleaves, our own soprano, to sing the song accompanied on the piano by Jon Payne who was on the lifeboat when Ben drowned.

Rachel came forward and sang, beautifully, the song 'Sailing'.

> *I am sailing, I am sailing, home again, 'cross the sea.*
> *I am sailing, stormy waters, to be near you, to be free.*
> *I am flying, I am flying like a bird 'cross the sky.*
> *I am flying, passing high clouds, to be with you, to be free.*
> *Can you hear me, can you hear me, through the dark night far away?*
> *I am dying, forever trying to be with you, who can say?*

Everyone in the church was deeply moved. Jim and Julia Lewis were in tears and many others unable to hold back their emotion.

There was a further hymn and the vicar then asked Ted to give the eulogy for Ben.

The coxswain rose and went to the pulpit, pulled out the notes he had written and looked at the congregation. He was unable to speak. His emotion through the service was now so high, he literally could not say a word.

Tina Harding saw that Ted was unable to say anything. She got up from her seat, walked up to the pulpit, stood beside him and quietly spoke into his ear.

'Ted, you can do this. Remember, we're a family. We're all together and you are the coxswain. Forget your notes and say what you think is right.'

Ted looked at Tina.

'Thank you, Tina. I just didn't know how or if I could start. I've struggled all week with my notes and now in this church it is overwhelming. I'll try and say just what I think is right. It may come out all wrong but I will try.'

Tina gave Ted a reassuring hug and went back to her seat.

'Thank you, Tina, for rescuing me,' he said to the congregation. 'She reminded me that we're a family on the lifeboat. We're a team and I can now see from the number of people who are here today, we are a much bigger family than I ever thought we were.

'Ben was family. He was a great guy who would do anything for others. He was the one that volunteered to get diving qualifications and he was the one that dived to rescue those poor migrants. I was the one that let him go on the dive and I will never forget that fateful decision.

'Someone told me, "Life is all about very fine margins and you've saved so many other lives." This is true, but today we are grieving over the life of one of our own crew. It's nearly eighty years since the Daymouth lifeboat lost the life of any of its own crew from the boat, but today we grieve for the loss of one of us. I will never forget this.

'My heart goes out to Jim and Julia who have lost a son and my heart goes out to our Daymouth lifeboat crew who have lost one of our family. Looking out now at the vast congregation here today, I also realise that Daymouth itself has lost a member of one of its own, larger family in such tragic circumstances.'

At this point Ted broke down in tears and began making his way back to his seat. The congregation spontaneously started to applaud him and continued for some time. Then there was silence.

The vicar waited a few moments before getting up.

'Thank you, Ted. We all know you've saved many lives and that you have been and hopefully will continue to be such a superb coxswain of our Daymouth lifeboat. Everyone in this church and beyond shares your grief and that is why so many people are here today. You are not alone.'

There were further hymns and a bible reading given by the mayor. At the end of the service, the vicar made a final announcement.

'After this service there will be a private family burial in the church cemetery and others are invited to a wake, or should I say celebration, of Ben's life at the Waterside Hotel. All are welcome and I don't want to stop anyone from coming; however, I'm not sure that the hotel can cope with all who are here. Perhaps the wake should be restricted to all who knew Ben. I think it's obvious from what has happened at this service today that we all deeply appreciate how so many people have attended to show their obvious support for Ben's life, for his parents and for the Daymouth lifeboat. There will be a book of condolence at the lifeboat station together with the opportunity to make an RNLI donation specifically to our local lifeboat.'

The coffin was carried out of the church on the shoulders of the lifeboat crew. Then it was taken to the adjacent cemetery where a small group of family, friends and lifeboat crew attended the burial. Ted Sandringham and his wife, together with Tina Harding, Laura Clift, Jon Payne and Adam Ranworth, were amongst those present as the coffin was committed to the ground below.

The burial, party then walked down the hill towards the Waterside Hotel where Adam found himself walking next to both Jim and Julia Lewis and Ted Sandringham with his wife Tessa. Adam broke the silence. 'These are difficult times for all of us, but for you, Jim and Julia, and for Ted and Mrs Sandringham, I can't imagine how difficult it is for you all. All my sympathies are with you and today we saw just how many people are grieving with you. Ben was a good guy and it's a tragedy. I do hope we'll be able to help you in the future.'

'Thank you, Adam,' said Jim. 'It's all like a terrible dream, but we know it isn't a dream. Everything's too raw at the moment to make sense of anything, but thank you anyway. Ted, you were very brave. I knew I wouldn't have been able to say anything today. What you said and did was great, really heartfelt, and we must stay together as friends whatever happens.'

'Jim,' said Ted, 'that was one of the most difficult moments in my life. I don't know what I said, but I hope it was OK. I do know how I feel inside but I can't find the right words. Of course Ben was a good guy and one of the lifeboat family. He's not with us anymore and I feel a deep responsibility. I too was amazed at the funeral attendance and you and Julia were very, very brave.'

The group continued their way to the wake in silence, all absorbed in their own thoughts.

*

The Waterside Hotel had been alerted to the large number of people at the funeral and they had prepared extra food and made available an outside terraced area. Over a hundred people eventually arrived and the atmosphere was very much less sombre than in the church. By the time the burial party had joined the wake, the wine, tea and beer and food were circulating generously.

'That was an amazing funeral service,' said Laura to Sarah Holberton. 'And I'm so glad the atmosphere here is less tense. Ted was fantastic, but it must have been a huge ordeal for him.'

'I agree,' replied Sarah. 'The service was very moving for everyone. I knew Ben a bit as he'd helped repair our boat. But for you it must have been tough. You were on the lifeboat at the time and you knew him well.'

Sarah continued. 'Tina was great. She and I have had quite a few battles racing the yawls and she's my own doctor. But today I saw someone doing the right thing at the right time. I was really impressed.'

'I agree,' said Laura, 'she was brilliant when the lifeboat came ashore after the French boat capsized. She took over from Ted and handled the press with great authority. Ted's a fantastic coxswain, but losing a fellow crew member was just too much for him.'

'Oh look,' exclaimed Laura. 'There's Jasmine Sanders with David Young. I thought David had gone back to London?'

'He had, but he came back for the funeral; he's staying

with Adam. I don't think Adam was too keen to have him back and I think I can see why. David only seems to be interested in Jasmine, which is sort of sweet, but Jack's still in Dartmoor and there's talk of a link between the migrants and the drugs. I tried to get something out of Adam about that but he said the police had told him to say nothing.'

Adam had been keeping clear of David during the wake and met up with a group from Eastside including James and Grace Holberton together with the Carbrooks and Admiral Tom, who was resplendent in his full naval uniform. 'Well, I haven't worn this uniform for years and thought it was the right thing to do to pay my respects to this poor chap who drowned. I found the service incredibly moving and I was amazed at the number of people that came.'

'Absolutely,' replied Grace, who also had dressed up in her finery for the occasion. 'Poor Ted was literally lost for words; however, what he finally said was very moving and we were all very proud of him.'

Adam was about to say something but caught sight of Detective Fraser who had come into the main room from the terrace and appeared to be looking for him.

'Adam, sorry to butt in, but could we have a quick word outside?'

Adam followed Fraser onto the terrace where he found an unoccupied corner overlooking the estuary.

'I didn't go to the funeral but Chris Thompson and Paul Barclay did and said the whole service was very impressive and moving. My job is to find the bastards that masterminded this disaster and I'd like to get you up to speed on the progress we've made so far. I don't need to remind you that this is totally confidential and somewhat irregular, but you seem to be a key person in the investigation and you may be able to help in the future. This is all strictly off the record and between you and me. That includes your mate, David.

'We've got Dan Pitcher for toast, although his father's fancy lawyer from London tried to make it difficult for us. But Dan, bless him, has been all cooperation and gave us everything he could about Frank Green. Green's a nasty piece of work and proved to be a much harder nut to crack; however, we've now got enough on both of them to be able to keep them in custody for the drugs and migrants offences until they come up for trial, where I'm confident we can secure long jail sentences for the two of them.

'Frank Green has been running, in Princewater, a county lines drug supply from London. Strictly cash. He paid cash on receipt of monthly supplies. Steady business that we think he has been doing for several years. The London supplier appears to have recently started to diversify into migrants and Green was tasked with collecting migrants from boats that come into Daymouth and transporting them to London for processing from there. Dan Pitcher was enlisted by Green to do the water transfer. All Green was prepared to say was that they had to be delivered to a location on the Mile End Rd in East London. He claims that was the only information the London end were prepared to give and they would give him the exact location when he actually had 'ownership' of the migrants and, of course, that never happened. All negotiations were done using throwaway mobile phones so the only clue we have for the London connection is the Mile End Rd area. We are working on this, but at the moment we've drawn a blank.

'We're also working with the French on the Cherbourg connection and there is some progress at that end. So yes, there is a connection between the drugs and migrants and yes, Green and his lacky, Pitcher, are both locked away. We fully expect that Green's Princewater drugs operation will be replaced by someone else who'll either use the existing supplier or another gang may move in. That could get messy, but what I really want is the London end of this business. Adam, your track record so far is you just "happen" to be around when "stuff happens", so that is why I am telling you all this. If more "stuff does happen", keep me informed.'

*

A few days after Ben's funeral, Adam was able to persuade David to go back to London. It was clear that both David and Jasmine wanted to be together; however, without revealing confidential information, Adam managed to convince them that the best thing to do was for David to go back.

The 'Fleur de Landemer' was successfully salvaged from where it had eventually sunk and most of the summer visitors had departed from Daymouth, leaving the estuary quiet and to itself. After an outcry of support from both locals and crew, together with a very strong push from the hierarchy of the RNLI, Ted had agreed to stay on for at least another year as the Daymouth coxswain.

*

The next major estuary event was the hearing of the Marlo Eco Park planning application. The migrant tragedy had previously dominated discussion around the town and the estuary, but as the day of the application hearing approached, there was more and more discussion on how an eco park could affect the whole area. The public were given the opportunity to register their views and at the closure date for public submissions there were 189 in favour and thirty-two against. The Planning Department published a report on the application and recommended the application should however be rejected, but it was up to the twelve elected councillors at the planning meeting to make the final decision.

On the day of the hearing, the Holberton family travelled together to the District Council office, although there was a family division of views, with Sarah and Grace as supporters and James strongly opposed.

'Whatever happens today,' said Grace in the car, 'I do want us all to be civilised to each other. There's going to be a winner and loser but we must stay together as a family. Ian Carbrook and you, Sarah, are the nominated persons to speak in support of the proposal and the chairman of the AONB team, Stephen Humphreys, and James will speak against it. So as a family we have one for and one against. I just don't know how this has happened but, quite honestly, I think it makes us look very silly having Holbertons on opposite sides.'

The meeting took place in a rather palatial council chamber room that looked similar to a law court. Councillor Jeremy Munday was chairman, sitting in a grand seat above everyone else. Just below him was the clerk and then the eleven councillors who together with the chairman would make the final decision. The opposing teams had their own sectors to the left and right of the councillors, and facing all of this was the public gallery, which was full. Prominent amongst the people in the gallery from the Daymouth side were Beryl, Laura and Harry Payne, the ferryman. From the Eastside of the estuary there was Jasmine Sanders, Adam, Admiral Tom and Bert Appleyard, the owner of Marlo Farm.

The chairman opened the meeting by saying that as the Marlo Eco Park proposal was so important to the region, he was going to allow two short presentations from both the objectors and supporters to the application. Each speaker would be allowed a maximum of three minutes after the chief planning officer had presented his own report.

The chief planning officer, Mr Anthony Drake, stood up and addressed the councillors. 'This has been a difficult application for us to consider; however, at the end of the day, we strongly oppose it and recommend rejection.' He then went on to say that the proposed eco park was currently agricultural land in a region designated as an Area of Outstanding Natural Beauty (AONB) and giving planning permission for this, admittedly carefully thought-out, proposal would be against AONB policy and would set a dangerous precedent for the whole area. He took the rest of his allocated time to give reasons why the application should be rejected.

The chairman then asked the first of the objectors to the application to speak and Councillor Stephen Humphreys for the AONB team stood up. He supported Mr Drake's recommendation to reject the application and said that the whole proposal was counter to the AONB remit of maintaining the beauty of the area, discouraging commercial development and protecting the ecology.

Sir James Holberton was the second objector and he said he was speaking as an individual resident of Eastside and also as an Eastside Parish Councillor. 'My family has lived in Eastside for many years and I am appalled at the idea that Marlo Farm could become Marlo Eco Park. We all know the whole

Eastside peninsula is an AONB and that is how it should stay. The peninsula has barely changed in the last hundred years and it represents some of the finest countryside in the West of England, and probably the UK. The Daymouth estuary is a jewel in the crown and any development of the type proposed here would be the beginning of the end for the whole estuary.' James continued in a similar vein until the planning clerk told him his allocated time was up.

'Thank you, Sir James. That now concludes the parties entitled to speak in favour of rejecting the proposal and so we now move onto the two speakers supporting the application. Mr Carbrook, I understand you wish to speak in support of your own application.'

'Thank you, chairman,' replied Ian as he stood up. 'I have very little to say as I hope that everyone has carefully read all the details of the application itself. I would just like to provide some background. I was in the business of importing fruit from the Mediterranean into the UK and retired some years ago to Eastside. I became a member of the Eastside Parish Council and through that, got to know Bert Appleyard who currently owns Marlo Farm and incidentally, Sir James Holberton, who has just spoken. I believe if status quo is allowed to continue, Eastside will continue to be what it is already, a retirement or holiday home area for the wealthy. There is no work or indeed scope for young families on Eastside. Bert and I came up with the idea of an eco park, and I'm prepared to invest my own money, at least thirty million pounds, in the project. I'm doing this because I believe it's the right thing to do. I suspect your local council don't have the financial resources to even contemplate this kind of venture.'

Ian sat down to a hushed council chamber.

'Thank you, Mr Carbrook,' said the chairman, and after a short pause continued, 'Would Miss Sarah Holberton please step forward as our last speaker.'

'Thank you, chairman. I too live in Eastside with my parents and I work as a teacher at Torden Primary School. Marlo Eco Park is a real opportunity for the Tordon peninsula to move into the twenty-first century and I was deeply saddened to see the Planning Office and the AONB team recommending rejection. The planning office appeared to pay no attention in its report to the dire situation of employment for the young on the peninsula and I know first-hand how pupil numbers at Tordon Primary School are decreasing fast. There is little work and barely any affordable accommodation available for young families. In relation to the AONB, I do hope everyone has very carefully read the environmental report written by Miss Paula Chase on the proposed development. In her report, she could not find any compelling reason why this project shouldn't go forward. She found no eel grass or seahorse issues on the foreshore and in fact praised the way the site was going to be managed, for example using electric vehicles and its own energy sources. I am therefore saddened that the AONB team seems unable to understand that the social and economic benefits of the proposal must surely outweigh any wish for status quo.'

Sarah sat down and there were murmurings of approval from the public gallery and, in particular, Bert Appleyard was heard to say, 'Here, here, well done Sarah.'

The chairman interjected saying, 'Ladies and gentlemen, this is a planning committee meeting and the public are allowed to be present but they must not comment.'

Then, talking to the councillors, the Chairman said, 'I'm sure you will all have read the submissions on this important planning application and you will also have seen that there are one hundred and eighty nine letters from members of the public supporting this application and thirty-two against. I will also remind you what I have said about previous applications and that is: "Every application should be considered on its own merit." If this application is passed, it does not mean that other similar applications will also be passed. Do any councillors have any questions or issues they wish to raise before the vote is taken?'

One councillor asked a technical question about a point relating to road access to the site both during any construction period and afterwards. Following this there was complete silence.

'If there are no further questions, we will now go to the vote. All those in favour of giving planning permission, please raise your hands,' said Councillor Munday.

Seven hands were raised.

'And those against.'

Four hands were raised.

'There being no abstentions, this planning application is passed. As chairman, I would have had a casting vote, but I'm pleased to see that it is not necessary. I'm sure the Planning Department will wish to raise a number of technical issues; however, I can confirm that this committee has given permission for the Marlo Eco Park to proceed.'

There were whoops of joy from the public gallery together with a few glum faces and the clerk moved forward to clear the gallery in preparation for the next application.

The Holbertons returned to Eastside and after a long period of silence Grace said, 'So it's over. Well done, Sarah; and James, I hope you're not going to sulk for too long. It was a fair match and Ian and Sarah won very convincingly. I thought the Chairman's final comment about the application not setting a precedent was the clincher. But, I was surprised it went through. Normally those councillors gang up together and I did think they would go along with the Planning Department's recommendation. But they didn't. We must now learn to live with each other and as far as James and I are concerned, we need to start looking forward to going to Monaco in a week's time with Ian and Susie, and of course Adam as well.'

CHAPTER 13

The plane was at an altitude of 38,000 feet with Adam looking out of the aircraft window at the snow-topped mountains of the Alps. The flight was coming in to Nice, the nearest airport to Monaco.

He wasn't sure why he'd agreed to the invitation to Monaco for an autumn break from Daymouth and he certainly wasn't sure whether the whole thing would work with the Holbertons and Carbrooks as company. To make matters even more complex, Grace had contacted him just before he left home saying that Robert and Jenny Harvey would be there as well. The positive aspect however on this latest news was that Jenny had arranged for Steve Mansell, their hot-shot professional sailor and general odd-job man, to collect him from Nice airport and then take him to his hotel in the Principality.

'Hi Adam, good to see you on the Côte d'Azur,' said Steve as Adam emerged from the arrivals gate at Nice. 'I wasn't sure you would recognise me and so I did my chauffeur bit with your name on my board.'

'Thanks Steve, it's very kind of you to come. I guess you know the airport well?'

'Sure. Monaco is maybe a half hour by car if the traffic is

OK, but it can take over two hours in the height of summer. Of course, there is a helicopter service, ten minutes in the air with beautiful views of the coast between here and Monaco; however, unless you are a real VIP there can be added time at both ends of the journey. Anyway, apart from collecting you, I've no daily orders from the Harveys or any of my other clients so I thought, unless you have your own plans, we could have lunch together at the Club Nautique de Nice. It's on our way and on a beautiful warm day like this we can eat outside at their restaurant on the top floor of the yacht club overlooking Nice and the harbour.'

'That sounds great, Steve, providing of course you let me pay the bill.'

Once in the car, they left the parking area and joined the traffic along the Promenade des Anglais, which stretches for several kilometres. The road is sandwiched between the City of Nice on one side and the turquoise-coloured Mediterranean on the other.

'What a wonderful sight,' said Adam. 'And the people look so happy! I guess the weather makes a difference, but everyone seems to be outside either promenading, cycling or skateboarding. There's so much movement.'

They drove past the impressive Negresco Hotel and then, after a circuitous route through part of the town, entered the Old Port of Nice.

'This is where the ferries go to Corsica,' said Steve. 'And sometimes the yachts race from here to Corsica and back. Today, the sea's quiet but it can be a very rough crossing with huge waves. Sailing on the Med is brilliant and the big difference to the UK is that there isn't any tide. Yes, it does rain here sometimes, but generally the sky is blue, not grey as I remember it living in London.'

Steve parked near the imposing and iconic Club Nautique de Nice and they made their way to the top floor where they were shown to an outdoor table with a panoramic view.

'Wow, that's incredible,' gasped Adam. 'That matches, or maybe even surpasses, the view I have of the Daymouth estuary. The blue, the sparkle of the sea and the coastal backdrop of Nice and the harbour. What a beautiful place. I'm not surprised that the rich Europeans discovered this area over a hundred years ago and it became a playground for the rich and famous. This is something special and thank you for bringing me here.'

Steve and Adam both found themselves very relaxed with each other and they were able to enjoy a very pleasant lunch with a carafe of wine followed by extremely good expresso coffee.

'What a great atmosphere,' said Adam. 'Everyone seems so relaxed. When you said Club Nautique de Nice, I was thinking it would be very posh, but no. The people seem quite normal and just happy to be eating well in a fantastic setting on a beautiful day.'

Steve looked at Adam and smiled. 'Yes, you're right and I wanted to take you here before we went to Monaco. This restaurant is in fact open to the public and so you don't have to be a member of the club to eat here. Few overseas tourists know about the place and so nearly everyone you see is probably a local. I like this place, it's special and I have to say very different from Monaco.'

'That sounds a bit like a warning as to what I am to expect.'

'That may be a bit strong, but yes, you could put it that way. Monaco's a very strange place. It's what is called a "Principality of France" and that means although it's a part of France, it isn't really! Does that make any sense to you?'

Adam looked at him quizzically and Steve continued. 'His

Serene Highness of Monaco is the boss and what he says goes. The Principality is a tax haven and attracts super rich people who don't want to pay taxes. It's a few square miles of a rich person's playground. There are very few true Monegasques and much of the population is made up of people who have bought their way into residency or are on a temporary resident's permit. I for example share an apartment with a Monaco police officer Pierre just outside Monaco in a place called Cap d'Ail. I've no hope of residency unless perhaps I become a sailing World Champion. Many who actually work in Monaco either travel daily from France or Italy. So, Monaco is pretty unique. A hot spot for the rich and famous. A tax haven in a geographical location very similar to here, namely very beautiful. It's a pressure cooker of wealth that makes even London look and feel quite normal. So, Monaco is Monaco. Different and absolutely full of moneyed people.'

Steve drove Adam to his hotel, the Hotel Bleu, where he had booked a room.

'You've chosen well. This is a good hotel near the sea and it's just outside the edge of Monte Carlo, which is the high glitz area. Here's my card and do contact me if you need any help, but I suspect I'll see you again as Jenny is planning a day for your party to go on "Invicta". I'll probably be enlisted into that. If you're not doing anything tonight, I'm happy to show you around and we can have a drink at the Monaco Yacht Club. I'm a member there, but beware, if you want to get in, you have to wear a tie!'

'Thanks, Steve, that would be great. I don't need to meet up with Grace and James until tomorrow morning so I'm free this evening. How about coming here at around 7pm?'

'Fine, see you then.'

Steve drove away, and Adam registered at the hotel. The room was quite small with a pleasant balcony that had one position where he could just see the sea. *Oh well*, he thought. *Not quite as good a view as Eastside Cottage or room 302 at the Daymouth Waterside Hotel, but it certainly feels a lot warmer.*

He spent the rest of the afternoon acclimatising himself with the hotel and its immediate surroundings. He discovered a swimming pool on the roof of the hotel and enjoyed some exercise doing many lengths. There was no one else in the water with only a few people around the edges sunbathing or sitting around chatting.

Steve arrived at 7pm sharp having established that he could leave his car in the hotel car park. 'This place is like the rest of the world only a hundred times worse,' he said. 'Finding a parking space is a nightmare and you're really better off on foot or using the trains or bus.'

They walked together from the hotel towards the Monte Carlo area. 'If we walk along the shore, we'll pass Lord Harvey's "Invicta"; it's moored at Port Poirot. If you follow Formula One motor racing, you may even recognise the area as it's close to the pit lane for the Grand Prix.'

Within a few minutes they were at Port Poirot. 'There it is, alongside a raft of other super yachts. Each of those would cost 10 to 100 million pounds with about a 10% annual running cost, so you can get some idea of the wealth around here.'

'That's certainly a lot of floating real estate. I'm beginning to get the idea. Monaco is in a different league to almost anywhere else. It certainly makes Daymouth seem modest although many British people think that it is a well-heeled place. After living there now for a bit, I've discovered that it's a real mixed bag of rich and poor.'

They walked on and Steve then pointed out a group of identical racing yachts. 'Those are the boats I race, they are called J70s. Each one's the same and you race them with a crew of three to five people. The racing's highly competitive and when we have regattas here, teams from all over Europe come to sail. Robert sponsors me as a helm of his boat and next year we go to the World Championships that will be held in Greece. We're a strong team on the boat and I would be looking for a top ten position and maybe even in the top three. It goes without saying that his lordship will be demanding we win.'

A little further on they reached the entrance of the Yacht Club. The security guard at the entrance checked Steve's membership card and required Adam to sign in as a guest. The building was very impressive, very modern and very everything.

'Let's go to the bar and have a drink. I sense you've already noticed the difference between here and Club Nautique de Nice!'

They sat down with a view across the harbour and drinks were served. 'Well done for wearing a jacket with your tie. I forgot to tell you about that. It's all part of the dress code, and there's another code for women. Welcome to Monte Carlo!'

Adam and Steve had hit it off right from the word go and they enjoyed just chatting to each other. They both shared a strong interest in sporting fitness. Adam talked about his triathlon experiences and Steve on the necessity for athletic strength whilst sailing. 'Even at Daymouth you need to be fit sailing those quaint local boats,' said Steve. 'I recall this year you sailed with Sarah Holberton in the regatta and you and she had a great race in the windy day stuff. Jenny and I filled up with water and had to retire, but I watched you both sailing brilliantly. Sarah's a very good sailor and that race showed just how fit she is. Are you going out with her?'

'No, I'm not really going out with anybody, although I have to say I have got a soft spot for Sarah. There was a recent planning application at Daymouth where she spoke brilliantly in favour of it. Her father, James, in fact spoke against it, but she won the day.'

They continued chatting over a further drink and then Steve said, 'Let me take you to see the Monte Carlo crown jewels: the Casino de Paris and the Hotel de Paris, Monte Carlo.'

They walked up together to the Place du Casino and Steve explained, 'You're now at the centre of the universe as far as Monte Carlo is concerned! In front of you is the Casino de Paris and in front of that is the usual array of super cars that vie for a prime spot. The trick is to drive up in your Ferrari or Lamborghini then pass or throw the keys to the concierge and walk straight into the casino. You then hope he'll park your car in one of the most prominent positions. If you turn up in a family car, they take it round the back. Now look to your right and you'll see the Hotel de Paris, one of the most luxurious and expensive hotels in the world. To the left of us is the Place du Casino's outdoor bars and restaurants. I guess we could try a find a table and just absorb the atmosphere, but be careful: you'll pay a high price for the privilege.'

They were fortunate to find a table with a clear view of the arriving and departing cars from the casino. 'Well, I have to say this is certainly different from Daymouth and I'm not even sure I've ever seen anything like this in London before. Is it like this every day?'

'Always; it's the key place where the rich flaunt their wealth and meet up. Now if you look over there at that table with six people around it you might also notice three other men standing a discreet distance away with their hands in pockets. They are probably personal bodyguards for someone in that group. Maybe Italian Mafia, maybe Russian or maybe just someone important who is just very, very rich; welcome to the hot house of Monaco.'

*

Grace and James Holberton had elected to stay at the Hotel des Pins that was located near to the Place du Casino and on the following morning Adam walked to meet them at their hotel.

'Adam, so pleased to see you in Monaco, isn't it fun!' said Grace in the reception area. 'We weren't absolutely sure that you would come, particularly after we told you Lord Robert and Jenny Harvey would be here. Anyway, here you are and it's wonderful to have you. We have a gentle plan for today. The idea is that you and I go off to Menton, which is just a few kilometres towards Italy, and have lunch with Ian and Susie Carbrook at their apartment. After that, we'll play some bridge and you can partner me as brilliantly as you did on that summer evening at Daymouth! James is going to stay here. However, you boys, that is you, James and Ian, are going off this evening to play a bit of poker. Ian has a couple of friends he plays with here and hopefully they'll join you at the Casino Noir et Blanc. It's a private club and you'll have your own table and dealer. Adam, I do hope that my plan is OK with you?'

'I guess so, the bridge sounds fine and I'm interested to see Menton, which I have heard is worth visiting. I'm not so sure about the poker bit. Is it black tie? Is it for real money? Are the stakes high?'

'Don't worry about any of that. Ian Carbrook will explain. He plays a lot and he knows the score. Yes, they do play for money but I don't think the stakes are particularly high.'

*

Grace and Adam arrived by taxi at number 5 Rue de Citron and met up with Ian and Susie in their top floor apartment.

'Welcome to Menton and our apartment,' said Ian. 'You've come on a sunny day, so we can enjoy our bridge outside on the roof terrace with a great view of the Med. But first, how about a walk along the sea front and maybe a coffee. This town is very different to Monaco and it's worth seeing.'

The party of four set off along the promenade, with Grace and Susie, and Ian and Adam having their own separate conversations.

'This is the first time we've really had the chance to chat,' said Ian as he and Adam walked side by side along the long and wide promenade. 'I saw you at the Marlo planning application meeting and wasn't quite sure which side you were on. And now here you are on the Côte d'Azur partnering Grace, and I also believe coming to play some poker with James, myself and a couple of friends.'

'Yes, curious, isn't it? Anyway, here I am, and in the end, I did see the positives in the Marlo project. People I know well at Daymouth such as Sarah Holberton, Jasmine Sanders and Laura Clift from the Smugglers Inn have all told me that the estuary has to move with the times and even Paula Chase who works for the AONB and who I met stranded on an estuary island was satisfied that the project was indeed eco-friendly. I can see that the peninsula needs to move on and requires more employment for the young all the year round, not just in the summer.'

'I'm glad you've said that Adam and thank you. Tonight, if you do play poker with us, you'll meet a chap called Jan Ziabicki. He is Polish but his parents were evacuated to Truro, in Cornwall, during the Second World War and he grew up and went to school in Truro. Since then he's made a lot of money but is continually saying Cornwall needs commercial investment.'

Ian continued, 'You just mentioned Jasmine. I know that her husband Jack's in jail for selling drugs, and I know that you were on the lifeboat when that terrible Ben Lewis tragedy took place and all those migrants drowned. Do you want to talk about any of that?'

'Sorry, Ian, I've been told by the police not to say anything about drugs and migrants as the investigation is ongoing.'

The mention of drugs suddenly brought Daymouth back into Adam's mind and he recalled Ben's concerns about Ian being involved in drug supply. Since the drowning and the identification of Frank Green and Dan Pitcher as the local drug source, he'd completely put to the back of his mind Ben's earlier concerns. Surely, Ian couldn't be involved? He seemed a nice chap and his wife Susie was charming. They were good friends of the Holbertons, who apparently were rock solid people. Ian also appeared to be undertaking the eco park project for all the right reasons.

He continued to ponder the situation in silence as they walked for some time along the promenade.

'Sorry, Ian, I was in a bit of a dream. Your mention of the

Daymouth tragedy brought back some disturbing memories that I have been trying to suppress. However, this chap Jan Ziabicki sounds an interesting person. How has he ended up here?'

'Apologies for raising the drugs stuff. The Côte d'Azur should be about enjoyment not concerns. Not sure I know the answer to your Jan Ziabicki question. For the last hundred years this area has always been a popular resort for the well-heeled and Jan is certainly that.'

Adam thought it best to change the subject and so he brought up the imminent prospect of poker. 'Ian, I'm concerned about this evening. I have played poker in the past, but poker in Monaco sounds pretty serious. Is it black tie? Is it for serious money? Maybe I should drop out right at the start?'

'Adam, we play for fun and by Monaco standards our stakes are very modest. We normally have a 5K euro pot for each player. The Casino Noir et Blanc is a private club and no, we don't do black tie. Jacket and normal tie are enough and we have our own room and dealer. Ladies are of course allowed, but we are basically a group of chaps that have made money in the past and who enjoy a game of cards and a modest flutter. None of us are particularly good poker players, but we do try.'

'That sounds sort of reassuring. I'll give it a go, but reserve the option of bailing out if it just isn't for me.'

They continued the walk with Ian explaining highlights of various buildings until they reached the Jean Cocteau Museum where they all had a coffee and chatted amongst each other. Grace was the liveliest of the group adding, 'Jenny Harvey has kindly arranged for us all to spend tomorrow on their boat and take a little trip, firstly to a nearby bay and then maybe even to Cap Ferrat or Cap d'Antibes. Us landlubbers will go on "Invicta" but Jenny thought it would be fun if the sailors amongst us, that is Adam and her, sail to the bay with Steve in their racing yacht. Isn't it wonderful how everything is working out so well!'

Adam was somewhat relieved to hear the plan. He liked Steve and was keen to view the coast from the sea. He then realised that the several days of bridge and poker he had signed up to was not something he was really looking forward to.

Ian and Adam walked back together along the Menton promenade. 'So, you've told me about Jan Ziabicki but I think you said there will be two friends joining us this evening; who will the other person be?'

'Thomas Giddings, and I do know quite a lot about him. Thomas worked for me when I owned my logistics company, Euro Fruit Imports, or EFI. I set up the company about twenty years ago to import Mediterranean fruit into the UK running a fleet of lorries that brought in fruit such as lemons, olives and tomatoes that are grown around here, and imported them to sell at the London fruit markets. We had a base near Bethnal Green. When I retired about five years ago Thomas bought the company from me and has done well. He's increased the number of lorries and now lives here in Monaco.'

'Sounds like a success story for both you and Thomas,' said Adam. 'But Ian, I'm still feeling uncertain about these poker games. I can handle bridge with Grace, but poker's different. What about James, who will be playing with us as well? Is he any good at it?'

'He does play poker at his club in London. Grace said he was keen to come and I think poker was the only reason he agreed to come in the first place. I've had a couple of chats with him since the planning application meeting and, on the surface, he seems to be OK, though I'm not totally sure about that. He really did think that giving planning permission for Marlo would mark the end of Eastside.'

After lunch in the apartment the group spent the afternoon playing bridge on the terrace in warm sunshine. The atmosphere was relaxed with both Grace and Susie thoroughly enjoying play. Adam had to work hard to support Grace as the Carbrooks were an accomplished pairing and at the end of play they came out clear winners.

'That was fun, even in defeat,' said Grace. 'Playing in the sunshine on a roof terrace in Menton is heaven. You two are so lucky to have lovely places in both Daymouth and here.'

'And don't forget we have Antigua too!' said Susie. 'But yes, of course we are incredibly fortunate, Ian really did work hard to build up EFI from nothing. I think he does deserve credit for that.'

'Well, so does Susie,' exclaimed Ian. 'In fact, I'm more than happy to say that she managed most of it, she was actually the brains. She did all the buying and scheduling in the early days before everything went digital and we worked the business together. It was a joint effort and fortunately we're still both here together to enjoy our reward.'

He went on, 'I think it's probably time for me to get you both a taxi. Adam, I'll meet up with you at the Casino Noir et Blanc at, shall we say eight o'clock this evening? It's very close to the Holbertons' hotel. James, Jan and Thomas will join us there. It's obvious from the way you played bridge this afternoon that you know your way around card games. It should be an interesting evening.'

*

Adam arrived at the Casino Noir et Blanc on time and was taken to the main bar area of the club.

'Adam, welcome to our club,' said Ian. 'Let me introduce you to our fellow players. Of course, you know James, and this is Jan Ziabicki who I have played poker with for a couple of years and beside him is Thomas Giddings who worked with me and now owns my old company EFI. I do hope you'll enjoy the evening. We each put five thousand euro into the pot and that limits our total evening's liability and covers the club costs including the private room, our house card dealer, Jacques, and drinks. Jacques has been doing this job for several years, he always deals, manages play and acts as banker. Of course, if you come out on the plus side, the money is for you to take away. Needless to say, if you are unfortunate enough to lose, you might receive some or none of your pot. Are you happy with those arrangements?'

'Sounds all right, but as I said earlier, I'm not used to casino poker and so it will be a steep learning curve for me, and yes, I'm happy to play tonight, but I might opt out of further games if it's just not for me.'

'Fine; let's all have a drink and get to know each other before we start.'

Adam used the time while having drinks to make a quick assessment of the people he was playing against. Ian was clearly the leader of the group and from today's bridge match at Menton, he was very sharp at cards. James was a bit of an unknown quantity as Adam now realised all his previous encounters with him had included Sarah or Grace. In their company, he had seemed quite grumpy, but tonight, surrounded by other men, he was more relaxed and at home with himself. Jan Ziabicki was unusual as he always had a smile on his face and Adam's first impression was of someone he liked. He had, however, learnt from the past that first impressions can be, and often were, wrong. Finally, there was Thomas Giddings who Adam took an immediate dislike to. He didn't know why and again thought to himself that first impressions can be misleading.

'Gentlemen,' said Ian, 'Jacques is at the table and ready to start play. He has randomly chosen our allotted positions around the table. Can you all please take your seats in the card room?'

The group walked in and the door closed behind them.

*

Two hours later, they emerged from the room and headed to the bar.

'Well, that was certainly a baptism of fire,' said Adam, 'I was lucky to get away with a relatively small mauling. I certainly learnt a lot and I'm up for another round. It's all quite addictive, isn't it?'

'You played really well, maybe a bit conservatively, but that's not necessarily a bad thing,' replied Ian. 'Well done, James and Thomas. You certainly cleaned Jan and me out tonight. I hope we can get our revenge on you both the next time we play, in two days' time. I gather that the Harveys have organised a trip on "Invicta" tomorrow and so we will meet the day after that. Lord Robert has said he would like to join us, so we shall have a very big gun present.'

Adam ended the evening with a large brandy sitting alone with Jan Ziabicki. 'Ian told me your parents brought you up in Cornwall, is that right?'

'Yes, it was during the Second World War that my parents came to the UK from Poland. We lived in Truro, which Ian tells me is about hundred kilometres from Daymouth. The people of Truro were so kind to my parents and then to me. I spent fifteen of the happiest years of my life there.'

'So how come you have ended up here in Monaco?'

Jan looked across at Adam and smiled. 'You know, Adam, you remind me of myself twenty-five years ago. I could tell from the way you were playing poker this evening that it was so similar to the way I would have played in your situation all that time ago. It's really strange, I hope you won't feel offended.'

'I'm flattered that you should say something like that. No one has ever said anything like that to me before.'

'Adam, all I know about you is that you're a colleague of Ian's who I've known for a couple of years through poker and that you and he live in a nice Devon place called Daymouth. Evidently, James, who played with us tonight, lives there too and there's been a planning application battle between Ian and James which Ian has recently won. I know nothing about your own background, but I'm happy to share with you a bit of my own story as to how I've ended up here. Who knows, you might end up here too?

'After living in lovely Truro, I went to Edinburgh University and did well. I then joined an oil trading company in Aberdeen when North Sea oil was starting to open up. I left the company and set up as an individual. I moved from Scotland to Norway to Russia, then to China and then Saudi Arabia doing much the same: keeping out of trouble and accumulating a lot of money. I'm a loner and someone who has kept my head down. My last move a couple of years ago was to Monaco. I suppose the tax haven bit attracted me and I now no longer need to work so I can live anywhere I want to. I have no family, no children, no wife, no mistress. I am just me.'

CHAPTER 14

The following morning, Steve met up with Adam at the Hotel Bleu and they both walked down towards the Marina pontoon where the J70 sports boats were moored. On the way, they saw Jenny Harvey who was waiting for them at Port Poirot on the Harvey super yacht 'Invicta'.

'Hello sailors!' she shouted from the stern of 'Invicta'. 'It's time you took me for a sail in a real sailing boat and not this motorised monster. What a lovely day and it looks as though a perfect breeze is coming in too.'

Jenny loved her sailing. She had spent many of her childhood holidays sailing at Daymouth, and that was the reason she continued racing in the annual yawl regatta. Lord Harvey had insisted that if she was to continue yawl sailing at Daymouth, she had to win, which was why he brought in Steve to helm the boat. Robert then decided Daymouth yawl success was not enough and this resulted in him financing Steve to sail a J70 at Monaco. The sports boat was a near equivalent to the Formula One racing cars that compete in the Monaco Grand Prix: expensive and professional. Although he would normally sail the J70 with a professional crew, today it was for pleasure and Steve, Jenny and Adam were greatly looking forward to the opportunity.

They left 'Invicta' and made their way to the pontoon. 'I feel so liberated,' said Jenny. 'Robert's been quite unbearable for the last few days. I know when business isn't going well. This morning he was absolutely horrid to the chef. The poor chap forgot to get any marmalade for breakfast! What a relief to come out with you guys for a real sail.'

They rigged the boat, sailed out of the marina and then headed towards the Baie de Saint-Laurent, which was adjacent to Monaco.

'OK, let's try the asymmetric spinnaker,' shouted Steve. 'Jenny, you know what to do. Adam, just hold on.'

Jenny pulled the crucial ropes and the wind filled the huge off-wind sail. 'That's fine,' shouted Steve. 'Now, let's have everyone up on the side deck and see what this boat can do. The wind's perfect and there're some great waves to play with.'

The boat took off as they sailed on an exciting three-sail reach with water and spray everywhere. Steve was in his element with both Jenny and Adam thoroughly enjoying the ride.

'Amazing,' shouted Adam. 'What an experience in such fantastic conditions.'

Jenny also had a big smile on her face and her mood was transformed from the breakfast crisis.

After several miles of high-speed sailing, Steve said, 'Let's take a gybe and power our way back to the Saint-Laurent bay. I expect "Invicta" will have anchored by now and they'll be waiting for us.'

Robert Harvey and his crew were indeed waiting for the J70 to arrive. The Carbrooks were also on board as well as Grace. James had declined the invitation, pleading potential seasickness as a reason for being absent.

Steve expertly brought the J70 up to the stern lower deck

of 'Invicta' and dispatched a rather wet Jenny and Adam on board. He then sailed off single-handed to take the boat back to the marina in Monaco.

Adam and Jenny were meet by Robert, who appeared to have recovered from his marmalade breakfast tantrum. 'Welcome aboard, Adam. I do remember you from our little Daymouth party earlier this year. You had a friend who I think was called David and we had a good old argument about mathematics. Anyway, here we are now on the Mediterranean on a lovely day. Jenny, you looked soaked. Go and get changed and make sure Adam has a change of clothes too.'

Adam was shown to a guest room on the boat and a crew member came with a range of clothes for him to inspect. After he'd changed, he went up to the main deck where both Ian and Susie were sitting with Grace.

'Oh Adam. You looked as though you were having a wonderful time sailing in that boat,' said Grace. 'We're having a great time too. Isn't this super yacht "Invicta" magnificent? Robert showed us round and, well, it is a bit like a luxury floating hotel. Aren't we all so lucky to be here?'

The Harveys joined the group and Lord Robert explained his plan for the rest of the day.

'I propose that we motor over to Cap d'Antibes; it's about forty miles away. That won't take long. We can have lunch close inshore at either the Plage de La Garoupe or the Baie des Milliardaires, depending on which is the most sheltered. Several Russian Oligarchs have chateaux on Cap d'Antibes and the only way to really see them is from the water. On land, high walls, fences and guards protect each one. Maybe when we get back, we can go and have a drink at the Monaco Yacht Club.'

There were general nods all round, Lord Robert gave orders for the anchor to be raised, and 'Invicta' got underway.

The trip across the Bay of Nice towards Cap d'Antibes turned out to be quite uncomfortable even in such a large motor yacht as 'Invicta'. The waves had increased in size after leaving the relative shelter of Monaco and there was a strong swell, known locally as a Houle, running almost exactly at right angles to the direction of travel. James had made a good decision to stay ashore and both Ian and Susie Carbrook were beginning to turn a bit pale.

'If you're feeling at all queasy, I suggest you take one of these pills and stay on deck,' suggested Jenny.

'Invicta' eventually lurched its way to Cap d'Antibes and Robert directed the super yacht into Plage de la Garoupe, a bay that was protected by a headland and where the water was calm.

'This will do,' declared Robert. 'Drop anchor and let's have lunch.'

Jenny realised that Grace, Ian and Susie were not really in a condition to want food and suggested that maybe they take the yacht's rib to the shore and have a short walk before lunch. Adam joined them, whilst Robert remained on the boat getting somewhat annoyed that his guests didn't seem to have any sea legs.

As the group walked along a path with the sea on one side and a high stone wall on the other, Ian Carbrook and Adam found themselves once again talking to each other.

'I guess this is one of those oligarch's walled fortresses,' said Adam.

'Maybe it is, but there are plenty of people in this part of the world that want to protect their ill-gotten gains. Talking of which, how did you get on with Jan Ziabicki and Thomas Giddings at the poker last night?'

'I liked Jan, but was unsure about Thomas; of course, first impressions can be misleading. Tomorrow's game should be interesting and goodness knows what Lord Robert Harvey will bring to the table. Chaos perhaps?'

After a short walk on dry land the group returned to 'Invicta' in better spirits and able to take on the specially prepared lunch served outside in the sun on the upper deck of 'Invicta'.

'What luxury,' said Grace. 'Thank you so much for inviting us,' she said as she sipped her glass of chilled rosé wine and ate some prawn canapés.

After a long lunch that went on well into the afternoon, Robert summoned his crew to pull up the anchor and he then conducted a coastal tour of Cap d'Antibes.

As they cruised along the coastline, Robert gave a running commentary. 'On your right you can see the magnificent building and grounds of Château de la Croe. This is currently owned by Roman Abramovich and was the home of the Duke of Windsor and Mrs Wallis Simpson during the Second World War, and then owned for a while by the Greek shipping magnet Aristotle Onassis. You can see for yourself the level of security. I can count at least three guards patrolling along the sea wall in front of us.'

Further along the coast, Robert could not resist talking about the imposing Hotel du Cap. 'That hotel is one of the finest on the Côte d'Azur and I've stayed there on several occasions. My hedge fund has used it for a number of our annual meetings. It's also one of the hot spots for the Cannes Film Festival.'

Much to the relief of Adam and his other guests, Robert finally ended his commentary and 'Invicta' turned round and headed back for Monaco. The other good news was that by then, the wind had dropped considerably and the journey back across the Baie de Nice was much more pleasant.

During the return journey, Adam found himself sitting talking with Susie Carbrook on the rear deck. 'Susie, I am afraid that bridge isn't really my game. I don't want to let Grace down but I'm wondering if it is OK if I drop out of tomorrow's planned match.'

'That's not a problem at all, Adam. In fact, it could work out quite well. I am sure Jenny will be very happy to pair up with Grace. She'll be delighted to escape from Robert, he's being a total pain at the moment, and it will give her an escape for a few hours. She was only saying to me a few minutes ago that her little sail with you and Steve today was one of the best things she's done in ages. Between you and me, I think the marriage is on the rocks.'

'Thanks Susie, I'm most grateful for that and of course I'll say nothing about what you've said. I'd be interested to have your views on both Jan Ziabicki and Thomas Giddings though. I met them at our poker game, but I've only met them for a few hours and can't make up my mind about either of them.'

Susie looked directly at Adam. 'How interesting that you ask me that question. I've been trying to work you out and you're really a bit of a puzzle and not quite the person I originally thought you were. Charming and friendly but someone with a bit of an edge. I have seen you looking at Ian a couple of times in a rather strange way. Are you some sort of secret agent?'

'Not at all!' replied Adam. 'Sometimes I don't quite know

what I am, but I can assure you I am not a secret agent!' As soon as the words had come out, he paused for a second and realised that he did hold certain secrets and was acting under instructions from the Special Branch. Perhaps he was a secret agent after all?

'Well, on the assumption you aren't a secret agent,' continued Susie, 'all I know about Jan is that he's very rich, very careful and always happy. I've only met him a few times when Ian's brought him over to Menton. He's a bachelor, good company and Ian says he's very good at playing poker. I do know Thomas as he worked for the company when Ian and I were running it. He was quite low profile when we were in charge and it came as a bit of a surprise that he raised so much cash to buy the company, but he's done very well indeed since we left and he's become a significant person in Monaco. Good luck to him. We left the business in good shape when we sold and he's clearly moved it up several gears since then.'

At that point, one of the crew came to the lower deck and requested they join Lord Robert and the others on the upper deck for high tea. This consisted of quite a lot of alcohol plus delicate cucumber sandwiches and delicious cakes. Jenny came over to Adam and told him she'd be delighted to take his place at bridge tomorrow and for any further days if needed.

After 'Invicta' had berthed, the group went up to the Monaco Yacht Club and Lord Robert ordered further drinks. By this stage, he was fairly drunk and speaking very loudly.

'Adam, returning to your Daymouth friend David, I recall he was extolling the merits of mathematics in terms of business deals. Perhaps you'd like to tell him when you get back to Daymouth that I'm close to completely shorting Plymouth Super Boats into bankruptcy. Just a few more days and they'll be gone. That was nothing to do with mathematics. I saw an opportunity and our hedge fund went for it. That's what finance is all about and today you saw the result of that. "Invicta" rules the waves!'

Adam was shocked and initially didn't know what to say. After a long pause he quietly said. 'Robert, thank you for your hospitality today and in particular the fantastic sail I had with Steve and Jenny; however, I think it is now time I should go.'

When he got back to the Hotel Bleu there was a message waiting for him to contact Jan Ziabicki. He phoned the number and Jan answered.

'Hello; is that Adam?'

'Yes. How can I help you?'

'I wondered if you were free sometime tomorrow and we could have a chat. I'd be happy to come and collect you from your hotel.'

'Yes fine.' Replied Adam. 'Would say ten o'clock be OK?'

*

The following day, Jan arrived at Hotel Bleu and met Adam.

'I find Monaco can be very claustrophobic, so would it be all right if I drive you up to Fort Revère? It's an old fort that overlooks Monaco and the Mediterranean. It's in the Parc de la Grande Corniche, which is a very beautiful spot and on a clear day like this we should be able to see Corsica on the horizon. The park around the fort is a peaceful mountaintop place where we can talk without any distractions.'

Adam was happy with the plan and Jan drove them along the twisting roads that took them high above Monaco to the small town of Èze and onto the nature reserve of Fort Revère.

They parked the car and walked along a path that brought them to a seat that overlooked Monaco and the Mediterranean.

'This is where I sometimes come to sit; to look and also to think. I've been here quite a lot recently and after meeting you two days ago I'd like to share some of my thoughts with you, is that OK? The one thing that I ask is that our conversation is totally confidential, just between you and me. But first: just look at the view, it's amazing from here and at this time in the morning there's no one else around. It's as though we've got the whole world to ourselves. And yes, look straight out onto the horizon, you can see Corsica, over a hundred miles away. They say it's something to do with a light refraction effect. I say it's amazing.'

They both marvelled in silence at the vista from the seat and then Jan continued.

'Yesterday I did some homework on you, the Marlo Eco Park proposal and also Daymouth. It all made interesting reading and I've been wondering whether maybe it could fit into my own plans. But, before I start telling you about that, I did have trouble trying to work out where Lord Robert Harvey fitted into the jigsaw puzzle. I understand he's joining us for poker tonight and yesterday you went off for a day cruise in his yacht. He seemed to be someone who didn't really fit into the world of Daymouth.'

'You're right, Lord Robert only tolerates Daymouth because his wife Jenny learnt to sail there and continues to race annually in a specific sailing boat during the Daymouth regatta. Last night at the Monaco Yacht Club he was particularly difficult as he was bragging about how he was close to shorting Plymouth Super Boats into liquidation.'

'Oh, he did say that, did he?' There was a pause and

Jan continued. 'Plymouth Super Boats is one of the largest employers in Plymouth and that was one area I wanted to talk to you about. Namely, providing basic employment levels for Cornwall and now possibly Devon. I could tell from his super yacht "Invicta" that Robert Harvey was a bit brash and I did have a look at his hedge fund on the internet. Adam, I think I can fix this one for you! After our talk, I'll go back to Monaco and buy a major part of Plymouth Super Boats shares. That will send the share price rocketing up and Lord Harvey will be left with a serious problem, having to sell his shorted shares at an inflated price rather than paying nothing.'

'But surely that would cost you millions of pounds?' exclaimed Adam.

'That is also one of the things I need to tell you about and it is the one thing you must keep confidential. You are in fact the only person I've ever told this to, but, if push came to shove, I could raise four billion pounds sterling in a matter of days.'

Adam was stunned and immediately said, 'But why tell me? You've only known me for a few hours.'

'That's something I've tried for the last forty-eight hours to understand myself. Maybe it was the way you played your cards at the poker game? Maybe I was seeing you as myself twenty-five years ago? Maybe I saw you as someone who could help me spend my money in the way that I want to before I die?'

They both sat together on the seat without saying a word for at least a minute. Adam was trying to take in what he'd just heard and Jan was working out how best to explain his plan.

'Perhaps I should start from the beginning. I think I told you after the poker game two days ago that the best days of my life were when I was a child at Truro in Cornwall. I've not been back since then but I know Cornwall and maybe Devon too has not enjoyed prosperity since then. Cornwall was special for me. The people were so nice to us and, remember, we were foreigners, not locals. Again, as I told you, I started oil trading in Aberdeen for an oil broker and then set up on my own. I made a lot of money there, paid my taxes and put the money in Scottish banks. I then went to Norway where oil and gas discoveries were in the process of transforming the fortunes of the country and from there onto Russia just after the collapse of the Soviet Union. It was chaos. I kept out of trouble and also made a lot more money. Then I went to China when that country was transforming into a super power. I kept out of trouble and made more money, which I invested and put in Chinese banks. Finally, I found myself in Saudi Arabia and did my oil trading around the Middle East. This was probably my most profitable time and at that point I had money in Scottish, Russian, Norwegian, Chinese and Middle Eastern banks. I've paid all my taxes in each of those countries and, most importantly, kept a very low profile and so you won't find my name on any rich list around the world.

'I'm now nearly seventy with a lot of money that I'd like to spend in a useful way. I've got my own ideas on how I can provide employment and perhaps revive the economy of Cornwall and when I heard about this Marlo Eco Park concept, I thought that too could be included and expanded across the whole of the West Country. And then I met you! Instinct told me that you might be able to help make these ideas become a reality. I now realise that I'm too old to do this on my own. Sadly, I don't trust any government in the world to spend my money in an effective way and I've learnt to be very wary of so-called charities.

So, Adam, this is a big opportunity for you to partner me

in what could be a very exciting period of life for you and for Cornwall and possibly Devon too. I certainly don't expect you to respond immediately; in fact I'd be very worried if you did. But I would like you to think about it and when you're ready, come back to me and we can talk further.'

'Jan, I'm left speechless and genuinely don't know what to say. Yes, of course I'll think about it all very seriously and yes, we should talk more to each other and find out whether your sudden and unexpected proposal would really work. I'm not without my own funding, but I'm literally millions of miles away from your own apparent resources.'

They sat on the seat for some time longer saying nothing and then Adam finally suggested, 'Let's take a bit of a walk here and then go back to Monaco where you've just said you have some business to do, putting a brake on the Robert Harvey grab of Plymouth Super Boats. I'll spend the afternoon either swimming or taking a walk and try to get my mind around what you've said. In the evening, I presume we'll meet up for the next round of poker.'

*

Adam gave Jan a parting handshake at the Hotel Bleu and headed straight for the bar. He was about to order a large whisky, but then held back, thinking to himself, *This is big. I need to have a clear head to sort this one out. It's not just big, it's colossal. Four billion pounds is just a huge amount of money and I can't imagine how anyone can have kept that much money under the radar. But maybe I can? Jan's obviously a very clever guy and he seems to have been in all the right places at the right time to do well. Oil trades are always done with seriously large sums of money and yes, I guess if large trading companies can do it, so can a single person, if he knows what he's doing. This is all going to take some sorting out.*

He decided that the hotel bar was not the best place to attempt to understand the morning discussion with Jan and he went to his room to try and collect his thoughts. After a few minutes he formulated a plan saying to himself, *Right, after this morning's bombshell, the best thing I can do is really try and clear my head. I'll do what I have done before: run and swim. Firstly, I'll run what I think is about 15km from Monaco to the Club Nautique de Nice where I had lunch with Steve, and then I'll go for a long sea swim there. That should clear my brain.* During the earlier lunch with Steve, he'd noticed that there was a small beach next to the Yacht Club where an enthusiastic group of Nice swimmers met and carried out deep water sea swimming from the sheltered bay.

The run to Nice went without incident and Adam was able to put all his thoughts and energy into navigating a complex coastal route to the Nice Yacht Club. When he arrived at the Yacht Club there were groups of people on the beach who were clearly serious swimmers.

A very tanned and healthy-looking middle-aged lady in one group said to Adam as he arrived on the beach, '*Bonjour, vous souhaitez nous rejoindre? Je t'ai vu courir et tu avais l'air très en forme.*'

'*Merci,*' replied Adam.

'Oh, you sound English. My name is Emma and I am American, but I've lived in Nice for the last twenty years. I haven't seen you here before?'

'No, I'm just on the Côte d'Azur for a short stay and have run over to here from Monaco.'

'Well done. You must be very fit.'

Emma and Adam got into easy conversation with each other whilst they sat on the beach. She explained that the beach was quite famous for extreme swimmers and also for sea diving from the surrounding rocks. The chat helped him clear his mind from events that were unfolding in Monaco and after about ten minutes he excused himself and said it was time for him to go for a swim.

'Enjoy,' said Emma. 'I may be gone when you come back. Make sure you have a great swim.'

Rather than dive into the water from the adjacent rocks, Adam took the easier route of simply walking in from the sandy beach. Once in the water, he felt a huge release of energy and pleasure. He was in his element and quickly used his powerful crawl to put distance between him and the shore. He'd been warned by Emma to keep his distance from the buoyed shipping lane that went into Nice harbour and he soon found himself in a coastal section that was both beautiful and perfect for swimming. The nonexistence of a tide was a huge bonus that he hadn't anticipated. Swimming from Daymouth had been good, but at every moment, the strong tide was a factor.

When Adam returned to shore, Emma had gone. He had enjoyed his conversation with her and felt a little sad that she'd left. He dried off sitting on the beach and thought about running back to his hotel in Monaco, but in the end decided he had done quite enough exercise and would take a taxi back to his hotel and prepare for the evening game of poker.

*

Ian Carbrook was the first to arrive at the Casino Noir et Blanc, followed by James Holberton, and Ian welcomed James with,

'You did well to avoid the "Invicta" trip, James, our crossing from Monaco to Cap d'Antibes was a bit sickly and then Lord Robert got drunk when we were back and was quite rude to Adam.'

'The rudeness doesn't surprise me,' replied James. 'I've always found Lord Robert hard work, but Jenny's lovely and we all like her.'

They continued their conversation and later, Thomas Giddings and Jan Ziabicki joined them at the bar. Adam then arrived too, shaking hands with everyone in turn.

Ian said, 'Congratulations, Adam, for coming back to play. I hope you found the last game interesting and you're ready for a bit more tonight. All we now need is Lord Robert. I was there when he had a bit of a dust-up with you at the Monaco Yacht Club yesterday. I do hope that won't spoil the evening.'

A few minutes later, Lord Robert arrived looking very hot and bothered.

'Are you all right?' said Ian.

'No, I'm not fucking all right! Some bastard has just bought a bucket load of Plymouth Super Boats shares and the price has rocketed. I was shorting them into liquidation and if this situation stays the same for the next month, I'm going to have to pay out millions. So no, I'm not all right.'

'Oh dear,' said Ian. 'Sorry to hear that, Robert, perhaps you'll have more luck this evening, but do remember it's a five-thousand-euro pot for each player and so millions aren't involved tonight. Let me introduce the two players that you probably haven't met before. This is Jan Ziabicki. He now lives in Monaco and is a retired oil trader.'

Robert muttered something but didn't seem interested in him.

'And this is Thomas Giddings who also now lives in Monaco. He bought my company Euro Fruits Imports, EFI, five years ago and imports fruit into the UK from around here. He's been very successful in the last few years.'

Robert seemed more interested in Thomas than Jan and asked him, 'Where are you based in the UK?'

'We supply London and our main distribution centre is in Hackney, close to the Mile End Road. We bring fruit into the UK, crossing the Channel at Dover and have also recently started deliveries from Cherbourg as the Dover route is getting extremely difficult to manage.'

Adam suddenly felt his mind begin to race. He realised he had just heard two locations that linked to both Daymouth drugs and migrant activities. He was almost in panic but managed to control his emotion as when looking around he saw that everyone else in the room appeared to be acting normally.

The EFI distribution centre near the Mile End Rd could well be the location Frank Green had disclosed to Detective Fraser and the 'Fleur de Landemer' migrant-laden boat had come out of Cherbourg. Surely this was too much of a coincidence? But then again, surely it was an indication that Thomas Giddings or possibly Ian Carbrook were involved in both the drugs and/or migrant traffic?

Adam's mind was working overtime trying to access the situation. This information, together with the morning meeting with Jan, was turning the day into a tumultuous event.

Jacques arrived and said the table was ready for play to start and they all went into the room.

Within an hour, Adam had lost all his chips. He was unable to hold his concentration and made several errors of judgement.

'I'm sorry, everyone, but you've cleaned me out. My apologies for playing so badly. I think I should leave and maybe return on another occasion when my mind is working more clearly. Thank you anyway for the invitation to play.'

Adam left, unsure of the state of play on his departure. He knew he had left with nothing and thought Ian Carbrook and Thomas Giddings were currently the greatest beneficiaries. As he left, he glanced at Jan, who said nothing and continued to have his permanent smile. There was no exchange of looks or words from him as Adam left the room.

As soon as Adam was out of the casino he felt a wave of relief and started thinking about what his next move should be. On arrival at his hotel, he went to his room, found in his English wallet the card that Detective Fraser had given him and rang the number on his mobile.

'Hello, who is speaking?'

'This is Adam Ranworth speaking from Monaco and I would urgently like to speak with Inspector Fraser, who gave me this number to ring if needed.'

'Thank you, sir, would you please hold the line while I try and get him. This may take several minutes and so please be patient.'

There was a very long silence; however, after about five minutes, Fraser came on the line.

'Hello, Adam, this better be good. I was just about to go to bed after a long day.'

Adam then went on to explain the background and also what he had just heard at the casino in relation to the possible EFI link with the Mile End Rd and Cherbourg.

'Oh, you have been busy again being the little detective, haven't you?' said Fraser. 'It won't be long before you have taken over my job. I find it very difficult to believe in coincidences, and I find it very difficult to believe that, at nearly every step in this investigation, you appear to be involved in some way. I think you need to run this past me again, so I get your story clear and then we can decide what to do.'

Adam retold Fraser in more detail about the sequence of events, although he held back from saying anything about the Fort Revère conversation with Jan Ziabicki.

'OK; I think I've got the message. You think EFI could be at the heart of possibly both the Daymouth drug and migrant investigations. At the moment, this chap Thomas Giddings and/or Ian Carbrook could both be in the frame and you have put Lord Robert Harvey also into the pot of possible suspects. That's a pretty big call on your part.

'I want you to leave this with me tonight and I will call you again tomorrow morning. In the meantime, I don't want you to speak to anyone at all about what you have told me. Stay put in your hotel and wait for my call. You've now given me work to do and I may well miss my sleep tonight. This better be useful information. If it isn't, you are not going to be popular with a lot of people.'

CHAPTER 15

The following morning, Adam waited anxiously until eleven o'clock when the telephone in his room rang and Fraser came on the line.

'We've decided that you must return immediately to the UK and we've reserved and paid for a seat on this evening's BA 6.30pm flight from Nice to Heathrow. You need to tell one of your group in Monaco that you've got to return urgently to the UK for personal reasons and say no more. Don't go back to Daymouth. Either stay in a London hotel or, if you prefer, see if you can stay with your friend David Young. Again, you shouldn't share any information you've given us, or that we've given you, with him or anyone else. We're now working with a number of agencies in different countries on this case and it's crucial that we know where you are and that you remain silent for however long it takes. It may be a few days or could be longer. Do you understand? Where would you prefer to stay?'

Adam was taken aback by the directness of the commands.

'Yes, I do understand and yes, I will take the flight to Heathrow. I'll phone David and arrange to stay with him. I do realise this is a serious matter, but I have to say I'd prefer to be asked rather than ordered to do this.'

'Sorry about that, Adam, but this is important. Don't forget that I am Special Branch and we do have certain powers. You've been most helpful so far and remember, these instructions are for your own protection as well. I must go now, there are lot of things happening that need sorting.'

The following hour after the Fraser conversation, Adam made various phone calls from his hotel room. David was very surprised to hear from him and immediately got excited about the possibility of a visit to Daymouth, and of course the prospect of seeing Jasmine again. Adam struggled with the right words, but explained that the police wanted him to stay in London for a bit and could he stay with him and also be collected from Heathrow tonight off the BA flight from Nice? David was of course very curious to know what was going on, but agreed to help.

The call to Grace Holberton was somewhat easier because at that time neither she nor James were in their hotel and so Adam left a voice message to say that he had been urgently called back to the UK on a personal matter and would be leaving in the evening. He gave no further information and hoped they wouldn't ring back.

Calling Jan was a potentially more complex issue and as he called the number, he was not sure exactly what he was going to say.

'Hello, Jan Ziabicki here.'

'Hi Jan, it's Adam. I'm afraid something's come up and I've got to go back to the UK this evening. It's urgent and a personal matter but I promise that I'll get back to you and talk through your proposal very soon.'

Jan asked, 'Was it linked to last night?'

Adam struggled to answer the unexpected response.

'Why do you ask that?'

'Well, for a start you played poker as though your mind was somewhere else and I noticed before the game that you seemed to react to Thomas Giddings when he mentioned the Mile End Rd, Hackney and Cherbourg in a conversation. I told you that I'd done some homework on Daymouth over the last couple of days and I read about the recent migrant tragedy involving a French boat that came from Cherbourg. Coincidence? I think not? So, Adam, yes you should go back to the UK and sort out your personal matter and I look forward to hearing from you after that.'

Adam was initially lost for words and after a long pause said, 'Jan, I'm amazed at your insight. Let's leave it at that for the moment and I will contact you again as soon as I can.'

After ending the call, he was in total shock at the way Jan had read the situation even to the extent that it crossed his mind whether he too was in some way possibly involved? He thought to himself, *I knew he was bright, but he must be super bright to have picked up on all those details. The guy's incredible; I can see how he may well have made billions without the rest of the world really knowing about it.*

Adam sensed things were getting decidedly tricky and that the best thing for him to do was to check out and leave Monaco straight away. He'd go to Nice, have lunch in a restaurant and then head off to the airport in order to catch the 6.30pm flight to London.

*

The plane arrived at Heathrow on time and the queue at passport control was quite short. However, after walking away from the control gate, a uniformed woman approached and spoke briefly to him before leading him to a side room.

'Welcome back to the UK,' said Fraser. 'We need to have a little chat and then you can go and meet your friend David who I'm told is already waiting in the arrivals area for you.'

The chat involved Fraser and a woman officer giving away very little information from their side but extracting as much as they could from Adam concerning the Carbrooks, the Holbertons, the Harveys, Jan Ziabicki and Thomas Giddings. They were particularly interested in the Casino Noir conversation where Giddings had mentioned Hackney, Mile End Rd and Cherbourg, and pressed Adam to recall verbatim what had been said. After a heavy interrogation, he was finally released from the clutches of Special Branch and allowed to leave.

'Where have you been?' exclaimed David as Adam appeared at the arrivals hall. 'It's over an hour and a half since your plane landed.'

'Sorry about that, Special Branch intercepted me and wanted information.'

They walked off to the car saying little to each other. The mention of Special Branch had made David realise that whatever was going on was serious.

On the journey back to the apartment, Adam explained his difficulties relating to the instructions he had received about saying nothing to others, including David. 'I'm afraid until they give me the all-clear, we're both going to have to keep off the subject of Daymouth and that, as far as you are concerned, includes Jasmine. I can't even tell you about Monaco either and so it's going to be tough. I hope we can do a few London runs and maybe some swimming. Perhaps I could borrow one of your bikes and we can cycle together?'

*

The days passed without any outside contact, until the evening of day five when there was a ring on David's doorbell.

'We have news,' said Fraser standing in the doorway with another officer. 'This is Elizabeth and she is from the communications section of Special Branch. Both you and David can hear what she has to say now. Tomorrow morning the news will be on the radio, television and in the daily press.'

Adam and David sat down in front of the two police officers and Elizabeth opened her file. 'Yes, as Fraser has just said, there will be a press release to say that arrests have been made in the UK, France and Italy in relation to both drug smuggling and migrant traffic in the Daymouth area. However, there are still issues that will have to remain confidential for some time.

'In addition to the previous arrests of two Frenchmen and two local Devon people, there have been further arrests of groups of people operating in the East London area and the small Italian port area of San Remo. A major drugs and migrant smuggling gang has been identified and further arrests in both the UK and Europe are expected.

'There will be some detail given about the Daymouth migrant tragedy of the 'Fleur de Landemer' and also how a county lines drug route has been broken up. We expect considerable interest in the story and our PR team will be using it as an example of the positives that we do. Special Branch will not be mentioned and Paul Barclay from Plymouth and a London Officer have been assigned the job of fronting any interviews. We would be grateful if both of you would continue to take a low profile for a little while longer and not talk to the press. Adam, you will be needed in the future to give evidence in court proceedings.'

Adam looked at Fraser saying, 'But what about people? Who was involved in all of this and how did it all happen? Surely you can tell us something more?'

'It's tricky,' said Fraser. 'But I guess you have a right to know some of what has happened so far. After all, you did give us two crucial clues in teasing out Dan Pitcher, which then led to the Frank Green arrest, and from Monaco, the link to EFI. So, I'll give you an outline, providing you both agree not to take it any further with anybody else?'

There were nods from both Adam and David and a scowl from Elizabeth.

'Basically, for some time, two lorry drivers employed by EFI have been transporting drugs with their fruit cargo from the San Remo area close to the Italian/French border, to a location on the Mile End Rd and, more recently, also transporting migrants from Italy to Cherbourg. We raided EFI in Hackney, East London and found the administrators there were very cooperative. They have records of all their lorry movements using smart tachograph data that is carried by each of their lorries. From a study of the EFI lorry movements, we established two lorries were consistently doing minor deviations from their designated locations in Italy, France and the UK. From that, we raided the tachograph deviated location in Mile End Rd and the Italian police went to Poggio near San Remo. Both locations were drugs storage bases and arrests have been made. The two lorry drivers are in custody and when they were made aware of the evidence against them, have confessed and provided further, very useful, information for both the drug trafficking between Poggio and East London and the migrant trafficking to Cherbourg. The London operation was pretty big and we're very happy with our catch. The Italian operation is more complex as the Mafia is involved in both the drugs and the migrant side. Maybe I shouldn't say any more about either end of the chain as both are ongoing.'

'So what about the individual links and all the people you were cross-examining me about at the airport five nights ago?' said Adam.

'This is where it gets very tricky for me to say too much at this stage and what I am about to say must remain strictly confidential. The Holbertons and Harveys are clear and your man Jan Ziabicki, although shrouded in a lot of mystery, doesn't seem to be linked with any drugs or migrants.

'We believe the Carbrooks are also probably clear, but from the lorry drivers' confessions, it appears Thomas Giddings was the mastermind in using his own company, EFI, to transport drugs and migrants. He alone appeared to have recruited the two drivers and paid them handsomely for their detours. From the evidence we've got so far, we're reasonably satisfied that no other EFI employers were aware of the scam. We currently believe the drugs and migrant trafficking has all happened since the Carbrooks left the company and at present we think they are in the clear.'

'We do however have a real problem as Giddings is currently in Monaco. Both the French and Italian police have been very helpful, but as Giddings is currently in Monaco that is where he may well stay, certainly for the time being. He knows he's in trouble because we've raided Mile End Rd, the Italians raided Poggio, and the French, Cherbourg. Monaco is a Principality and His Serene Highness controls everything, including the police. So getting access to Giddings in Monaco may take some time. He's been very clever. For the past five years he's made several significant donations to Monaco, organised charity events and has generally ingratiated himself into the upper echelons of the local social life. We just have to be patient. At the moment he's imprisoned in the Principality, which, as Adam now knows, is a very small place. If he goes to neighbouring France or Italy, he will be arrested. None of this will be made public knowledge and so you both must keep what I have said confidential.'

*

The next day, David and Adam watched breakfast TV reports on the Daymouth drug and migrant story and were amazed how high-profile it was. There were very few other topical international or national news stories for the broadcasters to focus on and so the Daymouth drugs and migrant story was the centre of attention.

'I think I should stay put here for a few more days before going home in order to let things settle down a bit,' said Adam. 'When I do go, do you want to come too?'

'You bet I do; Jasmine and I are now more than just good friends. I'm not sure how this latest news is going to affect Jack's position in prison, but I do know that I care a lot for Jasmine and I want to be with her.'

This news came as no surprise to Adam as, from everything David had said previously about Jasmine during his short stay, he knew that he was besotted with her, and in all fairness, he could understand why.

Three days later, they drove down together to Daymouth. By then, the drugs and migrant story had become short-lived in the national press and both of them were excited, for different reasons, at the prospect of returning to Eastside Cottage.

'It is quite remarkable how my trip to Monaco has changed so many things,' said Adam to David as they drove past Stonehenge on their journey to Devon. 'Monaco may have changed everything. I met a chap called Jan Ziabicki and he's really inspired me. I hope he'll come and see us, very soon, at Eastside and I want you to meet him too. He could change both our lives.'

*

Within minutes of their arrival at Eastside Cottage, there was a knock on the door and the Admiral appeared at the doorway.

'Welcome back both of you. It has been chaotic here with reporters trying to track you down. The Holbertons and Carbrooks have both come back from Monaco and I've had Jasmine, Sarah and Laura contacting me wanting to know if you're here. Added to that, all Daymouth and Eastside is buzzing with the national news about the drugs and migrant arrests. I've never known it so hectic and to think, I just came here to die!'

Adam enjoyed the Admiral's joke and proceeded to give him a potted version of the story, explaining that he was still under orders from the police not to give out too much information. 'Hopefully, everything will come out in due course and then I'll be able to tell you more,' said Adam. 'But now, if the Carbrooks are back, I need go and see them and I suspect David will want to go to Jasmine.'

It was low tide and so Adam was able to walk along the sandy beach to the Carbrooks' house. The weather was a bit grey and there was quite a strong breeze blowing down the estuary; however, he felt a wonderful feeling of freedom and realised that he had missed the simplicity and beauty of Daymouth, particularly when compared with Monaco. The contrast was huge.

Susie had seen Adam walking along the beach and she met him at the door with tears in her eyes.

'Oh Adam, you were a secret agent after all! What can I say? Ian and I have had a few nightmare days and we were also very concerned for you.'

She led Adam into the house and Ian joined them.

'Adam, it's good to see you in one piece. We've had a right grilling from your man Fraser and he gave both of us a very heavy interrogation in Monaco. I think he was sure we were suspects and I have to say it was very frightening for both Susie and myself. However, we're now back and it looks as though Thomas Giddings was the snake in the grass and was the one behind the transporting of drugs and migrants using rogue EFI drivers. We think all this was done without the rest of the EFI organisation knowing about it, which is some relief to us. But, just think, we were playing poker with this chap just over a week ago.'

They sat together for some time drinking and talking, trying to take in the whole significance of what had occurred in Monaco.

'Whilst you were in Monaco, did Jan Ziabicki ask you anything about your eco park project?' asked Adam.

'He mentioned it a couple of times. Why do you ask?' replied Ian.

'Nothing really, I think he may come back to us about it.'

'Oh, and did you know the gossip?' said Susie, trying to raise their spirits and move away from drugs and migrants. 'Jenny Harvey has left Robert. She said she'd had enough of him and came back with the Holbertons. I think she's staying with them at the moment. I have to say, I'm not surprised. Robert was an absolute pain in Monaco.'

The conversation continued for a bit before Adam left to go home.

*

When he got to Eastside Cottage, David, Jasmine and Sarah were there. Sarah wrapped her arms around Adam saying, 'It's great to see you, we were so worried. My parents and the Carbrooks have had a torrid time in Monaco, but now it seems to be OK. Did you know that Jenny came back with them and is staying with us for while? We're all meeting up at the Smugglers Inn later, you must come too.'

They all took 'Greta' across the estuary to Daymouth and met up with Grace, James and Jenny Harvey who had come earlier on the ferry. Laura was behind the bar and welcoming everyone. 'It's fantastic to see you all again. I'm so happy. Adam are you OK? There've been so many rumours going around the town.'

Adam leaned over the bar and gave Laura a kiss. The relief and release of emotion from all the group was evident and everyone wanted to say something at the same time.

'Let me start by saying all the drinks are on me this evening,' said Adam. 'It's great to be back amongst everyone here. It is all very emotional and I've never felt this way before. Can someone tell the lifeboat crew and friends, I want them to share the evening with us?'

Grace came over to Adam and put her arms around him. 'I just don't know what to say. The last few days in Monaco were a nightmare, but now I'm so happy to be back home, and we have a trophy! Jenny's come with us too. She has finally had the courage to leave Lord Robert for good.'

The party quickly got underway with conversations occurring in all directions. Ted Sandringham arrived with some of the lifeboat crew and also Jim and Julie Lewis. Adam made a direct line to the Lewis's and shook their hands. 'Thank you so much for coming, both of you. I'm so relieved that the police have been able to make multiple arrests. I know of course that none of this can bring Ben back, but at least some sort of justice does seem to have been done and you helped to make that happen. Ben's diary entry was key to starting the whole process off.'

The Lewis's both smiled at Adam and thanked him for his words. Ted came over, gave Adam a pat on the back and then took the Lewis's to the part of the bar where the lifeboat crew had congregated.

The party was well underway with the appearance of Beryl, the ferryman Harry Payne, the local policeman Chris Thompson and others arriving. Laura and her assistant were hard-pressed to keep the supply of drinks going and Adam went behind the bar to help and he thought it might also be a way to reduce the barrage of questions he was getting from almost everybody who was there.

The party went on for some while and at the end, Harry Payne said he would take all the Eastside people back on the ferry. Laura came over to Adam and whispered into his ear, 'Would you like to stay here with me tonight?'

Adam paused for a moment, smiled and then said, 'Laura, that's super kind of you, but I've some serious thinking to do tonight in order to sort something out for tomorrow. I've got to make some very big decisions and choices.'

*

Adam struggled through the night trying to sort out in his mind how he was going address the issue of Jan Ziabicki. Clearly, he would need to talk to Ian Carbrook, but in order for any plan to work, surely more people would need to be involved?

He came down in the morning to find David and Jasmine together around the breakfast table. 'We're going off for the day and staying overnight in Cornwall to talk things over. Jasmine's mum has agreed to look after the children and we just need some time together.'

Adam had resigned himself to the relationship taking its own course. 'I do hope it works out for you both, whatever happens. Today's an important one for me and the outcome could affect both of you too, so don't make any final decisions until you get back, when I should know more.' He then went for a morning run on the beach to try and clear his head for the day in front of him.

After breakfast, Adam phoned the Carbrooks, asking them for a meeting, and they suggested he come for an impromptu lunch. When he arrived, both Susie and Ian were pleased to see him and insisted he first have a drink.

'Thanks,' said Adam as Susie thrust a large glass of white wine at him as he sat in one of their lounge chairs. 'Perhaps we should talk now before alcohol gets the better of me. Last night at the Smugglers Inn was very intense.' There was a short pause and he then continued. 'What I want to talk to you both about is Jan Ziabicki. Ian knows him as one of the Monaco poker group and I've only met him a couple of times; however, one morning when I was there he took me to Fort Revère above Monaco and we had what I can only describe as a remarkable conversation. Some of what he said was in strict confidence but in order for you to make any sense of this I need to tell you about some of the things we discussed.

'Jan's been thinking for some time that he, in some way, wants to help Cornwall. He was brought up there and now apparently wants to put something back into the system. He then heard about your Marlo Eco Park project, liked the idea and thought it could be a template for other eco parks throughout both Devon and Cornwall. He has other ideas in mind too but didn't disclose them. For some reason that isn't entirely clear to me, he took a shine to me and thought I might be able to help him. I guess the bottom line in relation to yourselves is, would you be interested in being involved? I have to say I was staggered when he told me how much finance he had available and I was personally convinced his motives were genuine: that he really did want to put something back into the West Country.'

Ian and Susie looked at each other and smiled. 'Adam,' said Ian. 'Jan has just been on the phone and talked to us about this. What you've just said confirms what he's proposing. I know Jan from playing poker with him, but I must admit I didn't know that he was super, super rich. He's also incredibly clever, and yes, I think what he's proposing is for the right reasons, just as I hope you realise the idea of our eco park is for the right reasons too.'

'How did you leave things with Jan? Are you interested in joining him?'

'Yes, both Susie and I are very happy to be included, and from what Jan said, he very much wants you to be heavily involved too.'

Not for the first time in the last couple of weeks, Adam

was astonished at the unfolding events. 'That's brilliant and so fast,' he exclaimed. 'Things seem to be happening quicker than I can keep up with; but let me try something else too. Would you be prepared for there to be Holberton involvement also? I've said nothing to them so far, but as you know, Sarah spoke brilliantly on your side during the planning application and having Grace and James on your side would greatly help progress, certainly in the Daymouth area, where they're so highly respected.'

'Yes, that would be fine,' Susie immediately said. 'I like them both and maybe we could pull Lady Jenny in too. I got to know her in Monaco and, unlike her husband, she's very nice and an intelligent person.'

'I agree,' added Ian. 'If Susie approves, then it's certainly all right with me. You do realise, Adam that with Susie on board, this project, however it develops, will be a success.'

Adam couldn't believe how smoothly the conversation had gone. He had struggled all night trying to work out what to say and now discovered that Jan had already done most of the work, probably many times more effectively than he could have done.

Ian got up from his chair and declared, 'I think this calls for another drink, and then we can have lunch.'

*

On returning to his cottage in the afternoon, Adam picked up a message on the phone from Grace inviting him to supper at home that evening. She said she would have invited David too but had heard that both he and Jasmine were off for the night, which left her to do all the cooking. Adam phoned back accepting the invitation but saying nothing about the eco park or Jan Ziabicki.

That evening when he arrived at the Holbertons', he was met by James saying, 'I hardly had time at the pub last night to thank you for what you've achieved. Yes, our last few days in Monaco were a nightmare, but now we are back, Grace and Jenny are so happy.'

They went through to the lounge and were joined by Jenny and Sarah. Jenny was quite animated and wanted to tell Adam about her last few days in Monaco.

'I think it started with the marmalade issue on "Invicta". Then I had that fantastic sail with you and Steve and finally, Robert was so beastly about the shorting of Plymouth Super Boats. After that, together with having to put up with Robert ordering me about for so many years, I decided enough was enough and I have left him and am filing for divorce. I've plenty of ammunition over all his past infidelities and I've a powerful secret weapon! In the early days of the hedge fund, he thought it would be tax-efficient to put the fund in both our names and so I'm entitled to half of the value and I can assure you, I will go for it too and enjoy every moment of the chase.' Jenny had a radiant smile and added, 'I'm now back in Daymouth, very happy and very grateful to everyone here who is making me feel so at home.'

Grace eventually appeared from the kitchen a little flustered as she was without the help of Jasmine. However, she was very cheerful and they all enjoyed an aperitif before supper.

It was over supper that Adam raised the issue of Marlo Eco Park and Jan Ziabicki. He provided the necessary background and summarised the discussion he'd had earlier with Ian and Susie. 'So, in conclusion, I'd like to know how each of you feels about involvement in a possible project involving Ian and Susie together with Jan? Obviously, you may want to give the whole thing some thought before committing to anything, I'm not expecting an immediate response; however, a hint at this stage could help me a lot.'

Adam looked around the table at the rather astonished faces.

'Well, I'm up for it and very excited too,' said Sarah.

'Me too,' exclaimed Jenny. 'This is something I could really get my teeth into.'

Grace looked at James and was unsure what to say. James broke the silence with a smile. 'You know, even I'll go along with this. After all we have been through – drugs, drownings and migrants – I think it's time to try and do some good in the world and I can now see where both Ian and Jan are coming from. It appears this chap Jan Ziabicki has the cash to make a difference, and trying to bring Devon and Cornwall together a bit would be a great positive. I love the idea of doing something that's not reliant on the whims of politicians and the government and, in the end, I was persuaded by my own daughter's arguments about the eco park. Grace, what do you think? I would only be involved if the family moved together on this.'

Grace looked up a James and went across and kissed him. 'You great beast. Of course I'm in too. How wonderful to have something that we can all work with together.'

When the evening drew to a close, Adam started walking away from the house and Sarah came out and spoke to him. 'Adam, I just wanted to say that you have been great and I think you're wonderful.' She gave him a huge kiss and went back into the house.

*

The following day, David returned to Eastside Cottage having left Jasmine at her mother's home with the children.

'Welcome back, David. How did you get on?'

'Thanks, Adam, we had enough time to sort ourselves out and whatever you have to say to me won't make much difference. We want to be together. Jasmine went to see Jack a couple of days ago and he still isn't prepared to tell the police who was the source of drug supply. He's still afraid of repercussions both in and out of jail. Jasmine says she just cannot live like that and she wants to be with me and I want to be with her. So: have you got any news?'

'Well yes I have and I think I'm relieved that you two have made a clear decision,' replied Adam. 'Now sit down and I'll explain what I've been doing.'

He summarised both the meeting with the Carbrooks and the Holbertons and then said, 'It's my turn to ask you. Do you want to be involved in this venture? It will almost certainly mean that you would have to leave London and your current job and come to live somewhere in Devon or Cornwall.'

CHAPTER 16

Jan Ziabicki was introduced to everyone around the large dining table at the Carbrook home and then the Admiral stood up and spoke.

'Adam has given me the dubious pleasure of chairing this meeting and I have to say it's a very great honour. As a long-retired Royal Navy Sea Lord, I thought my days of saying or doing anything important were well and truly over; however, here I am presiding over what could be an astonishingly imaginative plan for both Devon and Cornwall. My only job is to simply say welcome and to wish the ship every happiness and success for the future. Many of us have been through recent turbulent waters but now, if all the ideas we are going to hear about today can be brought to a reality, then something very special will emerge and I wish the ship a very safe passage.

'My next-door neighbours, Adam and his friend David, have agreed to act as overall managers for these proposed projects. Ian Carbrook will first speak about his Marlo Eco Park concept and then Jan Ziabicki will explain his own proposals.'

Ian stood up and gave a summary of the Daymouth Marlo Eco Park project and how Jan had then proposed that the concept could be used as a template for further eco parks around Devon and Cornwall. The plan was to initially build the Daymouth park and if that was successful, Jan would finance the extension of the concept to other locations. The objective was to create genuine all-year local employment and raise the overall profile of the two regions.

Jan Ziabicki then stood up and gave everyone present a brief summary of his life, explaining that his happiest times were as a child living with his Polish parents in Truro. He wanted to bring a little prosperity back to Cornwall and Devon by financing two projects and supporting the Marlo Eco Park expansion. One project was to build a factory in Camborne that would make modular homes. It would be called Affordable Modular Homes and would manufacture genuinely affordable homes, in a substantial factory, which could then be assembled throughout the West Country and if successful even further afield. It would provide both significant employment for the area as well as much-needed local affordable housing.

His second project was more speculative. He had spent time in Russia and seen a trial drilling operation to drill deep into the earth's crust, but their equipment was not state of the art and they also ran out of money during the operation. He would form a company called Deep Earth Energy and, using his financial resources together with modern technology, the company would drill deep into the Cornish earth's crust through granite and, if necessary, towards the earth's mantle. They would drill an annular pipe that would pump water down the outer annulus; the water would return as steam up the central core of the pipe in order to run steam turbines and produce electric power. If successful, Cornwall could become a twenty-first-century 'energy gold mine' and he had already formed a team of geologists and engineers who all had agreed that his ideas were possible in the chosen Cornish sites.

He then went on to say that there were still many aspects of all the proposals that needed to be firmed up and Adam, together with David, would be masterminding this, probably from Daymouth. He added that, in the last week, he had bought a farm near Truro and would be moving there soon; however, his main job was to provide the money that would make all this happen. He was really happy to have everyone around this table onboard and, as a confirmation of his commitment that this was not just a dream, he had asked a publicity company to take photos of the group and circulate the news to both the local and national press. In this way, it would show to everyone that the proposals were not just ideas; they were a reality.

*

Three weeks later, Adam and David were sitting in Eastside Cottage when the doorbell rang and Adam got up to answer it. He opened the door and saw two men.

'Hello, my name is Keith Thompson-Smith and this is my partner, Michel Navard. I saw your name and photo in the paper recently and recognised you as the person that saved my life at Putney earlier this year. Is it all right if we could have a chat?'

'Yes of course,' replied Adam, totally shocked.

Adam led Keith and Michel through the cottage to the waterside terrace where David was sitting.

'David, these are two people who heard about me from the recent press release and this is Keith, who is the man I rescued from the Thames at Putney earlier this year.'

The four men sat round the table on the outside terrace and Keith immediately spoke.

'Firstly, Adam, I must apologise for not contacting you until today. At the time, I was a total mess and yes, I was suicidal when I jumped off Putney Bridge. However, as soon as I actually jumped, I realised I didn't really want to die. You saved my life and I cannot thank you enough for doing that. For a month after you rescued me, I was still a mess and it was only when I meet Michel that my full perspective of life changed. Michel and I are now partners. We love each other and the discovery has transformed both our lives. We met at a counselling session as Michel was also going through a very difficult time and since then, both our lives have changed. We love each other. We also love the world and, in particular, both of us are so grateful for you saving my life and maybe indirectly, Michel's too.'

Adam was lost for words and it was David who spoke.

'That's brilliant; I am so happy for you both. My name's David. Adam and I have known each other from our university days. We're not in love with each other, but we are very good friends. We too have been through something of a roller-coaster period; however, I suspect it's nothing as traumatic as that which both you and Michel have experienced. I'm sure we're both delighted that Adam's brave rescue was so worthwhile.'

'Yes,' Adam replied, having recovered his composure. 'I'm so glad you came and found me. I worried when you didn't made contact. The rescue, in fact, changed my life too.'

The four of them spent the next hour discussing how the last six months had changed all their lives. It was an intimate conversation where Adam, David, Keith and Michel shared their private thoughts in a way that none of them had shared them before. It was absolutely clear to all of them that the event on

Putney Bridge had changed all of them in positive ways, although there had been some considerable bumps along the way.

*

After Keith and Michel left, Adam went and knocked on his neighbour's door. The Admiral appeared somewhat surprised to see him.

'Hello Adam, you look a little shell-shocked. Have you had some bad news?'

'No Admiral, it isn't bad news, but it is interesting news, and I need your thoughts on how best to go forward.'

'I have to say, Adam, that since you've arrived here six months ago, my life has changed from someone who was just quietly waiting to die, to being thrown into an action-packed arena involving drugs, migrants, romance and very much more. Yes, of course we can talk, but I'm not sure that I'll be able to help you.'

The Admiral opened a bottle of wine and they sat down to talk.

Adam explained the meeting with Keith and his partner Michel, during which the Admiral consumed a glass of wine. When Adam finally paused, the Admiral replied, 'You have been on quite a journey in the last six months. I too went on a journey that was of course totally different to yours, but life-changing for me. The Falklands War was my moment of truth and I think this last six months at Daymouth has been yours.

'I don't know whether to work backwards or forwards on what I've seen of you. Maybe backwards works best, although I apologise if I get things wrong.

'I've been fascinated by the turn of events since your arrival and of course astonished by your recent Monaco trip and the discovery of the source of drug and migrant smuggling. Your meeting with this man Jan Ziabicki was another totally unexpected drama. The uniting of the Carbrooks and the Holbertons, yet another very surprising event.

'Your lifeboat experiences brought back deep memories of the sinking of my ship in the Falklands War. Something I knew I would never forget, but your rescues, where someone lost their life, and then more recently the tragic drowning of Ben Lewis and those poor migrants, brought it all back to me in a very real way.

'Amongst all of this, I've followed your relationship with Jasmine and, as you know, I've a particularly fond of her. I admired the way you went to see Jack Sanders in Dartmoor but also hope she and your friend David will eventually hit it off together as, in my view, they are a more suited couple. I've been fascinated about your own relationships with Laura at the Smugglers Inn, and Sarah Holberton, and was interested to know which direction you were likely to take.

'And then, I go back to one of our early meetings when you told me why you came to Daymouth in the first place; the chap that you saved under Putney Bridge. The way that you said you saw a look in his eyes telling you that he didn't really want to die after all. Very powerful stuff and, from that moment, I felt you were searching for something that was missing in your own life. Now you tell me, that very man has reappeared into your life, happy and eternally grateful for your actions.

'When my ship went down with so many lives lost, I knew, from that time, that I had to do something and change my own life. It may just be that you have also reached that moment in your life too.'

ABOUT THE AUTHOR

Malcolm Mackley studied Physics at Leicester and Bristol Universities, then later moved to Chemical Engineering at Cambridge University, where he devoted thirty years to teaching and research. He lectured on his specialist subjects throughout the world as a Fellow of Robinson College, a Professor of Process Innovation and a Fellow of the Royal Academy of Engineering.

In 2011, he moved, with his wife Margaret, to Devon and experienced first-hand the very exciting and different challenges of living in an iconic estuary town. Writing the book Daymouth was a liberating opportunity for him to move away from the constraints of scientific work and create an original fiction story about people, places and drama from an entirely different perspective.